Murder Plain and Simple

"Look Gale, as far as I'm concerned, he was just an out-sider who got caught in some bad mess and ended up dead. People get unlucky sometimes, and sometimes the price is very high," Ella finished.

"What kind of bad mess?"

Ella's voice grew shrill and loud enough so that out in the yard Katie Pru turned to stare at them. "So you're a detective now, too? I don't know what kind of bad mess. But it was bad enough to get him and the oth-ers all killed, wasn't it?" She stopped, her face flushed, her breathing strained.

Gale stood up and tried to guide her grandmother to a chair, but Ella shook her off. "Ella, there's some-thing you're not telling me. I want you to tell me right now. What is bothering you so much?"

Ella's mouth was a tight line; she stared hard at her granddaughter. "This is a very small town, Gale. I can count on one hand how many murders we've had since I've been alive. You think this was a random act? This was not an accident. And it damn sure wasn't because they were in the wrong place at the wrong time. They were in the middle of a patch of woods so remote that no one ever goes there, and they got shot. That was planned, Gale. And in a town this small, that means we're all in danger . . ."

The
Mother Tongue

Teri Holbrook

BANTAM BOOKS

New York   Toronto   London   Sydney   Auckland

The Mother Tongue
A Bantam Crime Line Book / February 2001

Crime Line and the portrayal of a boxed "cl" are trademarks of
Bantam Books, a division of Random House, Inc.

ISBN 0-553-57719-0

Published simultaneously in the United States and Canada

Bantam Books are published by Bantam Books, a division of
Random House, Inc. Its trademark, consisting of the words "Bantam
Books" and the portrayal of a rooster, is Registered in U.S. Patent
and Trademark Office and in other countries. Marca Registrada.
Bantam Books, 1540 Broadway, New York, New York 10036.

PRINTED IN THE UNITED STATES OF AMERICA

OPM   10   9   8   7   6   5   4   3

In memory of Darien Bogenholm
who gave me gifts I could never repay,
not the least of which was showing me
that I had both roots and wings.

Mythic connections exist between the weaver and the writer, as if fibers and phonemes were parallels. We both work in threads and yarns; when we both draft, it is furiously, the movement of the spindle, like the movement of the tale, twisting tighter and tighter until we risk snapping the whole in two, its end lashing out of our control. I learned early after my husband's death that there was comfort in the steady rhythm of spinning wool. I could watch the fibers disappear like smoke from my hands, only to remove them later as a firm skein from the spool. Now, as I write these memoirs, I find equal comfort in spinning words. . . . Each chapter is a skein I can hold in my hand. Ultimately, they will be woven into whole cloth. And that, finally, is what I want—a sense of the whole, a tapestry of words that reveal the missing life.

— Introduction, pg. i
A Missing Life: Memoirs of a Grass Widow
by GALE GRAYSON

PROLOGUE

In Statlers Cross, Georgia, everyone was white. A black couple lived five miles out of town in a clapboard house with trimmed boxwood hedges and rows of daffodils along the walkway; they were respected. William could fix all the engines brought to him by the men of Statlers Cross, and Jackie had made every wedding cake consumed in the Methodist Church fellowship hall for twenty years. But they never shopped in town, preferring to drive to the county seat of Praterton, and if they were missed, it was rarely commented upon. The one notable time was when Andy Vaughter, finishing an article on multiculturalism in *Time,* tossed the piece to the floor and hollered to his wife in the kitchen, "Good thing we have old Dobby Dobbins. If he didn't walk down the road talking to cars, we wouldn't have any diversity at all."

Reebe Vaughter responded by throwing a dish towel at her husband. "You know I don't approve of you making fun," she said. But in truth Andy had hit upon a reality of Statlers Cross that few bothered to notice. The town was astonishingly homogeneous. Of its 362 residents (623, if one counted the new subdivision outside the city limits, which no one did), all were of either Scottish, Irish, English, or Cornish descent. All were Baptist or Methodist, with a handful of Pentecostals claimed by both denominations during revival weeks. Until 1981 they were all Democrats, although after Jimmy Carter's second presidential race an increasing number concluded that the Republican Party of the 1980's was more like the Democratic Party of the 1950's and switched loyalties. By the 2000 election, Ted Stevens could accurately grumble as he screwed the legs on the Democratic polling booth: "Not worth chipping my fingernails for. Only a handful's gonna use it and they'll probably do it out of meanness."

So it was a testimony to expectations that Ilene Parker walked past the Epson place and saw an unfamiliar child playing in the front yard for three consecutive days before she slowed, put her hand to her throat, and turned to examine the little girl carefully. Straight black hair fell like pillow fringe across the child's forehead; folds of skin came down over the far edges of her eyes. The little girl smiled when she saw Ilene and waved her pinky. Ilene hurried past, but for several seconds, she saw that pudgy hand in her mind. The skin color was not white. It was not black. Instead it was milky beige like the cap of a mushroom, and it delighted and alarmed Ilene.

She continued to the center of town and entered the old-fashioned comfort of Langley Drugs, where Cooper Langley stood behind his cash register, opening a can of Diet Coke. Ilene dawdled in the aisles, picking up a loaf of bread and a jar of instant coffee, and took them to the counter.

"Good morning, Cooper," she said. "Heard anything about the new family?"

Langley took a swig. "Probably just what you've heard, Ilene. John"—referring to John Watkins, the new preacher at the Methodist Church—"John went to meet them yesterday. Says they seem like a nice family— mother, grandmother, and a little girl. Spell their name

N-g-u-y-g-e-n. 'Nugent,' I guess. John knows how to pronounce it."

"I didn't even realize the Epson house was for sale."

"You knew when Mary went into the home the kids were going to sell it eventually. Besides, it needs someone living in it. Nobody to take care of it, it'll go to seed real quick."

"True," agreed Ilene. "Thank you, Cooper. I think I'll go introduce myself to them."

She was at the door before Langley finished his second swallow. "They don't speak English," he told her. "I don't know what they do speak, but it ain't English."

Ilene Parker thought about this as she walked the quarter mile to her home, across the railroad tracks that divided the town, down the side street with its five neat houses—the Stevenses' tiny 1970's frame bungalow and the Vaughters' 1960's red brick ranch both squashed onto a single lot that had belonged to their grandparents; then the grandparents' five-room clapboard, built in the 1940's. Fifty feet beyond that stood the old Epson house, a nice home by Statlers Cross standards, two-story with three spindly columns and a one-person balcony in the center. It had been built in the twenties, before the Depression, when the town's cotton mill was still healthy and James Epson was one of its floor managers. Not a fancy house, but a good house, and one that Ilene Parker, cozy in her well-tended cottage beyond it, had been proud to have as a neighbor.

As she passed by, she saw the child peeking shyly from behind a plum tree. Ilene slowed. Should she speak to her? What should she say? The little girl didn't speak English. Would she frighten her? And if the mother and grandmother came out, what would she say to them? Would they misinterpret her motives? Would they be defensive and think she had come to complain about their noisy child? Would they yell at her in a language she couldn't understand that would forever ring in her ears—high-pitched, angry, foreign? And what did she have with her to offer in lieu of language—a loaf of store-bought bread and some instant coffee? No, no, that would be awful. She'd go home and bake them something, and then when she returned, they would know without words that she was trying to be their friend.

But when she got home and pulled out her cookbooks, she realized she didn't know what they would eat. What if they had religious restrictions against the Crisco in her mother's pound cake recipe? What if, where they came from, homemade bread was an insult? What if the flavors that were so special to her—the lemon in her chess pie, the sweet potatoes in her biscuits—made them gag? What if they accepted her food but laughed at her, or worse, were so affronted they took her on as an enemy? In the end she put her recipes away and the next day changed her path to town.

Despite this, the idea of living next door to diversity settled quietly into the accommodating mind of Ilene Parker. The mother took a job as the cook at the local café—she walked down the sidewalk to town every morning neatly dressed and returned every evening looking tired but composed. The ragged quince bushes beside the front door were trimmed back, and in the spring, pots of azalea bushes appeared by the driveway, waiting to be planted. All summer the Nguyen girl climbed trees and jumped off the front porch as any child would do. Ilene Parker decided that distance, like fences, made good neighbors, and in the evenings, she sat in a plastic chair by her porch and looked out at the Epson house as the twilight tinted it a peaceful shade of heather.

One Saturday morning in August, as Ilene sat outside snapping the last of her garden beans, she glanced across the ground separating her from the Nguyens and saw a pickup truck pull into her neighbor's driveway. Out of its back crawled four small men. They unloaded the truck in efficient movements—tarpaulins, bags, ladders, planks, and finally, can after can of paint.

Ilene continued to snap her beans. "What a nice family," she said aloud, "to have bought the old Epson place and to care about it enough to keep it from disrepair."

At first she thought the color the men smoothed over the side of the house was a base coat. It had been so long since her own house had been painted—and even then her late husband Bobby had taken care of it—she couldn't remember if houses required a base coat or not. But days passed, and the color got deeper and brighter as first one coat, then another was added. By week's end the men had disappeared and the old Epson place, so fine with its three white columns and its proud balcony, glowed near the heart of Statlers Cross like a giant, pulsating, screaming blue police car light.

"What the hell do they think they're doing?" Ted Stevens asked preacher John Watkins during the Ways and Means Committee meeting at the Methodist Church. "My children have toys that color."

"That's not the way Americans treat their houses," said Reebe Vaughter from her desk as the city clerk.

"Well, that's the problem, isn't it?" said Mayor Tim Murphy. "Those women ain't Americans."

"Well," Reebe said, feeling vaguely uneasy. "They don't have to be *Americans*. But they do need to respect us. I mean, they came here voluntarily. They need to understand how we live and how we feel."

"Maybe someone should go talk to them," suggested Ted. "Maybe your wife should, John."

"And say what?" asked Reverend John Watkins, new, untested, and afraid of dispute. "I've checked. They haven't broken any law. They can paint their house any color they please. Besides, they don't speak English."

"Like hell, they don't speak English," muttered

Mayor Murphy to Reebe. "Those kind of people don't speak English until they need something."

"Now you don't know that, Tim. Maybe we could get an interpreter . . ."

"Yeah, if we knew where they were from to start with."

For weeks the tempest grew, subsided, then grew again as Statlers Cross wrangled. Some suggested offering to repaint the house in a more suitable color. Others wanted to form a committee to escort the Nguyens on a trip to a hardware store to help them make another choice. But all plans stopped unfulfilled because no one could say with any certainty what nationality the women were and what language they spoke.

In the midst of all this, few noticed the slim British man who rented Zilah Greene's deserted house on the edge of town. He, after all, was very white.

1

Monday

Alby Truitt didn't relish the idea of eating dinner at Ella Alden's house at the east end of Statlers Cross. For starters, the place was too full of dead things—dead fish, dead crows, dead snakes—all God's smaller creatures caught and made arty to fill in the white spaces of the Alden clan's peculiar enclave. It was also, Alby knew, too full of more ambiguous deaths, both of others and himself, but that was a thought he pushed to the back of his mind as he trundled his truck over the railroad tracks and up Ella's gravel drive. No, it was neither taxidermy nor memories that pissed him off: Ella Alden's house disturbed him because it was too damn full of Ella Alden.

The truck's headlights settled on a stretch of barbed wire fence as he pulled to a stop. As he stepped into the cool evening air, a pecan branch, overladen and much too long for health, slapped his face, and the bitter smell of pecan grime filled his nostrils. He wiped his face and came away with a smear of blood on his knuckle. Crap. The only reason he had agreed to come tonight was because Ella's granddaughter, Gale, had issued the invitation, and he owed her. He started for the entrance, down a row of worn stepping-stones barely visible in the faint glow of the front-door light.

"Alby?" The voice came from the rear of the house. "Alby Truitt? We're around here."

He left the stones and waded through calf-high weeds to the back porch. It was late October, and the first crispness of fall had finally come to the Georgia night; nevertheless, the overhead back porch light was on and the fan spun slowly. Behind the mesh screens he could make out the figures of two men seated in rocking chairs.

The man on the left rose and unlatched the screen door. "I took a chance you were Alby." The accent was British. "Don't tell me I'm wrong."

"No, sir, you're not wrong." The handshake was firm, welcoming, as Truitt mounted the porch steps. Alby lifted his head to look the Englishman in the eye. "You must be Daniel. An honor to meet you in person. We talked once over the phone . . . awhile back. . . ."

"I remember. It's good to have a face with the voice. Gale speaks highly of you."

She rarely talks of you, Truitt thought, although, interestingly enough, this English visitor was exactly as he had imagined him—soft-voiced, dark, with a hint of humor behind his eyes. So while Gale might have spoken of him infrequently, she must have done so vividly. He shook his head. "Gale never mentioned you were so tall. You didn't sound tall over the phone."

Daniel Halford's laugh was deep. "You don't exactly fit my idea of a Georgia sheriff, either. No sunglasses and no paunch. A business suit, no less, but there you are."

"Better keep an eye on the movies you watch. They'll give you all sorts of bad impressions." Truitt let the door swing closed behind him. "Seriously, it's good to finally meet you, Daniel. Hope the trip over was a good one."

Alby Truitt pushed aside the questions he wanted to ask, the questions that had pestered him since he first heard that Chief Inspector Daniel Halford, a respected homicide detective with New Scotland Yard, was visiting Gale Grayson in the U.S. He liked Gale, but she came bundled with troubles, not the least of which was her own complicated past with New Scotland Yard. What claim did Truitt have to ask any questions? Besides, the evening promised to be long and if he wanted to wear thin his stay, he could always bring them out.

He turned his attention to the second man, slightly built, blond-headed, still seated in his rocker. "Dr. Goddard, I presume?"

Goddard rose, his full height a good six inches shorter than Halford's and a few inches shy of Truitt's own. "I'd rather you call me Ron." This man's accent, too, was British. "I find 'Doctor' just gets me invitations to look in people's mouths."

"I can imagine. Not many doctors in these parts unless they're the type that can tell angina from heartburn." Truitt nodded toward the closed door that led to the Alden kitchen. "So what, have we men been relegated to the back porch? Should I check in with Ella and Gale and let them know I'm here?"

"Actually," Halford said, "we're supposed to take care of you while dinner is finishing. Care for a drink? Ella said if you wanted a shot of something we could drive to the liquor store outside of town as long as we didn't tell her about it."

"I bet that's exactly what she said. Naw, I'll wait." Truitt took a seat on a wooden bench shoved against the wall of the house; the sharp edge of a clapboard pressed into his shoulder blades and he shifted until he was more comfortable. Halford swung his rocker around to face him. Damn, the man was tall—his long legs stretched out until they came within a couple of feet of Truitt's on the opposite side of the porch. He was one of those men—and Truitt knew others like him—who absorbed all the ease in a room. Some would take it in and not give any back; those were men Truitt had learned not to trust. But this man cast the ease back, and the sheriff found himself relaxing. He caught Halford's eye and the detective gave him a brief smile. Well, well. They were each sizing the other up.

"So," Truitt said cheerfully to Goddard, "I hear you're a linguist. Afraid I don't know what that means exactly, unless you're like Henry Higgins, trying to teach other folks how to talk."

Even in the tricky glow of the porch light Truitt could tell Goddard was blushing. Or growing flush—the two indicated different emotional reactions. He grinned. "Understand that if I don't see it in movies or read it in a book, I don't know much about it. This is a pretty quiet part of the world."

"Not to worry. I'm afraid old G.B. Shaw did a bit of damage to people's perception of the field. No, Sheriff—"

"Alby."

"Sorry. No, I'd be a pitiful scholar if my goal was to 'teach' people to talk. What does that mean, anyway? Actually, I'm a historical linguist—I trace the development of dialects."

"No joke. I heard you've rented the Greene place next door. So you've decided to become part of this little community here? We must have some pretty intriguing dialects for you to have left the comfort of the University of Leeds to come so far."

Again the blush. Goddard gave a short laugh. "Somehow, I thought I'd be able to slip in quietly, be the good social scientist and observe without making much of a mark at all. Judging by what you just said, it seems that I underestimated the local grapevine."

"Folks usually do. I've noticed that if you're born and raised here, you could murder people and dry their hides on the roof of your house and people might decide to look the other way. But if you're from out of town . . ."

"And I'm a little more than from out of town."

"I'll say. Old Mrs. Daily, just last week, said, 'You know we have a British linguist living in Statlers Cross. I hear he's such a nice man. And he pays to keep the grass at the Greene house mowed.' So you're off on the right foot. Take care of the house and you'll be everybody's favorite outsider."

Goddard smiled. "I'll have to remember that. It's never a good idea to offend your study group."

Truitt rested his head against the clapboard siding, enjoying his role as storyteller and, he admitted it, mild provocateur. He glanced at Halford and saw that he was watching him, reared back in his chair, his legs casually crossed.

"Ron and I were just discussing his study when you came, Alby," Halford said. "Interesting stuff. He believes that maybe some of the people in Statlers Cross have dialects closer to native English than Brits do themselves."

"Really? I've heard that in parts of Appalachia they still speak Elizabethan—or they did before cable. But nothing like that around here. We all sound pretty Southern to me."

"Yes, you do," Goddard agreed. "But there's this idea in historical linguistics that says the mother tongue of a language keeps evolving while the offshoots—the dialects that developed when speakers moved to other parts of the world—contain purer elements."

"So we talk more like your great-grandfather talked than you do?" Truitt asked, intrigued.

"Perhaps. That's along the lines of what I want to find out. You have several families here in Statlers Cross who immigrated from the coast of Cornwall in the mid-1800's. They originally came for the Dahlonega gold rush, then settled here in Calwyn County to farm. I'm trying to interview them and see if the theory holds true."

"Huh. Which families?"

"The Keasts. The Craddicks. A few others, but those are the ones I'm focusing on."

"So have you met 'em all yet?"

"Some. You know I've been here almost two months. Met James Craddick. Several of the Keasts—Stuart and his grandmother Rosen. She's very promising. I've had a couple of taping sessions with her."

"Taping sessions?"

"I tape the interviews to have a record of the speech. Always audio, sometimes video to get the facial movements."

"So even linguistics has gone high-tech. No more scribbling on pads with pencils?"

"Well, I do that, too."

"I have to say I'm surprised you've talked with Rosen," Truitt said. "The Keasts are fairly close—and closed."

"I noticed. Darrell Murphy, the mayor's son, introduced me to Stuart. I think that helped clear the way."

Truitt shook his head and waved at a moth that darted past. "Darrell must be a persuasive fellow to get Stuart Keast to let you talk to his grandmama. There are a number of tight clans in Calwyn County, but in my experience the Keasts are the tightest. They don't like friends, much less strangers."

"I'm willing to wager that's why Rosen has such a wonderful sound to her. No television in her house, no radio or telephone, although I noticed a cell phone in Stuart's truck, the sly puss. Her house is quite isolated—on a hill at the top of an overgrown drive. Passed several houses that were abandoned and covered with vines before I reached her place."

"That would be the Keast homestead, all right. They've let that road go. But I'll let you in on a little secret—they got a back road they keep cleared and graveled. I think they were probably sending you a message. You can get close, but not too close."

"Ah. That actually makes me feel better. They'll be happy to know I have no intention of getting too close. Not good science. All I want to do is listen a bit. I just want my recordings and my notes, then I'll quietly leave."

"And return to the relative hustle and bustle of Leeds," Halford offered.

Overhead, the fan pumped the air; Truitt rubbed his arms. "October's an iffy time of year around here. Some days are still hot enough for the air-conditioning, then the nights'll be cold enough for blankets." He stood. "Don't suppose Ella would mind too much if we hollered uncle and went inside where it's not as chilly."

It had been over a year since Truitt had been in the Alden house, and those last visits, taking place in the course of a murder investigation, had been strained. The sheriff had an old history with the Alden family—Ella had home-nursed his mother to her death from cancer when he had been too cowardly to do it—and it irritated him that even a back-door entry into the house filled him with unease. His first impression of the kitchen was one of domestic warmth—a copper-bottomed pan simmered on the stove; in one corner, next to a microwave, an automatic coffeemaker sputtered liquid into its pot. The kitchen plumped with the smells of cinnamon, tomatoes, and cornbread. It should have been welcoming, but as the three men filed into the room, Truitt's elbow brushed a large wooden desk pushed against the wall and knocked over a taxidermied crow. Its beak hit a stack of papers that slid to the floor as Truitt made a scrambled save for the bird.

"I've been doing that all week," Halford said as they stooped to gather the papers. "Knocked a trout off the wall yesterday. I believe the ladies are used to it."

"No, I'm afraid we're not. Men are interesting, but it seems to me they don't have any concept of their bulk."

Ella Alden stood in the doorway that separated the kitchen from the main hall. She was dressed as casually as Truitt had ever seen her in what looked like black linen pants and a white cashmere sweater, covered by a green Williams-Sonoma apron that reached past her knees. Tucked under her arm was a silver tray.

"Alby, I'm glad you made it." Her voice sounded bemused, and as she entered the room, he was uncomfortably aware that she was teasing him. "To be honest, Gale and I had bets on whether you would come."

"Ella Alden, you are renowned as the best cook in Calwyn County. I had another night of canned beans and hot dogs looking me in the face. How could I not come?"

"Flatterer."

"Not at all. I'm being sincere."

"Prevaricator."

Truitt turned to Goddard. "You see, Doctor? This is how we communicate in the South. The guest pays compliments, the hostess demurs. It's a two-hundred-year-old tradition that has seen us through all kinds of social turmoil."

Goddard looked at a loss for words. "Don't worry," Truitt continued sotto voce. "I was just yanking Ella's chain. Very gently. That's part of the tradition, too." He raised his voice to conversation level. "We've been having a fascinating talk, Ella. Ron was telling us how Rosen Keast has such an interesting dialect because she's so isolated."

Ella shifted the tray so that it covered her torso. "The Keasts have managed to keep to themselves, all right. Of course, you could say that about all of Statlers Cross, and until recently you would have been accurate. Before that new subdivision was built—what in the world do they call it? Sag Harbor something?—anyway, used to be coming here from Atlanta, Gale and I were what passed for outside influences."

"That's right," Truitt said. "You brought all the evils of the big city with you."

Goddard raised his index finger, a classroom gesture that Truitt found amusing. "But it's not just the big-city influence now, is it? The world seems to be coming to little Statlers Cross."

Ella frowned. "You mean the Nguyens. Nice enough people. But they're causing problems. You would think people would try to fit in."

"Ah, Ella," Truitt said, "I think the Nguyens are going to do just fine. Let that house sit in the rain a few seasons. The color will dull. Folks'll forget."

Ella shot him a strange look that nonplussed him, and for a moment he had the sensation of having forgotten something important. She shook her head and made her way to the refrigerator.

"Daniel," she said over her shoulder, "Gale's upstairs getting Katie Pru ready. Would you mind showing our guests into the dining room?"

As the men walked single-file down the narrow hallway toward the dining room, Truitt's cell phone rang in his pocket. He excused himself and quickly made his way to the front of the house and the empty parlor. Closing the door behind him, he flicked open the phone. It was his evening off; if he was getting a call it was because his able deputy had encountered something too tough to handle alone.

Despite the crack of the transmission, he could hear the contained excitement in Craig Haskell's voice. "I hate to bother you, Alby. . . ."

"What've you got?"

"A problem. A call came in about a car down in the woods off Fairly Road. I'm down here now. Three bodies."

"Accident? Only one car?"

"Only one car, but I don't think it's an accident. I count five bullet holes and Alby—I haven't even opened the door."

Gale Grayson sat back on her haunches and looked in exasperation at the rat in her daughter's hair.

"It's not a rat," Katie Pru said. "Don't call it a rat."

"It's not a rat with teeth and a tail, but it's a rat, Katie Pru. It's what happens when you don't brush your hair well before you go to bed at night. It looks like you've grown a nest on your head."

"Call it a nest, then," said Katie Pru. "I don't like it when you call it a rat."

Gale sighed. "Rat or nest, I'm going to have to cut it out. If I keep trying to brush it I'll just end up pulling it out hair by hair."

Katie Pru walked to her mother's desk, which sat between the room's two windows, and took a pair of blue-handled safety scissors from the top drawer. "Cut it," she said, handing the scissors to her mother. "But don't call it a rat. And don't let me see it after you've cut it out."

"Deal."

Gale sat cross-legged on the floor and pulled her daughter into her lap. At five, Katie Pru had started insisting on having more say-so in her personal grooming. But say-so hadn't yet translated into action, and throughout the day Gale had caught glimpses of the clumped *rat* flopping on the side of her child's head. She had left it alone as long as possible—what parent relished the idea of attacking problem hair in a preschooler?—but downstairs she could hear the rumble of male voices, punctuated by Ella's higher-pitched warble. Wincing, she took a firm grip of the massive tangle and cut.

"Done," she announced, palming the hair. "Go use your brush one more time and then we'll be ready to go down."

As Katie Pru solemnly stared in the mirror and whacked at her head, Gale eased herself up onto the double bed. She could hear the distant exchanges from downstairs, muffled by the thick beams and 135-year-old planks of floor and ceiling. The room next door, where Halford was staying, was empty, but beyond that she could hear a soft lyrical voice. Nadianna Jesup was singing her baby to sleep. Not for the first time, Gale marveled at their little household. Eighteen months ago, Ella had inhabited this rambling old structure alone. Then Gale and Katie Pru had moved back from England and filled two bedrooms. And four months ago, new to motherhood and ill at ease in her father's house, Nadianna had nervously approached Gale with a proposition: She'd change her part-time position as Katie Pru's babysitter into full time if she and her baby could live rent-free in one of the spare bedrooms. Initially Ella balked. She had always been suspicious of Nadianna, the "little Pentecostal mill girl," as she derisively called her. But even Ella's critical eye could see how much Nadianna cared about Katie Pru. In the end, an accord was reached. Ella and Gale would provide Nadianna with insurance, Social Security, room and board, and a generous stipend in exchange for six hours a day in child care.

The result was this family of three women and two children. The arrangement hadn't been without tension. But the book Gale and Nadianna had produced from their research trip to England—*Mill Strands: The Story of Two Villages*—had been a regional success. Nadianna's photos had been stunning, and even by Gale's tough critique of her own work, the accompanying text had been balanced and evocative. The Calwyn County Council for the Arts had held a well-attended launch party at the restored arts center, and the Atlanta press and arts community had treated the book with a genteel respect. The first printing, admittedly modest, had sold out in less than a month, and six weeks later, the publisher was making noises about a third printing. Buzz was starting that Nadianna would be nominated for a national photography award, butso far the buzz was just that. Nevertheless, the notoriety was proving good for both women. Careful planning and wise follow-up projects could help both their careers.

And that was the rub. While Gale was ready to rush forward, Nadianna lingered behind, nuzzling her baby, nurturing Katie Pru. But Gale sensed it wasn't the lingering of a new mother infatuated with the children in her life. It was a young woman with her life on hold while she tended to other responsibilities, namely the raising of a fatherless child. Gale had been there. It was a treacherous and hard-formed place to be.

She sighed and rolled onto her stomach, watching Katie Pru lean into the mirror to examine her teeth. The housing arrangement had been beneficial for Gale—with six uninterrupted hours a day, she had been able to make headway on her latest project. But she wasn't sure what the arrangement was doing for Nadianna. And she worried about how the gradual return to a child-centered life was impacting Ella as well.

She rose and made her way to her desk. The papers were stacked in piles—they really were piles, despite their haphazard arrangement. She shuffled through them and found the first page.

I did not marry a terrorist. I married a poet.

It was a weak beginning and she knew it. She also knew that those first sentences would be written and rewritten over the next year, pounded and tweaked until they conveyed precisely what she wanted the reader to feel. The difficulty was at this point she wasn't sure what that was. After eight years, she wasn't yet convinced how *she* felt.

She gently replaced the first page on the top of the stack. She was still amazed that her book proposal had found a publisher. How many people truly wanted to read a memoir about a woman, naive by any standards, who had exhibited the bad judgment to leave her native country and marry a man who ended up a murderer? Who wanted to hear the sad story of her stubborn abandonment of home, her sheltered life abroad, the little clues she overlooked, willfully, until the day her husband committed suicide, knowing he'd leave behind a pregnant wife to deal with his crimes?

She didn't know yet at what point she would end the story—the book proposal stopped at the birth of Katie Pru, that lonely act serving as the final punctuation in her life with Tom Grayson. But as she watched her daughter mug in the mirror, Gale knew that was inaccurate. If the story had a beginning, middle, and end, Katie Pru was part of the long, complex center. She was more than her father's legacy; whatever energy had compelled Tom to act as he did would forever find muscles in his daughter's strong body.

It was a depressing thought. Gale picked up the brush and, coming up behind Katie Pru, made one last attack on the child's head.

"Time to go downstairs, Miss K.P."

"Nadianna and the baby going to be there?"

"I don't think so. Not the baby, anyway. I don't know about Nadianna. Best behavior—deal?"

"Deal."

Together they descended the stairs. As they reached the bottom, the door to the parlor opened, and Alby Truitt walked out, grim-faced.

He stooped and chucked Katie Pru under the chin. "Hello, cutie," he said. "What has my favorite five-year-old been up to?"

"Rats," Katie Pru answered. Gale started to explain, but the look on Truitt's face as he straightened silenced her.

"I'm gonna have to leave, Gale. Will you give my apologies to Ella?"

"Sure." She knew enough not to ask questions. Instead, she walked to the front door and opened it.

"Be careful," she said. "If I thought it would do any good I'd offer to save you a plate."

"I wish I could take you up on it. Tell the chief inspector the extra piece of pie's on me."

2

Statlers Cross crouched in the far southeast corner of Calwyn County, a good thirty-minute drive from the more cosmopolitan and politically savvy county seat of Praterton. In Praterton, the old-money families, proudly bolstered in their antebellum homes, supported a reputable arts center, an innovative living-history museum, several growing industries, and a pricey Christmas house tour that drew people from three states. Statlers Cross was four points east of Jesus on all those accounts, and Alby Truitt knew it well. He had grown up outside of town, the son of a drug dealer and his widow. It had come to no real surprise to anyone that Dwight Truitt had dabbled in drugs—the area around Statlers Cross had been known for its "elements," dating back to the moonshine days and earlier, when Confederate Army deserters hid in its oak and piney backwoods. It might have surprised some that young Alby—awkward, ashamed—had returned from college and gone into law enforcement, but everyone knew this corner of the county bred a rough lot; the fact that one of its sons would decide to use his roughness in the name of the law was a rational and, the voters decided, a comfortable thing.

Although Truitt hadn't been down Fairly Road in fifteen years, it hadn't changed. It started as a wide gravel swath at the west end of Statlers Cross. After a hundred yards it turned to dirt and snaked northward past the town's communal Dumpster, which was visited by the county sanitation department every Tuesday afternoon. From there it dwindled, curling through dense woods and past red earthen banks until it fizzled out into a pinestraw-covered path that led to what used to be the best moonshine still in the county but was now just a hollow in the trees.

It was at the mouth of this path that Truitt came upon what passed for a platoon of official vehicles in Calwyn County—an ambulance, two police cars, and his deputy's navy Saturn, all with their headlights on, creating an eerie pattern of beams and trunks in the dark. He also recognized the battered red Ford Escort belonging to John Bingham, the county coroner. Inside the nearer of the police cars he could see two figures, one in the driver's seat and one in the rear. As he climbed from his truck, his flashlight beam whipped over the side of a sixth car, an aging, dull-finished Chevy Malibu pulled far off the path. The automobile was wedged so tightly between several trees that at first glance, it didn't seem possible for the driver to have gotten out through the doors. It wasn't a car Alby recognized. He glanced at his watch. It had taken him ten minutes to weave through these back roads in the dark; by his estimation, the Alden house was only three miles away as the crow flies. It should have taken the rest of the crew, coming from the county seat of Praterton, at least forty minutes. Evidently he had not been the first person called.

Deeper into the woods to the east, he saw the swaggering sweep of flashlights and the steady glow of stationary lamps. As he headed toward them, one flashlight beam separated from the rest and jostled forward.

"Alby." In the beam's illumination, Haskell's dark-complexioned face seemed skeletal, his jaw working under the skin. "What can I tell you? It's a mess."

"Looks like the personnel are all here. Tell me the story."

Haskell had worked under Truitt for three years; the only African-American in the sheriff's department, he had come to Truitt guarded and careful. Now the two men shared a camaraderie that Truitt highly valued. He respected Haskell more than anyone else on his staff. Haskell's wife Geri joked that the two communicated like a married couple—a nudge here, a look there, and all had been said. Each even knew how the other liked his coffee.

The look here, even in the dark, revealed his colleague was troubled. His jaw continued to work, as if it couldn't quite choose its words.

"Craig," Truitt said quietly, "tell me the story."

"The story. The Praterton P.D. got a call about six P.M. that a car with three persons with injuries had been found in the woods behind the Kirby property. That's all, and the caller hung up."

"This Kirby land?" Truitt mentally constructed an image of the local property lines, a configuration of barbed wire and poles. The Kirby property bordered Ella Alden's place on two sides. These woods occupied a dark little bowl on the edge of both holdings.

"The directions weren't too clear," Haskell continued. "The police and the ambulance spent a good hour trying to locate the place. The call came from the pay phone at the Jiffy Mart up on Highway 441."

Truitt nodded toward the Chevy. "That car belong to your caller?"

"Right. Marcus Siler. He lives in one of the trailers in that park over off 441."

"So what was Siler doing here?"

Haskell shook his head. "I think you should ask him, Alby. I'm getting a damn stone wall."

"He the one in the cruiser?"

"Yep."

"You call Bingham?"

"Yessir. And GBI. The crime scene techs should be here soon."

"Okay. Let's have a look at the car."

He followed Haskell into the woods, passing by the police cruiser with Marcus Siler in the backseat. Alby flicked his flashlight at the window; Siler flinched and drew back, leaving Truitt the impression of a skinny man with dark hair and an insignificant mustache.

"Know anything about Siler?" he asked Haskell.

"Other than his address, not a thing. Don't know his mama's name, if that's what you're asking."

"Yeah, that's about what I was asking. I don't recognize him."

"He *sounds* like he's from around here."

Truitt acknowledged the joke with a grunt. To Haskell's Baltimore ears, all Georgians sounded the same.

The car, illuminated as if for a photo shoot, sat in the center of a shallow dip in the ground. It was hard to understand how it had gotten there—this was well off the path, and a quick sweep with his flashlight indicated to Truitt that the driver had engaged in some hard right-left steering to maneuver through the trees. The car itself didn't appear damaged—no obvious dents or remarkable scratches—although it would soon undergo a strenuous examination by the crime lab. He walked slowly around the vehicle, nodding to the state police officer and two medics standing off to one side. No exterior bullet holes, from what he could see.

At the driver's seat door he stopped to address the bulky man leaning into the car's interior. "Good evening, John. What's the news?"

Bingham pulled his head out. "Evening, Alby. It's a mess."

"So I've heard. What kind of a mess're we talking about?"

The coroner stepped aside, gesturing for Truitt to take his place. Truitt squatted down in front of the open door and peered into the car.

"Jesus God," he said.

The bodies of two men slumped in the front seat. Truitt didn't know who the driver was—the man's face was pulped, only his lower jaw intact. His chest had also taken a hit; his shirt, the ubiquitous brown plaid that Truitt had seen on the back of almost every man in Calwyn County, blossomed red. Next to him the second man sat still restrained in his shoulder harness. A shot seemed to have blasted the pulmonary artery in his neck. Blood covered the seat, the dashboard, the windows. Except for spatter wounds, however, this man's face was untouched. Truitt recognized the blond hair and well-chiseled features of Stuart Keast.

Truitt turned around to Haskell. "So this is Siler's idea of 'injuries'?"

"That's what the dispatcher said he said."

"What kind of childhood did that man have?" Truitt rose and looked over the driver's shoulder into the backseat. Squinting, he leaned farther in and picked out the dark blue shirt of the figure curled up on the car's rear floor.

Shooting Haskell a hard glance, Truitt walked around the open rear door to get a closer look. The figure was male, small, wrapped in a fetal position. Truitt steadied his flashlight beam on the man's hands and amended the observation: He was *tied* in a fetal position. Duct tape encircled his wrists and ankles so that he looked like a child about to leapfrog. One small bullet hole burned a circle into his temple.

"You know the one guy's Stuart Keast," Truitt said.

"I don't know about the other two. You recognize the one in the back, Craig?"

"Nope."

"Neither do I," said Bingham. "But I can tell you he ain't from around here. Asian. Maybe Cambodian or Vietnamese."

"You saying that because of his size or because someone whispered in your ear?"

Bingham took off his eyeglasses and rubbed the condensation from them. "Both, Alby my friend. I found his wallet." With gloved hands, he pulled the wallet from the dead man's trousers and, flipping it open, held it up for Truitt to see. "Nguyen. Address is Chamblee, though. Boy's a fair piece from home. Chamblee's a healthy fifty miles from here."

Truitt grabbed Bingham's wrist to steady it and shone his flashlight on the driver's license. *Tuan Nguyen. Birth Date:*—Truitt did a quick calculation. The man was 26. *Weight: 125.* Truitt glanced back at the figure rolled into a ball small enough to fit on a floorboard. Close enough.

"He got a green card in there?"

"Not on your life. I bet we get this license under good light we'll see it's not legal, either."

Truitt once more caught Haskell's eye. He knew what his deputy was thinking. *Rednecks come in all sizes, shapes, and education levels.* Truitt let go of Bingham's arm and motioned to Haskell.

"Bag that, will you, Craig?" He waited while Haskell pulled on gloves and placed the wallet in a plastic bag. "So what do you make of it, John?"

Bingham blinked behind his glasses. "You got yourself three corpses, Alby. All suffered gunshot wounds. We'll send them down to the GBI crime lab, but you can bet your bottom dollar they didn't die sniffing glue."

"Any sign of a weapon?"

"No. But there're plenty of shells around for your crime scene techs."

"Any thoughts about how they're positioned?"

The coroner stretched and shook his head. "I dunno. You've got two gentlemen in the front seat as comfy as if they were commuting to work. Then you have a third guy—possibly an illegal alien—"

Haskell interrupted: "You don't know that, John."

"All right, I don't know that. But I know the address on his driver's license is in a part of Atlanta known for its immigrant population. You've heard of 'Chambodia,' haven't you, Craig?"

"I've heard of it. I try to ignore it."

"Fellas—"

"Like I was saying, these two guys could be sitting in traffic, while Mr. Nugent—"

"Nu-wen . . ." Haskell said tersely.

"—is tied up like a hog in the back."

"Craig," Alby said, "I'm going to want to talk with Mr. Siler in about five minutes. Could you go see one last time if you can tumble that stone wall before I get over there?"

There was no subtlety in the direction, and Haskell didn't pretend there was. "Certainly, Sheriff. I'll be waiting for you in the cruiser."

Truitt waited until his sergeant was out of earshot before turning back to the coroner. "John, I'm your colleague, not your boss. But I really wish you would be more aware of how you phrase things."

"Sorry, Alby. Craig's a good man. But I'm a fifty-five-year-old country boy and about as tolerant as they come. I didn't mean to offend him. I'm just setting a plausible scene up for you as I see it."

Truitt accepted the apology for what it was—no apology at all. He turned back to the bodies. "Two different guns used here."

"Does seem to be. I'm not a ballistics expert, but I've done my share of hunting." Bingham pointed to the driver's pulped face. "That's got shotgun wound written all over it. Tuan's head would be all over the backseat if someone had used the same weapon on him. That bullet hole in his head is a dainty little thing."

Truitt studied the small man huddled on the floor. "Remember that famous photo from the Vietnam war, the one of the prisoner getting shot in the head?"

"Reminds you of it, doesn't it? That's because an execution is an execution."

"And Mr. Keast and his companion here just happened to be driving through the woods and became the victims of a wayward executioner?"

"That's what I like about being coroner, Alby. I get to observe the crime scene, pontificate, fill out the paperwork, and tell the voters I've done my job. You get to do all the hard work."

"I want to put that on my posters come election day. 'John Bingham says Sheriff Truitt does all the hard work.' "

"It's yours to use, my friend."

Truitt slapped the coroner on the back. "All right, buddy. Finish up. The GBI techs should be here soon. I'm gonna go talk to our witness."

Marcus Siler's face looked stretched and gray as Truitt opened the cruiser door and smiled in at him.

"I'm Sheriff Truitt, Mr. Siler. Thank you for waiting for me. I really appreciate that you're helping us like this."

Siler frowned. "When can I go?"

Truitt looked surprised. "You can go now, Mr. Siler. I thought you were waiting for me so you could help me figure this out." He nodded in the direction of the crime scene, out of sight of the cruiser except for the lights. "I understand you found the car."

Another shrug. A hesitation. Then a nod.

"I can't imagine coming upon that. Must have been a shock to you."

Another nod. This time, however, Siler met Truitt's eyes.

"Listen, are you comfortable in there? It's a bit chilly out here. Would you mind if I got into the car with you and you could tell me what happened?"

Siler shot a glance at Haskell, who was sitting in the front seat.

"Guess I've got to make a phone call," Haskell said as he hauled himself from the car. "Here, Sheriff. Take my seat. It's nice and toasty."

Truitt made a show of settling in. "Now, Mr. Siler," he began, "take your time. I need to know exactly how you came upon that car. I need you to tell me why you were here, but also I want you to take me into the woods with you. I need you to be my eyes for now. I want you to tell me what you saw so that I can see it. Do you think you can do that for me?"

Siler shrugged. "I guess."

"That's great. Now, tell me, why did you decide to come here today?"

"I was looking for a good hunting spot . . ."

"So you've been here before?"

"Nossir. That's why I was down here. The Kirbys said sometimes I could come down here and hunt."

Truitt looked through the window into the dark. "I bet there's lots of good hunting around here. Nice and isolated."

"That's what Joe Kirby says. Lots of squirrels—and deer."

"Do you always check out a site before you hunt it?"

"Yessir. I like to walk a place over."

"I see. So about what time did you come down here?"

"About four o'clock."

"Come by yourself?"

"Sure. I don't like to hunt by myself, but I don't mind checking a place out by myself."

"Who were you planning to hunt with?"

Truitt thought he detected another hesitation. "My brother Ross."

"Ross Siler, is it? Okay." Truitt made a point of writing down the name. "So you came around four. Which route did you take?"

"You mean from my place?"

"Is that where you started from? Or did you come from work?"

"I don't have any work. I been out since the poultry plant laid me off last spring."

"Ah. Then what route did you take from your home? Start me from 441."

If Siler picked up on the fact that Truitt already knew where he lived, he gave no indication. "I come down 441 and turned onto Nora Road—"

"That would be the road that runs through the Alden land?"

"Yessir. Then I just come down all those little roads till I got here."

"Pass any cars?"

"Not once I left 441."

"Notice anyone turning onto 441 from Nora Road?"

"Nossir."

"This the way the Kirbys told you to come?"

Siler wrinkled his brow. "Pardon?"

"Joe Kirby told you about the woods, right? I was just wondering if he told you to come this route, or if he suggested a road that cut through his property. I'm sure there must be one."

"Nossir. He never mentioned any other roads."

"Okay. So you're driving down the trail through the woods. What did you see?"

"I pulled over and parked the car and got out to walk around."

"Mighty tight space you parked in."

"I wanted to get off the trail."

"Have any problem getting out of your car?"

"Nossir."

"Trees weren't in your way?"

"I managed."

"Okay. So you were walking around . . ."

"I noticed that dip in the ground. That's the kind of thing I was looking for—didn't want to be breaking my leg out here in the dark one morning . . ."

"Absolutely."

"So I walked over to the dip, and there was the car."

"You walked down to it?"

"Sure. It wasn't right for a car to be there."

"And what did you see?"

Here the skin on Siler's face seemed to sag, as if his muscles had abruptly let go. "Just what you seen."

"And what was that?"

"Them men. All bloody."

"How many men?"

"Three."

"Where were they in the car when you saw them?"

"Two in the front. One in the back."

"The one in the back on the seat?"

"Nossir. On the floor."

"Did you touch the car? Open a door?"

"Nossir."

"You didn't open one of the doors to see if the men were alive?"

"Nossir. I knew they were dead."

"You told the dispatcher there was a car with injuries. We thought it was an automobile accident."

Siler began to shake. "You mean it wasn't?"

"Hard to imagine how. Can't figure out how a car

could have gotten out here and in that hollow in a way that would cause injuries like that."

"I thought they got banged up real bad when they fell into the dip."

"Don't think so. Did you notice anything about the man in the back?"

"Just that he wasn't moving."

"You didn't notice anything that would indicate how he died?"

"Nossir."

"Did you open a door to get a look at him?"

"Nossir."

"Where were you standing when you saw him?"

"I was looking in the window."

"Rear or front?"

"Driver's window."

"You looked in the driver's window and saw the man on the floor of the backseat?"

"Yessir."

"Then what did you do?"

"I ran back and called the police."

"Ran? Why didn't you use your car?"

"I don't know. Scared, I guess."

"Scared of what?"

"I don't know. Scary to come across something like that."

"I can imagine, Mr. Siler. It would have scared me, too."

Truitt studied the man, the way his eyes widened as he talked, the way his hands kneaded his jeans at the thigh. Too many inconsistencies in this boy's story, he decided.

"Just one more thing, Mr. Siler. You've been very open about answering my questions. Why wouldn't you answer any questions for my deputy?"

Siler looked at him, the thin mustache drooping further as his jaw worked.

"You know why," he said at last.
"No, sir, I don't."
"Because I don't know him, that's all."
"And you reckon you know me?"
"Yessir, I reckon I do."

3

Tuesday

The Monday Morning Militant Moms—militant about
schools, zoning, and all things additive—met every Tuesday at the very noncombatively named Rose Cross Tearoom, where yards of cabbage roses covered the tables
and lace curtains fluttered in the air-conditioning like
surrender flags. It wasn't exactly a comfortable place—
one had to set one's rear end a little too daintily on the
chintz chairs—but then comfort, along with Formica and
pork rinds, could be had for lower costs at the barbecue pit outside of town. At the Rose Cross Tearoom one
got elegance and the edgy camaraderie that only occurs
among soldiers far from home. And the Militant Moms
were acutely aware that they were soldiers far from home.

Sally Robertson dipped her pink-shellacked fingernail in her iced tea, crossed her legs, and shot out her
words.

"Bobby Sherman," she said.

Donna Crow rolled her eyes. "Oh, come on now.
That shows no imagination at all. What kind of child
were you?"

"A *Tiger Beat* child. I had a huge crush on Bobby
Sherman. So, what, Donna—you going to tell us you
had a crush on the Pope? Who did you fantasize about
in high school?"

"It certainly wasn't one of those 'girly-men' the rest of you drooled over. Okay. I don't mind telling you. I had a crush on Dean Martin."

The tearoom was silent for three full seconds before the Militant Moms, numbering three, burst into laughter. Donna shrugged as she broke open a biscuit and jabbed a piece into her mouth. "What can I say? I had father issues."

"More like," retorted Honey Johnson, "you had *grandfather* issues."

"You're right. My grandfather was a cold and distant man. Never there for me."

"Died before you were born?"

"Absolutely. Sally, we're out of lemon curd."

"Damn, Sally," Honey echoed. "What kind of gin-joint you running here?"

Smiling, Sally took the empty jar from Donna without a word and sauntered into the kitchen. Behind her, the MMMM's reverted to murmurs. *Dean Martin wasn't so bad. Sure, if you could get past the lurch. And the hair. And the . . . well, middle-aged creepiness. Ladies, I hate to inform you, but middle age . . .* The kitchen door swung closed behind her. When Sally had opened the tearoom six months ago, it had been on the heels of the first wave of residents moving into Sag Harbor Estates. Like lost souls to a lighthouse, they had found her, parking their shiny SUV's and Volvos in front of the cracked walkway of the Main Street stores. Sally had often wondered what would have happened if she had opened earlier; if all the headaches and mistakes inherent in renovating the town's old photo studio into a café had evaded her and she had started her business on time, a full two months before the first moving van pulled into the new subdivision. More than likely she'd be out of business now, the cabbage rose tablecloths cut into dust rags in her house. As it was, the Rose Cross Tearoom was a modest hit. Brunch to lunch six days a week, dinners on Friday. And friends. The subdivision inmates (their word, not hers) turned out to be upscale, upbeat, and up-to-date. After two years of living in Statlers Cross and pretending she had a life, Sally Robertson had finally found friends.

She scooped up a jar of lemon curd from the pantry before noticing the small figure dressed in a black cotton shirt and white apron hunched over the stove.

"Everything going okay, Le?"

The figure didn't turn around.

"Everything is okay, Mrs. Robertson."

"Nothing much ever happens on Tuesday. A quiet day."

"Yes. Tuesdays are quiet."

"I'm going to get back to the customers."

"Good, okay."

Sometimes their conversations were longer, but the sentences never were. Sally was glad she had found Le—the young Vietnamese woman was hardworking, and she had picked up the recipes and Southern/English cooking style quickly—but she was equally glad Le kept to herself. Sally had been a teacher before moving to Statlers Cross, and while she occasionally missed the intimacy of women working together, she found herself relishing the division between boss and worker. The principal at her last school had been the mothering type, and Sally, having neither father nor grandfather issues, had responded. Late-night chats, advice on clothing, even a couple of antiquing trips together. Not very professional, and when Sally made a mistake and taped a child's hands together to keep him from touching the girl seated next to him, the disciplinary action had been both humiliating and devastating. Sally had learned not to mix business with friendship. So she was glad Le rarely spoke. She was glad she rarely even turned around.

Back in the dining room, the women had relaxed into their chairs; the schoolgirl chat had taken on a more mature languor.

"You know there're two of them now, don't you? Gale Grayson has one staying with her."

Sally set the lemon curd on the table. "Gale's got what staying with her?"

"An Englishman," Sue Matthewson replied. "Donna was just saying that in addition to having a crush on, ahem, Dean Martin, she was infatuated with Alec Guinness."

"It was his accent, lovey."

"Right. So we were just saying that now we have two Englishmen in Statlers Cross—the man who's renting that house on the edge of town, and Gale Grayson's friend. Have you seen him? Hunky."

"You know Gale used to live in England," Sally said.

Donna popped open the jar lid. "I knew she sometimes did work there."

"She was married to an Englishman. Katie Pru was born there."

"I had no idea. I always figured her daughter was born out of wedlock."

"Donna . . ."

"It seems to be the theme over there."

The four women looked at each other. "Donna . . ." Honey repeated.

"I'm not passing judgment." Donna stuck her finger into the lemon curd. "I'm just saying . . . you know . . . you leave the city . . ."

"No place is uncomplicated." Sally picked up the lid from the table. She'd have to take the jar home, offer it to Mal, see if it wasn't too prissy for him to eat. Chances are it would be. "The Aldens are wholesome enough. Nadianna and her baby live there because her family moved out of town. She didn't have a place to live. Besides, she helps look after Katie Pru."

"You have to admire the Aldens for inviting her in," Honey remarked. "I couldn't have a woman and baby living in *my* house."

"So what does that make—five of them?" Donna ran her finger along the jar's rim and stuck a gob of curd into her mouth. "In the metro area, there are ordinances against too many unrelated people living under one roof."

"This isn't the metro area," Sue said. "So I guess moving out to the country is a mixed bag. You get cows, but you get other stuff, too."

"Besides," said Sally. "Ordinances like that are to prevent overcrowding and illegal renters. The Alden place is huge. And Nadianna is not a boarder—she's practically family."

"Maybe they're gay." Donna raised her eyebrows. "Maybe old Ella Alden was one of the first liberated lesbian women in Statlers Cross. Now, that would be something to respect."

The MMMM's fell out laughing. The surrender flags fluttered in the windows. Sally stood unsmiling. Despite their newly graying hair, she thought, her friends were young soldiers. The bell on the tearoom door tinkled, and as she turned to greet her new customers, the Monday Morning Militant Moms lapsed into chatter about David Cassidy.

The two gentlemen at the door weren't exactly regulars—no men were exactly regulars—but Sally nonetheless knew them. They stood by the cash register, the younger in a brown deputy's uniform, the older in a dark blue suit. The suit was typical for Alby Truitt—

Sally had gathered from gossip that although he was local, Truitt worked hard to foster a careful mix of shrewd good ol' boy and well-schooled sophisticate. But this usually meant that the tie was kept loose, the slouch practiced. Today, the tie was knotted precisely at Truitt's neck, and he stood erect. Craig Haskell held his hat in front of him with both hands. The sheriff and his deputy, Sally decided, had not come for tea.

"Good morning, Alby. You look like you mean business."

"Morning, Sally." He didn't toss a joke back at her, and Sally felt her stomach clench. "Do you have an office? I need to talk with you a second."

Her mind swiftly went through the list, the way it did when she heard of a car accident on a familiar highway or, God forbid, a plane going down. Mal wasn't flying today—he had a layover in Tokyo. Her mother? Her sister? She could handle it if anything happened to them. Not callousness. She just knew she could handle it.

Truitt must have read the panic in her face because he laid his hand on her arm. "No, Sally. It's nothing like that. I need to talk with you, that's all. Your office?"

With the MMMM's watching, she directed the two lawmen through the dining room and past the Employees Only door that led to the kitchen. Directly to the left was her office, a cubicle no larger than six feet square, barely big enough to hold her desk and one extra chair. Truitt and Haskell moved to one side as she closed the door behind them.

"What's wrong?" she asked.

"Does Le Nguyen work for you?"

Sally felt a wave of relief, followed by guilt. She put on a voice of concern.

"Yes, she works here. Is she in trouble? She's a wonderful employee, Alby. If she needs someone to vouch . . ." Another thought struck her, and she opened her mouth in astonishment. "I assure you I checked her papers, Alby. I wouldn't employ someone illegally—"

"It's not that. I need to talk with her." He paused and although his voice softened, his face remained stern. "Listen, Sally. What I've got to ask her isn't going to be easy on her. She may need some support. Do you know her family well?"

"There's just her mother and her little girl. They live in the blue house."

"Do you know if there is anyone else Ms. Nguyen's close to? Any cousins? Or maybe friends?"

Sally shook her head. "I don't know much about her personal life, Alby. She's a good worker, and she's never missed a day of work, not even for a sick child. She's very responsible. That's all I know."

"Okay. Then I'm going to ask a favor of you, Sally, as her employer. I need Ms. Nguyen to come down to the hospital morgue and look at a body. I believe it may be a relative of hers. She's going to need someone with her. Can you come?"

Sally sank against her desk. "A body? What's happened?"

"We have a body that needs to be identified. I'm going to ask Ms. Nguyen to come with us. I'd like you to accompany her. Sally? Do you understand what I'm saying?"

She nodded. She understood. The wife of an airline pilot, she had an image bank that contained nightmares of identifying bodies. Burnt bodies, bits of bodies, bodies still strapped into their plane's upholstered seats—she had envisioned every imaginative scenario in her head. It was a game she played to build up her strength. She could do this. If Le needed her to come, this was something she could do.

"Le's in the kitchen," she said softly. "Should I get her?"

Haskell already had his hand on the doorknob. "I'll do it, Mrs. Robertson. Please wait here."

Le Nguyen still wore her white apron, smeared with a red concoction—raspberry filling?—and spotted here and there with crusty splotches. Flour smudged her dark hair at the temple. With her hair pulled back in a bun, her face looked even more delicate than usual. She kept her eyes down, but Sally could tell by her hunched shoulders that she was scared. Sally's own eyes watered as she fought the urge to throw her arms around her employee and comfort her.

"Miss Nguyen. Would you care to sit down?" Truitt motioned to the chair.

She did so, but only on the edge, her small feet balancing on her tiptoes. She clasped her hands in her lap.

Truitt knelt beside her, and Sally was taken aback by the amount of gentleness in the sheriff's face.

"Le," he said quietly. "I need to ask you something. Do you know a young man by the name of Tuan Nguyen?"

Le lifted her head, her eyes widening. Her nod was barely perceptible.

Truitt fished into his coat pocket and pulled out a plastic bag that held what looked to Sally to be a driver's license. "Is this him?"

Le's hands trembled as she took the license from him. Tears filled her eyes.

"My brother," she whispered. "Is he okay?"

Truitt rested both his hands on Le's. "We found this driver's license on a man when we were called to investigate an automobile accident. The man is dead,

Le. I need you to come with me and tell me if he really is your brother."

The tears spilled down her cheeks. She looked at Truitt, panic filling her face.

Truitt glanced up at Sally. She came around the desk and crouched on the floor next to them.

"It's okay, Le," she said. "I'll go with you. We'll go together. I'll be with you."

It was the mantra she had imagined she wanted to hear if airline officials ever came to her with the news of Mal's death. Of course, she also knew that, unlike the military notifying a family of a soldier's death, airline officials would never get the chance to notify her. The news media would beat them to it. So this was the mantra she would say to herself, over and over, until she could reach the phone and call someone for help. It was a damn pity, she realized now as she fought back tears, that her friends here in Statlers Cross would really offer her little more comfort than she could offer Le now.

Le didn't move. Truitt continued to clasp her hands, the driver's license sticking up between her fingers.

"Le, did you understand what I said?" Truitt asked, his voice still soft. "Is there someone you would like me to call? Is there someone else who can do this for us?"

The tears were running into Le's mouth. Tenderly, Sally reached up and wiped the flour from her hair.

Finally, Le shook her head. "No," she said. "There is no one. I will go."

"Okay. Sally here is going to close down the shop and come with us."

"No!"

As sudden as the panic had been, the fury was more immediate. Sally stood back, confused at the abrupt hardness in the small woman's eyes.

"No," Le repeated. "I don't want her to go with me. I will go alone."

She stood and carefully lifted the apron over her head. She handed it to Sally.

"No need to close the restaurant. You do what I do for a change."

Writing is not linear. It doesn't move readily from A to B to C. I'm not sure it can be divided into stages at all—how neat it sounds to say that writers incubate their thoughts, write their thoughts, edit their thoughts. In reality, writing is constantly doubling back, repeating, surging forward only to retreat. This is the nature of memories, too. Memories don't march; they dance. The job of reconstructing is to pick out and follow the steps. They are not always obvious, which is why memory is such a treacherous terrain.

— Introduction, pg. ii
A Missing Life: The Memoirs of a Grass Widow
by GALE GRAYSON

4

Daniel Halford set a plate of cheese sandwiches on the table and looked through the porch screen at the little girl squatting in the backyard. Her head was bent over so that hanks of dark hair fell forward, and he thought for a moment that she was about to topple. But she shifted her position, steadied herself, and, walking crab-fashion, moved three feet to the right.

"Katie Pru," Halford called. "What are you up to?"

She didn't lift her head. "Looking for owls," she yelled.

It didn't seem the most likely position for "looking for owls," but Halford knew Katie Pru well enough not to question. If she thought there were owls in the dirt, there were no doubt owls in the dirt.

"Why don't you take a break? I've got some lovely cheese sandwiches for you."

The head popped up.

"With pickles?"

"You bet."

"Oh, all right."

She sprang up, and with one last glance at the ground, darted toward the house. He was still struck by the changes in her. He knew children changed rapidly at this age—their legs lengthened, their sinews grew prominent. They moved from plump bundles that ran into things and needed constant attention to leggy hard bodies anxious to control their world. But it seemed to him that Katie Pru had made the transition inordinately fast. Then again, perhaps it was his own reluctance to see this small child vanish so permanently. There were no children in his life; his sister had sworn off motherhood and his own marriage had ended, thankfully, before a conception could take place. At thirty-nine, he sometimes wondered about his own biological clock, if he truly wanted to be childless, if the advantages of a life free of the ultimate responsibility offset the nagging thoughts that he was missing . . . something.

She hiked up the steps and slid past him. "Find any owls?" he asked.

She dug into her pocket and held up a dirty clod. "Just one. See?"

In her palm lay half a walnut shell. Halford flipped it over to reveal its inside face; staring up at him were two sad eyes and a pointed beak, slightly turned down at the ends, as if in sorrow. It was, without question, the head of an owl.

"I've never found an owl in such a way, Katie Pru. My hat is off to you."

She closed her hand and pocketed the shell. "That's because you didn't know to look."

"That's the truth. Thank you for showing me."

"It's not a good spot to find owls."

"No?"

"No. It's better further out, where those trees are."

He looked to where she pointed. "Are those walnut trees?"

Katie Pru nodded. "That's where the most owls live. I hear them at night. But Mama won't let me go there alone."

"It's awfully far."

"Not that far. We could walk there."

Halford grinned. "Miss Katie Pru, would you like to take me to where the owls live? Why don't we go after lunch? Will the owls still be there after lunch?"

"They might be. We could see."

"It's a plan, then."

The door that led to the kitchen opened and closed, and Halford looked up to see Gale carrying a tray of glasses and a crystal pitcher.

"What's a plan?" she asked.

"Katie Pru and I are going owl hunting."

"Hmm. Right now, I suggest Katie Pru goes inside and washes her hands."

Katie Pru looked down at her hands. "That's the problem with owls. They do get your hands dirty."

Gale set the tray on the table and plopped down in the rocking chair beside Halford.

"You know," she said, as Katie Pru disappeared inside the house, "Ella thinks Katie Pru's not disciplined enough. She says I let her run wild. But that imagination of hers is one of the things I find most fascinating about her. I can't fathom reining it in."

"You keep a tight rein on her physically. She let me know that she couldn't go out to 'where the most owls live' by herself. I'd say you've done a good job enforcing her physical boundaries. And as far as her imagination goes—well, I'd say with children like Katie Pru you just sit back and gawk."

"I wish you'd tell Ella that. It gets so wearing sometimes."

Gale lifted the pitcher and let tea and ice gurgle into a glass. Halford took the drink and settled back in his chair. "This may be prying, and if you don't want to answer, tell me so, but do you really still need to live here anymore?"

Gale slid a plate in front of her and picked a sandwich from the stack. She tore the crusts off and laid them in a bundle on the placemat, frowning. "Do I really still need to live here? I did at first. When I came back from England I had almost nothing. But now, you're right. I have royalties coming in from the mill book—and the advance on my memoirs was healthy. Creative nonfiction is hot. Creative nonfiction by widows must be even hotter. I've had several offers to teach, which I might do eventually. So, no, financially speaking, I don't need to stay. But it's not just the finances . . ."

She picked up a crust and nibbled it, staring out the screen toward where the owls lived. Halford doubted she saw the walnut trees. He felt the old tug, the one he'd felt five years earlier as he held this young widow's hand in his own while she struggled to comprehend that she was a young widow. The ensuing years had been melancholy ones for him. He knew that Gale's reasons for staying in Statlers Cross, for putting up with Ella's carping and the dry-dirt limits of such a small place, had nothing to do anymore with money. It had to do with family. With Nadianna and the baby, Ella and Katie Pru, Gale had built her family. And it didn't revolve around a male agenda of politics or business. It was both a haven and a coven.

"You fit here," he said.

She laughed. "I believe, sir, that I heard that line in a movie once. Something about the red earth of Tara."

"No, I'm serious. Something about that cold little cottage of yours in Hampshire—you never belonged. But here . . ."

"Yes, here, where my delicate white skin so beautifully shines and my bare feet are calloused in all the right places." She crumbled the end of the crust. "I don't fit here, either, Daniel."

"That's what you keep telling me, Gale. But now that I'm here, I don't think I agree with you."

"Ah, well."

He recognized it as his own *ah, well,* soft and ironic. She pressed her finger into the crumbs and absentmindedly brought them to her mouth. He still found her beautiful. There was no doubt she was her daughter's mother—the dark eyes, the round face finely narrowed at the chin, the mouth that, when she laughed, lifted in a quirky way at the corner. Not a perfect face, but he sometimes wondered if the idiosyncrasies were what gripped him. His ex-wife had been gone for less than a week before her face broke up into fragments he couldn't recombine into a memory. Gale's face had stayed with him, intricate, whole, all these years.

If her yearning for him was as strong, he had no way of knowing. He suspected not. Their communication over the past two years, when she left England for the first time, had been sporadic—first some drawings from Katie Pru, then a couple of phone calls. The last six months had seen a change, however. They had started telephoning one another once a week, exchanging E-mail more often. And then, out of the blue, the invitation. The next time he had some time off, would he like to come visit them in Statlers Cross? His work at New Scotland Yard had become less compelling. In order to broaden his expertise, and with an eye toward promotion to superintendent, his superiors had loaned him to the Dirty Squad, the pornography task force. And while, yes, he had learned quite a bit, his job had become less of a mission than a requirement. He went to work because it was expected of him. He was getting damn weary.

So a holiday had been in order. He had no idea what would be waiting for him when he returned. And at this point, he couldn't say he cared.

"Ah, well," he repeated to her. "Not a good fit. At least this gives us one more thing in common."

She brought her knees up to her chin, the rocking chair listing forward slightly. Her eyes held his.

"You've never told me what you thought about it— about my making money off Tom's death."

He shrugged and took a sip of tea. "I don't see it as you making money off Tom's death. I see it as you structuring the memories of your life. You're a writer— if someone wants to pay you to do that, then I think it's great." He smiled. "Just make me brilliant and intimi-datingly handsome in them."

To his amusement, she blushed. "Just the facts, ma'am," she said. "I'm sorry to say you don't come into it much. Not until the very end, when I could sense everything was unraveling but I couldn't tell why or even in what way. It was such an . . . ambiguous time. Then you appeared, the detective on the case, to tie up all the threads and explain it all to me." She stuck her hands into her hair and shook her head in exaspera-tion. When she looked up again, her eyes were moist. "God, I was so lost. You were a lifeline those first weeks after Tom killed himself. You scared the hell out of me— everything scared the hell out of me—but you *steadied* me. Even when I knew I was being investigated, I was positive that you were fair. Maybe I just needed you to be fair, and it turned out I was lucky. Had another detec-tive been assigned to the case, I might have been treated like crap."

"You wouldn't have been treated badly by anyone, I don't believe. But I did come out of that whole case feeling I had let you down."

"I know. But you didn't. Tom did."

"And that's what your book is about."

"That's what my book's about. . . . When I started this, I thought it would be a good way to sort things out, to understand the whole mess by putting it down in words and giving it a structure. But what I found out is that English is a damned inadequate language. Some-times I wish I was a painter and could just paint my memories. It's odd, but having Ron move next door has actually been a help. He seems like such a fussy old maid of a guy, but he listens well, and he has good suggestions. So much of what I'm doing is reconstructing Tom's words—his language, his poems, all the things he said to me. It's been nice to have Ron come over some nights and we just sit out here and talk about the English language, about what this word means, about the differences between how I might have interpreted a word as opposed to how Tom, as an Englishman, might have meant it. It's odd how life gives you what you need. Besides, I have to admit part of me's enjoyed having an English accent to listen to again."

"Well." Halford leaned forward to cup her knee in his palm. "Allow me to do the English honors for at least a few days. I'll do my best to avoid the fussy old maid label."

She grinned and rested her hand on his but removed it when the door opened, and Nadianna walked onto the porch, the baby straddled on her left hip. Tight in her grip was Katie Pru's wildly waving green hand. Halford glanced twice at the child's hand. Yes, definitely green.

"Mama told me to wash my hands," Katie Pru wailed.

"I don't think she told you to wash them in food coloring." Nadianna's voice was exasperated.

"I need them to look like grass. I want the owls to think I'm part of the grass."

As the baby took up Katie Pru's cry, Nadianna shot Gale a frustrated look. Rising, Gale grabbed Katie Pru's fingers, holding them aloft as a couple of green droplets hit the floorboards. "You, ma'am, are in trouble. Let's go out in the yard and hose those hands off."

"You don't want to see the bathroom," Nadianna warned.

"Great." Pushing the screen door open, Gale guided Katie Pru into the yard and out of sight around the side of the house.

Nadianna shifted the baby to her chest and hugged him. She looked at Halford over the squalling head.

"What do *you* think, Daniel? Gale doesn't believe in spanking. I'm going to have to come up with my own plan soon."

Halford smiled and motioned her into a chair. "I am a childless old fart, Nadianna, and I haven't a clue."

The baby was yelling so energetically, the back of his head had turned red. Nadianna began rocking him.

"Come on, now, Michael," she cooed. "There ain't no reason for this. Come on, now."

Odd, he had been in the house for three days and this was the first time he had heard her call the baby by his name. He had heard Gale talk to him by name, and even Katie Pru, but not Nadianna, and once he thought about it, not Ella either. Halford struggled briefly to find a significance in that, but he didn't have a point of reference. Babies were a rare occurrence for him. He'd have to remember to ask Gale.

Beyond the squall, he heard the faint sound of a car on the gravel drive. Nadianna lumbered to her feet.

"Ella's back from the store," she told him. "I better get this one settled down and quiet."

Mother and child disappeared into the house. The howls diminished to a faint wail. Halford took half a cheese sandwich, bit into it and recoiled. Mayonnaise.

As soon as Gale and Katie Pru rounded the corner of the house with Ella, he knew something was wrong. The older woman looked tired; Gale's face was grim.

He held the screen door open for them. "Ella? Is something wrong?"

She let the grocery bag she carried drop on the table. "I just saw John Bingham hanging around Cooper Langley's store."

Halford looked questioningly at Gale. "The county coroner and the local store owner," she translated. "Miss

K.P., you run inside and see if you can help Nadianna with Michael. I can still hear him crying."

Once Katie Pru was safely inside, Ella sat in a chair, her spine rigid. Her clasped hands worried each other on the tabletop.

"Okay, tell us, Ella," Gale said. "Did you talk to John Bingham? What did he say that upset you?"

Ella did something that seemed out of character even to Halford's unfamiliar eye—she slumped against the back of her chair. "Stuart Keast's dead. I never thought much of the Keasts, so I'll say a prayer, but it doesn't bother me much. But Darrell Murphy's dead, too. And that I mind a great deal."

5

It took no more than an hour from the time Ella left Langley Drugs for the goodwill of Statlers Cross to descend upon the Murphys. As Gale drove her grandmother up the driveway to the neat brick ranch where the mayor and his family had lived for three decades, she counted eight cars pulled onto the lawn. Living on Highway 441 with all its whizzing traffic had its disadvantages, Gale thought as she took a frozen casserole from Ella and helped her from the car. The Murphys' professionally manicured yard would pay the price for this sudden display of support.

It was a caustic thought, and Gale felt a twinge of guilt as she followed Ella to the front door. She had nothing against the Murphys, really. In fact, she didn't know much about them except that Darrell was her age and that, during her summer visits to Statlers Cross as a child, she had gotten the impression that his parents didn't like her. It had been a vague feeling, just a fleeting discomfort, that she experienced at church when the youth group went out together or the few times the Murphys had come over for dinner at the Alden house. Ella's maiden sister Nora had lived here then, with Ella and Gale coming from the plush greenery of Atlanta to spend the hot Georgia summers in a place that had few trees. The two sisters had pushed Gale into what social activities they could, and those activities invariably included Darrell, the older son of one of the town's most influential families. Gale always suspected that Mr. and Mrs. Murphy's discomfort had nothing to do with her in the particular as much as in the general. The Murphys were a company family of the highest order—in addition to serving in the unglamorous job of mayor of Statlers Cross, Tim Murphy was an executive of the county's largest employer, a plastics manufacturing firm. The Aldens, on the other hand, were commonly perceived as old money gone bad or, more charitably, as eccentric. The Murphys' sons were prizes, and Gale, with her dead mother, absent father, and city upbringing, was not a suitable companion for them.

"What do you remember about Darrell?" Ella asked, pausing at the doorway.

Gale shrugged. "Not a whole lot, I'm afraid. I remember he was blond. And skinny. A little goofy. He tried to get the girls' attention by making body noises."

Ella made a scoffing sound deep in her throat. "That's because he was a teenager. But he grew up to be a good man. He cut the grass for Nora for years and minded the house after she died and before I moved in. I used to get barn owls in the attic. Horrible, screeching things. He caught them, took them to the other side of the county, and let them loose, then fixed up the hole so they couldn't get in again. The only payment he asked was spoon bread and muscadine jelly." To Gale's surprise, her lips plumped as she battled back tears. She grabbed the casserole from Gale and knocked on the door. She smiled wanly. "And he wasn't as skinny as you remember when he died."

The woman who opened the door was not someone Gale had ever met. Of this Gale was certain, because having once seen the woman, she knew she would not forget her. Vivid green eyes looked out from a pair of oversize red glasses—"real estate lady" glasses, Ella had derisively called the style—which matched in color the shining gloss on her lips. Powder filled the fine wrinkles on her face, making her look older than she probably was. Silver hair leapt from her head, the tips stiff and pointed like egg whites. Gale self-consciously tucked her own straight hair behind her ears. Whoever this woman was, she certainly wasn't typical for Statlers Cross.

Ella, however, wasn't fazed. "Reebe," she said. "It's so good to see you. I feel like I haven't seen you in years."

The two women pressed cheeks. "Ella. This is so sad. Isn't this so sad? I came as soon as I heard." She turned to Gale and gripped her in a hug. "Shug, it's been so long. I remember when you were a tiny thing."

"Gale, you remember Reebe Vaughter," Ella said. "She's now the society writer for the *Calwyn County Courier*, in addition to being the Statlers Cross city clerk."

Gale remembered Reebe Vaughter, but not like this. The last time she had seen her, several years ago at a town barbecue, Reebe had been a brown chipmunk of a woman with pudgy cheeks and nondescript hair. Now she looked like, well, a spoof of a society writer. Gale nodded mutely as Reebe grabbed her hand; scarlet lacquered nails bit into her flesh.

"Oh, you two are such sweet things to come. We've got such a crowd and the word is only just getting out." Her voice dropped to a whisper. "It's so terrible how it happened."

"What do you mean?" Ella asked. "All John Bingham would say was they were found dead in a car."

"That's only the half of it, Ella. Y'all come in and join everyone. Myra and Tim are upstairs with the pastor— Myra is a mess, I tell you, but I suspect I would be, too, if it were my son. I'll take that casserole to the kitchen. Go on in the living room and I'll join you presently."

Reebe teetered away in high heels, her knee-length

skirt flouncing. Gale glanced at Ella to judge her grandmother's reaction to the exchange, but Ella's face was somber. There would be no humor in this gathering.

They entered a living room that was well appointed, if conventional. A long mahogany-and-velvet sofa faced a picture window, which was in turn sided by two wingback chairs. The last time Gale had been here had been the summer between tenth and eleventh grades, when the Murphys hosted a youth weenie roast on their lawn. Gale and her cousin Sil had slipped into the living room to get away from the mosquitoes and the loutish attention of the boys. Myra Murphy had come upon the two of them whispering on the sofa and shooed them out.

Seated on the sofa now were Sally Robertson and Ilene Parker, an elderly woman who lived by herself near the middle of town. The wingback chairs were occupied by the Methodist minister's wife Joile Watkins and the room's solitary male, Ted Stevens, the Statlers Cross Methodist Church's lay leader.

When Sally saw Gale, she rose and met her in the doorway.

"I'm glad you're here," she said, her voice barely above a whisper. "I feel so out of place. I don't know the Murphys that well. But I felt I should come." She crossed her arms, hunching her body. She looked pale, bright pink dots high on her cheekbones. "I can't believe it, can you? I mean, it's just so awful."

"What happened?" Gale asked. "We were under the impression that it was a traffic accident."

"They were shot. In Darrell's car. A hunter found them in the woods out by the Kirbys' place."

"My God. How awful!"

"I don't know how to react," Sally said. "It's just so stunning. Alby Truitt came by my tearoom this morning and I heard about it. God. I just don't know what to say."

Behind Sally, Ted Stevens stood abruptly. "Here, Ella," he said. "You take my seat. We're all shocked by this."

The look on Ella's face as Stevens gently lowered her into the chair stunned Gale—the jaw slack, the eyes downcast. She knelt beside her grandmother and clasped her hand. Ella's palm was moist.

"Ella? Are you all right?"

Ella shook her hand loose and pressed her fingertips to her forehead. "I'm fine, Gale. That was just something I didn't expect to hear. John Bingham should have had the decency to be more precise in his gossip."

"I'll get you some water," Gale said, concerned.

She had found the kitchen and was turning on the faucet before she noticed Sally had followed her.

"Gale. I need to talk with you. There's more to this."

Gale set the filled glass on the counter and grabbed a paper towel to dry her hands. "More than Darrell Murphy and Stuart Keast found shot to death in their car?"

Sally nodded, her blue eyes wide. "There were three men in that car."

"All shot? Who was the third man?"

"You know Le Nguyen, the woman who works for me?"

"I know of her."

"Alby came to my tearoom to ask Le to try to identify the third body. He thought it might be her brother."

"Did she identify him?"

Here Sally hesitated, her arms crossed protectively. "Alby asked me to go with Le to the morgue, but she didn't want me to go. I can't say I blame her. I mean, Christ, she works for me, but I don't know her that well. You know how it goes. But Alby had the dead man's license. It must have been Le's brother in the car."

"When was this?"

"This morning. About eleven. We were still in the middle of our MMMM's meeting—"

Sally broke off, obviously uncomfortable. Gale nodded impatiently. Everyone in Statlers Cross knew about the clique of exurban women who met weekly at the tearoom to bitch about the blunt rurality of their rural idyll. Was Sally's discomfort due to the fact that she was embarrassed by her subdivision friends? Or was she embarrassed because she had never invited Gale to join? Either way, Gale had no patience for it.

"Have you been over to the Nguyens to see how they are doing?"

Sally's face flushed. "I should've," she said quietly. "But I haven't. I'd like someone to go with me."

Gale studied the other woman, who hastily glanced away. They hadn't known each other long. Sally had moved to Statlers Cross with her husband little more than two years before, hellbent on renovating the old dogtrot house that had been in the Robertson family for generations. In that time, she had succeeded in that project, nursed and buried a long-ailing great-uncle who had resided in the house, and tackled the job of opening the only restaurant in town. From their first meeting Gale had instinctively liked her. There was something infectious in this blond former kindergarten teacher, a kind of optimistic energy that Gale had at times gratefully fed from. But in the past few months she had noticed a change. Sally Robertson was tired. More to the point, she suspected Sally Robertson was depressed.

"Sally," she said gently. "Le is your employee. You two work side by side almost every day. You need to go see her."

"You think I don't know that, Gale? Of course I do. But you should have heard her this morning when I said I'd go with her to the morgue. She was so . . . harsh."

"She was in shock. . . ."

The other woman's face grew more red. "I offered to help and she about spit in my face. The truth is I'm afraid to go see her alone. I don't want her to be hostile toward me again."

"I don't think it matters. You need to go see if she needs help."

"Then you come with me."

Gale picked up the water glass. "I need to see to Ella."

"You're as scared as I am." Gale could feel the tension in Sally's body. "You try to act more liberal than us, more open-minded than us, because you've been 'abroad,' but you're no different. You feel awkward around them, too."

"Them? Listen, Sally, Le isn't 'them.' She's your co-worker. If you don't want to go out of personal feeling, then you need to go out of duty."

"She was so cold," Sally said. "I know it's my duty, but I don't want to face her again by myself. Please come with me."

From the corner of her eye, Gale caught a movement; she turned to see Reebe Vaughter standing in the doorway of what Gale now saw was a screened porch.

"If you want my opinion," Reebe said, "you should go with her."

Gale kept her voice calm. "I'm sorry, Reebe. I really wish you had let us know you were listening."

"You're right. I should have. It was bad manners. But after a certain point, I wasn't real clear on when was a good time to interrupt."

"Any time would have done." Gale turned back to Sally, whose face showed a mixture of confusion and anger. "I'll go with you, Sally," she said. "But let me see to Ella first."

"Thank you, Gale." Sally's voice sounded fatigued. "Really. I can't do this alone."

Baloney, Gale thought as she left the kitchen, glass in hand. Sally Robertson had refurbished a house alone, nursed a dying man alone, started her own business alone. Whatever fear she had in comforting the Nguyens, it didn't have a damn thing to do with solitude.

6

Gale and Nadianna had been out of town on a two-week publicity tour throughout the Southeast when the Nguyens painted their house blue. It had been in the earliest days of the mill book's publication, before the positive reviews, before the buzz started, and they had hobnailed the tour together themselves, contacting bookstores, staying in the cheapest hotels and eating instant oatmeal and Vienna sausage sandwiches made on the side of the road. They had both children with them; the children were cranky and they were all hungry and exhausted by the time they returned to Statlers Cross. They had all spied the house at once, its blue as luminous as . . . Here Gale had faltered as she slowed the car to take in this new addition to the town. There was no describing the color in natural terms. It was like the blue of a stained-glass window. Or a bright blue marble. Or the blue sector of the gaudy tri-colored wheel Ella had used to illuminate her white plastic Christmas tree back in the sixties. It hurt to look at it.

"Oh, my word," Nadianna had said softly. "Do you suppose anyone's still living in it?"

"Why wouldn't they be?" Gale had asked.

"Because if they haven't been run out of town on a rail, just give folks time."

They had learned of the turmoil from Ella, who related it with a toss of her hand.

"I decided long ago that foreigners will be foreigners," she had said. "That's what makes them so delightful."

Now, as she accompanied Sally Robertson, Gale looked up at the house and winced. She thought of her own little cottage in the English village of Fetherbridge, where years ago she had almost defiantly let the hedges overgrow the front garden and vines overtake the walkway. It had been her way of secluding herself, but it had also been an act of assertion. She, the American widow too stubborn to return home to her own kind, hadn't belonged there, and she let her garden be her public notice that she didn't care. Yet, how much more courage was needed for a Vietnamese to settle in the United States than for an American to take root in English soil. What must the Nguyens' bright blue cocoon mean to them?

"I don't know what possessed them," Sally murmured.

"Did you ever ask Le?"

"No. It was none of my business. But I heard all about it at the tearoom, I'll tell you that. You can see the house from the tearoom windows. I got a lot of 'Here we finally have a nice place for people to come and eat and just see what they have to look out on.' Odd, really. As if people thought the tearoom could turn Statlers Cross around and this house would prevent it."

"Chamber of Commerce hocus-pocus," Gale said. "If we just spruce up our main streets and keep our lawns nice, folks will want to spend money on us. I wonder if Le heard the talk."

"She must've. How could she not? But she never said anything to me."

Gale wanted to ask: *And what did you say in her defense?* But she kept silent. If the third murdered man in that car had indeed turned out to be Le Nguyen's brother, this was not the time to start challenging Sally. Gale knew from experience what violence did to the intimate circle of its victim. And an ocean away from their homeland, the Nguyens' intimate circle surely included Sally Robertson.

"I think we've procrastinated enough," Gale said instead. "Let's go see what we can do."

They started up the three wooden stairs that led to the front porch, all painted blue—no contrasting trim here, thought Gale. The shine was still in the paint; as they stepped upon the porch boards, the heel of Sally's pump slipped, and she yelped and grabbed Gale's arm to keep from sliding.

The yelp must have been audible inside the house because the curtain across one of the first-floor windows fluttered, and the door opened almost immediately. Le Nguyen stepped out and closed the door behind her.

"What do you want?" she asked. Her small face looked pinched. An angry furrow creased her forehead.

Sally glanced at Gale. "We wanted to see if you were all right, if there was anything we can do."

"No."

"Le . . . I . . . Please let me help you."

"I don't need help."

"Then at least let me offer you a leave of absence . . . I'll continue to pay you . . . I just want . . ."

"I don't want the job anymore."

"Don't make a decision like that now. I'll hold the job for you. You take as long as—"

Le took a step forward as Sally shrank back. "I don't want the job," she said.

Sally looked at Gale, desperate. Gale slipped her hands into her coat pocket but moved closer to the Vietnamese woman.

"Le," she said softly. "My name is Gale Grayson. We haven't met—"

"I know who you are," Le interrupted. "The woman who takes in sluts with babies. The woman who married a murderer. I know about your grandmother, too. A witch. People are scared of her. I'm not scared of you. You are bad people. This whole town is bad. We tried to tell Tuan. You are all bad."

Le stared at her, dark eyes piercing. Gale knew this kind of fury. For her it had come days later, when the reality of Tom's suicide had finally sunk in. But she had never been sent to a morgue to identify a body. She couldn't imagine the shock and grief that could come from that. Fury might be the tamest reaction.

"Le," she pressed. "Is Tuan your brother? Was he one of the men they found in the car?"

The slap hit her before she could protect herself. Gale staggered backward to the steps.

"Bitch slut," Le said. "American bitch slut. You leave me alone. You leave us all alone."

Alby Truitt stared down at the collection of crime scene photos that covered his desk. The bodies of Stuart Keast, Darrell Murphy, and Tuan Nguyen were at the Georgia Bureau of Investigation's crime lab in Atlanta, waiting their turns for an autopsy, which meant the results of the various tests wouldn't be back for weeks. This was one of the prices paid by counties too small and poor to afford their own forensic department. Nevertheless, Alby didn't need to wait on tests to know what had killed these men. They had all been breathing with hearts pumping until the second they were shot close range—a blast obliterating Darrell Murphy's face (but not the distinctive scars on his hands which had left his father collapsed and gasping when he identified the body), another ripping Stuart Keast's jugular, and a third leaving a nice neat hole in Tuan Nguyen's left temple. All living men done in by gunshots.

But not done in by the same gun. Truitt picked up a picture of Nguyen and tilted it. It was a close-up shot—the corner of Nguyen's swollen eye was visible on the left-hand side of the photo. The wound was round, with characteristic black burns around the perimeter. Judging from the size, his guess was .22-caliber. Glancing at what was visible of Nguyen's eye, he searched his desktop for a full-face shot. Damn. The crime scene photographer, also part of a unit sent up from the GBI, hadn't taken one, or if she had, it hadn't come out. He'd have to wait for the autopsy photos sometime tomorrow. He usually made sure one of the local officers also took photos as a backup, but he was honest enough to admit that there were too few murders in Calwyn County for his people and the police department to have a standard procedure for homicides. The scene had been secured and the proper technicians called in from the state. Realistically speaking, that was as much as he could expect.

He looked again at the photo in his hand. The bruising around the eye was evident, but he couldn't detect any obvious bruising elsewhere on the man's face. Whether that bruise was the result of the bullet or was already there would be something the state medical examiner would have to tell him.

"I didn't get into this job for this," he hollered. "I got into this job because I knew there wouldn't be a lot of this."

"So how many does this make?" Haskell's voice sounded from the adjoining room.

"Four before. This makes seven. So in the past twenty-four hours I've had a seventy-five-percent increase in my murder cases. Damn."

"Well, I've had a three-hundred-percent increase," Haskell responded. "If that were a batting average I'd be into some good money."

"You'd be too rich and Geri wouldn't have any patience with you."

"Who said I'd stay with Geri?"

Truitt whooped, and Haskell's rich laugh sounded in response. "You know that's not leaving this building," Truitt said. "I'd be looking at number eight if Geri heard you say that."

"Naw. You'd rule it suicide. Hell, I might commit suicide rather than leave it to Geri. Woman's too damn creative."

"You don't deserve her."

"You tell the truth, Sheriff. I most certainly do not."

Still smiling, Truitt let his gaze wander over the photos. The driver's side window was rolled three quarters of the way down. Not to be expected on a cool October evening. The front passenger window was up, but the glass was in jagged pieces.

"You've seen these photos, right, Craig?"

"Yep."

"Got a preliminary assessment?"

"Trick question, boss? I was taught not to theorize in advance of the facts."

"The facts are waiting in line in Atlanta. Just give me your impressions."

Truitt heard the scrape of a chair and in a couple of seconds Haskell's sizable frame entered his office. The deputy stood over Truitt's desk, hands on hips.

"Okay. The car was registered to Darrell Murphy, and the mayor confirmed that it was his son's car. So I'd say Murphy drove into the woods voluntarily. Keast was there voluntarily, too—can't see a scenario where you'd stay buckled up in a car if you were in it against your will. Now, Mr. Nguyen is a different matter. I don't know if he was shot before, during, or after the other two, but unless we're talking something really kinky, he wasn't tied up in the back of that car because he wanted to be."

"Kinky happens. In fact, I was talking to an M.E. not long ago and he said he was seeing more kinky deaths these days."

Haskell looked at him and scowled.

"We're talking about a member of a minority, an immigrant, tied up and shot in the head . . ."

Truitt waved his hand. "I know. I agree. Just testing. Interesting we didn't find any weapons in the car. If Nguyen was shot at the site, someone disposed of the gun."

"Enough blood on the floorboard to suggest that he was killed in the car."

"Agreed. But if the same person who shot Keast and Murphy shot him, they used a different weapon."

Haskell nodded. "Bizarre, isn't it."

"I'll say. I'm guessing from the size it's a .22. Know who likes to use .22s? The mob. Some of the drug rings. Small, easy to hide and done right it doesn't make an awful mess."

"You think this is drug-related?"

"Don't know. I haven't heard of Murphy being messed up with anyone, but being a mayor's son doesn't make you immune to that kind of thing. Some might suggest that it makes you more susceptible. It's something we need to consider. But if the killer wanted discretion, he surely missed the boat with Murphy and Keast." Truitt was silent a moment, pondering the photos. He pointed to the shot of the open car window. "What do you make of that?"

"Murphy rolled down his window to talk with someone. And that someone stuck in a shotgun and blew him and Keast the hell away. Someone who met them in the woods."

"Or someone they unexpectedly encountered. There are a lot of holes in Siler's story. First of all, I don't understand why his car was parked the way it was. Then he says he saw Nguyen's body without opening the back door, which wasn't possible—Nguyen was so small, Siler would have to either have leaned way over the seat from the front or opened the back door to see him. And I'm having a hard time believing he thought those men were in a traffic accident."

"So we need to interview him again."

"So we need to interview him again. See what he can offer as an alibi up to the time he entered the woods."

Haskell took in a deep breath and let it out slowly. "It doesn't make sense. If Keast and Murphy abducted Nguyen with the idea of taking him to the woods and killing him, then how did they end up dead? You'd think the person on the losing end of an unexpected encounter would be the poor sap who came across them in the middle of murdering someone."

"Unless the other person was well armed."

"So what, Keast and Murphy kill someone in their car, then roll down their window to converse with a hunter who happens by? Can't see it, Alby."

"Me neither," agreed Truitt. "But something happened. I doubt we are looking at a murder-suicide here."

7

Ron Goddard had a sixth sense about things, although he discredited any notion that it was less than a logical phenomenon. It wasn't a gift, he always told people; instead, it had come from years of watching people's mouths—the way their tongues touched the soft and hard parts of their palate, pressed against particular teeth. He had thousands of audiocassettes in his library that captured the linguistic blueprints of hundreds of people, and these he played the way some people played recordings of their favorite singer or orchestra. He also had videocassettes, the tapes revealing the tics and rolls of his subjects' facial muscles. By observing both, he always said, the linguist could come as close as possible to witnessing the human soul. And having been privy to the workings of so many souls, he had fine-tuned the ability to sense what others couldn't. In some ways, Ron Goddard told himself, he was a bit of a divinity—in a purely secular sense, of course. He was a purely secular man.

His sixth sense had told him something monumental was happening over at the Alden house. It wasn't simply that the sheriff had left shortly after he arrived last night for dinner—Gale had dismissed Truitt's departure with a lighthearted "Duty called," and the remaining parties had sat down to enjoy their meal. In fact, the entire household had acted as if departing law enforcement was as natural and as momentarily annoying as the lights flickering, and he had realized that this would certainly have been the case. His temporary neighbors were not friends with the local sheriff and a London policeman by serendipity. This was a family that had a troublesome history to it. This was a family to be wary of.

He took a sip of coffee from his mug and looked out his kitchen window. Something had been going on at the Alden house since mid-morning. Ella—now that she had cooked for him he had to remind himself to stop thinking of her as "the old lady next door"—had driven up in some agitation, and an hour later had left with Gale bearing a foil-covered dish. An hour after that, the two had returned, emerging from their car empty-handed and walking, deep in conversation, to the house. It might be a leap to say that the events of last night and this morning were related, but he didn't need his well-developed instinct to tell him they were.

As he peered out the window, the back porch door swung open and Daniel Halford stepped out, the little girl with him. Goddard put his coffee mug on the counter and quickly left by his own back door.

"Hallo," he called, squinting at the harshness of the afternoon sun. "Going for a walk?"

Halford stopped, the little girl's hand—which to Goddard's child-deprived mind looked a touch greenish—in his own. "We're heading for that tree line. Want to join us?"

"Certainly." He hurried over to the rusty gate that offered the only egress in the barbed wire fence that separated the two properties. The gate stubbed the ground as he swung it open. Like the house he had rented, the gate showed less than careful maintenance. Not that it mattered. The rent was cheap, and the house served his purposes well.

He joined Halford and Katie Pru at the edge of a long wall of chest-high grass that spread across the back of the Aldens' land.

"Could use a good clipping," he said cheerfully.

"It's broom grass," said Katie Pru. "Grandma Ella doesn't cut it 'cause it keeps the varmints out."

"Ah. It serves a good purpose then." Goddard pointed to a break in the grass that revealed a red dirt path. "Is this what you use to get to the trees?"

Katie Pru frowned and readjusted her hand in Halford's. "It's a path. Don't you have paths where you're from?"

Goddard blinked. His instinct told him that this child didn't care for him. Truth was, he didn't care for her, either. He had little tolerance for children, even when they struck him as well contained. Independence in a child was a bothersome thing.

"Mr. Goddard lives in a fairly large city, K.P.," Halford explained. "Lots of paths in Leeds, but not many through grasses. Why don't you show us the way?"

Katie Pru dropped Halford's hand and led them through the thickets. Here the grasses grew less dense; brambles rose on either side. Soon they found themselves lifting their feet high to step over tendrils that crossed the path.

"Muscadines," Katie Pru said. "It's what keeps the varmints here instead of in the yard." She reached her hand into the thicket and plucked two large purple berries. Popping one into her mouth, she handed the other to Goddard.

"Bite it," she instructed. A flat piece of purple skin emerged between her lips, and she held it out for him to see before flinging it into the thicket. "Don't swallow the skin and the seeds. Just eat the squishy part. It's yummy."

Yummy wasn't the word he would have used to describe the bitter-then-sweet taste that hit his tongue. Instead of spitting out the skin, he spat out the entire berry plug, fighting to keep the grimace off his face.

"Thank you, Katie Pru," he said mildly, removing his handkerchief from his pocket to wipe his hands. "Interesting flavor. I'll have to get used to it."

If she felt slighted that her peace offering had been rejected, she gave no indication. Taking Halford's hand again, she led the men deeper into the thicket.

Another hundred yards and the thicket abruptly fell away, revealing a clearing of old walnut trees. *Clearing* wasn't the right word, Goddard thought. Yellow and brown leaves littered the ground, spattering the fallen logs and granite outcroppings. It struck him as neglected and wild, and he wondered if Katie Pru knew what kept the varmints out of *here*.

The child darted among the trees, feet crunching leaves. Bending and making a scooping motion with her arms, she sent a shower of leaves cascading through the air.

"The owls are under here," she announced. "You have to scoot the leaves out of the way to find them."

Another cascade fluttered, and she turned away from them, her interest intent on the ground. Goddard had no idea what she was looking for, and in truth, he didn't care.

"So," he said casually to Halford. "Seemed to me there were some goings-on around your place this morning."

Halford nodded, his focus still on the child. "The call Alby got last night. Three men were found shot in the woods not far from here. In fact, it happened on property that borders Ella's." He pointed westward. "She knew one of them rather well."

"Shot. My God." Goddard was silent a moment,

letting the news play in his head. Americans were mythically violent. They revealed it in their speech— "shotgun wedding," "loaded for bear." But he had suspected that it might be more tall tale than reality. Sure, their crime statistics looked bad, but they were a whopping big country. And he had always perceived Americans to be bighearted, if a little overheated. For violence to happen in as quiet a village as Statlers Cross . . .

"Is there anything I can do?" he asked. "Ella seemed all right this morning, but . . ."

He noticed that Halford was watching him with a curious expression, and he felt himself color. "It's the damn kitchen window," he explained sheepishly. "It invites you to watch. I'll have to put up curtains."

"Ella's all right," Halford said. "She's tough, and she's lived long enough to have seen a great deal. But evidently one of the men, Darrell Murphy, had helped her out quite a bit and she was fond of him." He paused, glancing at Goddard. "He was the mayor's son. I think you said you knew him."

Goddard's limbs went cold. "Darrell Murphy. Yes, I had met him. Quite a few times, actually. Nice man. He introduced me to the Keasts. God."

Goddard stared at the little girl, now leapfrogging through the leaves, her eyes on the ground. Yes, he had met Darrell Murphy. For Goddard, Murphy had been what social scientists called an informant. The name sounded sinister, and sometimes, in his darker moods, Goddard admitted it was. Murphy had been his escort through the linguistic circles of Statlers Cross— his Virgil, as it were. Goddard had told Darrell whom he needed to meet, and Darrell had introduced him. Darrell had been the first to take him up the overgrown trails to the Keast place, had walked him around the house until they had come upon Stuart Keast . . . with a shotgun slung over his arm. Goddard blinked and felt Halford's eyes on him.

"I believe you knew one of the other men, too," Halford said quietly. "Stuart Keast. I believe you said last night he had been helping you."

Goddard's legs buckled. He had slumped to the ground before Halford could reach out to steady him.

"My God. My God." It was all he could say. His hands lay limp on his knees. He couldn't move them.

Halford knelt beside him. "I'm sorry, Ron. I should have walked over to your house and told you. I didn't put you together with them, but of course you knew them."

Goddard looked at Halford, incredulous. "Shot, you said? Who would have shot them? Were they hunting?"

"No, it doesn't appear so. They were found in Darrell's car. And a third man was with them—a Vietnamese. Tuan Nguyen. He had family here in Statlers Cross. Did you know him as well?"

"Vietnamese. Yes, I had heard of the Nguyens. But they're a family of women. You say this was a man?"

"Yes, a son. And a brother. He evidently didn't live in town but visited them sometimes. Did work on their house. But it seems he kept a low profile. At least, that's Ella's assessment."

"So all three are dead? Stuart and Darrell and this other man?" At Halford's nod, Goddard squeezed his eyes shut. "What in heaven's name happened?"

"I'm sure it's too soon in the investigation to know. From what Gale was telling me, the bodies have to go to the state crime lab, and the tests could take weeks."

Halford's eyes were boring into him now; he could feel them without opening his own eyes. "What is it?" Goddard asked.

Halford shifted, his shoes crunching the leaves.

"Ron, can I ask you your impression of Darrell Murphy? What kind of man did he strike you as being?"

Goddard weighed his words before he answered; he knew his answer, to this policeman from his own country, was being noted. "Honest," he said, finally opening his eyes. "Helpful. And definitely earnest. His father, Timothy, is mayor, you know, and I had talked with him before I arrived, just to establish a contact and to make sure the town would be amenable to my study. Of course, Timothy was very supportive, but it was Darrell who proved to be a godsend. He aided me from the first day. He was like a manservant—no, that's derogatory. He was like a first mate. Whatever I needed, whomever I needed to talk with, he immediately arranged it. It was glorious, really. So often in this line of work, you can take months building the confidence of your subjects. With Darrell, it took me only weeks. I don't know what I would have done without him."

"And Stuart Keast?"

Here Goddard shifted, resting his rump on the dried leaves. "Stuart. Well, there is a different story. You ever see the movie *Deliverance*? It's a cliché to say that the mountain people in that movie represented the American South, but they came close to representing Stuart Keast. All the Keasts, in fact." He tried to rub the chill from his hands. "The truth is, the Keasts scare me. I'm never comfortable around them. Rosen is a superb subject and I'll swallow any number of misgivings to analyze her dialect, but I would be less than honest if I said I felt safe in their company. I felt watched. I felt that at any time one of them would have no compunction about taking off the back of my head with a shovel."

"That's strong language, Ron."

"It's accurate language. I've had this feeling one other time, Daniel, with a family in Cornwall. Isolated, as the Keasts are. Families that isolated—that don't have factory or office jobs, don't attend church, don't have an extended network of friends—make up their own rules. They don't feel a part of society because they're not a part of society. They are wild families. I did a case study of the Cornish family that lasted six months. As here, I lived in a cottage not far from them, visited them weekly. I gained their trust gradually. But I was relieved to leave them behind. A year after I'd gone, I came across a newspaper article. The father, a big, patriarchal type of man, had been arrested for killing his daughter. He had impregnated her, waited until the baby was born, and upon seeing that it was a girl, murdered them both." He glanced at Halford. "It was only about five years ago. Do you remember that case?"

"Yes. Horrific."

"I remember thinking it was horrific, and then realizing with a shock that I didn't find it surprising. He had struck me as exactly the kind of man who would do such a thing. He made his own rules. He ran his own universe. He tolerated me only because he saw me as a recorder of his unique ways. Well, I got the same sense with the Keasts. Stuart tolerated me because I could legitimize him. I was basically saying, 'Look, how you speak sets you apart, but it also makes you special. It makes you so special I'm willing to move here to listen to you.' So he let me in."

"So you sometimes felt in danger?"

"Not so much in danger as on probation. I got the distinct impression that if I stepped outside the boundaries he had set for me—and only he knew what those boundaries really were—I would have disappeared. But he and I both understood that I accepted that. For the honor of listening to him and his mother. That's how Stuart saw it."

"You need to tell this to Alby."

"You think so? It's only impressions. And besides, Stuart was the one who got shot. He wasn't the killer."

"He was killed. Someone either feared him or hated him enough to kill him. If a man is as threatening as you seem to indicate Stuart was, then Alby needs to know what kind of person he was."

Goddard was silent. The little girl was singing, the pockets of her coat now bulging with God only knew what. "Alby probably knows what kind of person Stuart was. I got that impression talking with him last night."

"Probably. But you've spent a lot of time with Stuart recently. Perhaps you can lend some insight."

"Perhaps. Or perhaps I'm better off letting it go. I could also be naive enough to say the wrong thing. And maybe I am wrong. Perhaps Stuart was the damn salt of the earth. I am a foreigner here, you know. Foreigners tend to be paranoid."

"True. But that's up to Alby to figure out. You need to talk to him."

"Fine." Shakily, Goddard tried to stand, but Halford had to grab his arm and help him up. "All right. I'll give him a call. But I expect he'll dismiss me."

"He won't. He's good. But let it be his judgment call."

The child was running back to them, bits of leaves clinging to her pants, her hands full of dark orbs.

"Daniel, you wouldn't believe the owls I found! Tons and *tons*."

Goddard looked down at the hard black nuts Katie Pru offered up to Halford. Her little green fingers were blackened and grimy. In addition to being disciplined, he reminded himself vaguely, children ought to be *clean*.

But Halford had no such concerns. "Terrific, K.P. What shall we do with them?"

"Take them back to Grandma Ella's house," she

decided. "They're going to make their own rules. They're a *wild* family."

And she was off down the path, scrambling over the vines. Goddard and Halford looked at each other. The damn child had listened to their every word.

8

The conversation—if it could be called a conversation—with Le Nguyen kept playing in Gale's head. Her own hesitancy, the tentativeness of her approach: *My name is Gale Grayson. We haven't met . . .*

Then the cutting words, as if Le were spitting at her feet: *I know who you are. The woman who takes in sluts with babies. The woman who married a murderer. I know about your grandmother, too. A witch. . . .*

I know who you are. . . . The words circled like moths in the night. They hurt more than the obscenity Le had leveled at her: *American bitch slut.* Cloistered in her isolating blue house, separated from the town by language and culture, Le Nguyen still knew who Gale Grayson was. An old shame burned Gale's cheeks. The sharp pain that gnawed in her stomach wasn't guilt—if she had ever felt guilt for what Tom had done, she had forgotten it. What she would never forget was the humiliation. Sometimes, amid the whirl of child-rearing and work, she managed to push it aside. But it was always there, reminding her to keep her head down. Le Nguyen had aimed her words, and with the precision of a poet, slashed and slashed.

She sat on the back porch, wrapped in a bulky cardigan she had found at the bottom of an old chest. She pressed her nose into the oversized rolled neck. She had a vague memory of her great-aunt Nora in this sweater, an image of her standing at the end of the front yard, looking east toward the center of Statlers Cross, her fist raised in the air and her turkey-wattle neck shaking in anger and defiance. Gale had the sense that Nora was yelling something, but she couldn't remember what. Quite possibly, she had been too young to understand. She understood now, however. She wondered if at seventy she would be still wearing this family relic, her shriveled chicken body a pathetic silhouette in the yard, squawking at real and imagined humiliations.

She fought back tears, pissed at herself for crying. She had come too far to let Le Nguyen get to her. She was too damn strong now for *this*.

The hand on her shoulder made her jump. She looked up to see Halford standing behind her.

"You shouldn't let this bother you," he said. "You know everything she said was out of anger and grief."

"I know that. It's not Le, not really. It's knowing that . . ." She wadded the drooping wool in her fist, pulling, twisting. She couldn't find the words.

"It's realizing that Le shouldn't have the faintest idea in the world who you are, isn't it?" Halford asked quietly.

The tears fell from her eyelashes and she angrily blotted her face with her sleeve. "Dammit, yes. It's not like I'm little Miss Junior League around here, out doing good for the dispossessed in the community. I'm not the damn Welcome Wagon. I'd never spoken with her until today. She shouldn't know me. But she's sure as hell overheard the gossip down at that tearoom."

Halford didn't say anything as he pulled a chair out from the table and sat down. He crossed his legs so that his knee pressed against hers. The pressure felt warm, comforting. Even as the tears rolled down her face, she reached over and took his hand.

"God, I want to leave here," she whispered. "I'm so tired of being ashamed."

"You've done nothing to be ashamed of."

"I know that, too. But it doesn't make any difference."

For several seconds they were silent, Gale aware of Halford's eyes on her wet face, the warmth of her hand buried in his. It was always with a small shock that she saw he didn't have delicate hands. She didn't know why—his body tall and solid, square hands matched him. But when she conjured up an image of his hands, they were elongated and sinewy. The reality was more dependable. She looked at him and smiled.

"I just realized something," she said.

"What's that?"

"You're the only person in the world I trust."

His hand tightened around hers. "That's a start."

Behind her Gale heard the door open and the thudding footsteps of a small child. With a clank, Katie Pru dropped a metal bucket on the tabletop. Gale shook herself free from Halford's grasp.

"I need some help," Katie Pru said. "I have a family of owl heads in the bucket. I need to turn them into a family of owls. They need bodies."

Gale peeked into the bucket at the collection of opened walnut shells. "I can see that. How are you going to do that?"

"With glue. And your socks."

"Hmmm. I need my socks, K.P. Besides, do you think socks might make big bodies for these owls?"

Katie Pru picked up one of the shells and held it up, musing. "I think you're right. Maybe the fingers from your gloves."

"Maybe something else."

The small face frowned. Gale glanced at Halford to see him fighting a grin.

"Pine cones?" Katie Pru asked.

"That's a good choice."

Another pause. "Alum'num foil?"

"Good again."

Katie Pru's face lit up. "What about Grandma Ella's jar of spools? I could glue corn on them to make feathers."

"I dunno, K.P. Grandma Ella's had that jar for quite a while. It's hard to find wooden spools these days. You'll have to ask her. And as far as the corn goes . . ."

But Katie Pru had snatched her bucket and disappeared into the kitchen.

"By the way," Gale said to Halford, "thank you for taking her this afternoon. She enjoyed the walk. I better warn Ella that if she doesn't want Katie Pru to use those spools she better hide the jar. Once that child gets an idea . . ."

Halford smiled, but he didn't move his knee to let her up. "Let's go out tonight," he said.

"Out?"

"Yes, Gale, out. I've been in America for three days and you've yet to take me out. Statlers Cross is lovely, and I find your family delightful, but I've only a few more days here and I'd like to go out. Dinner. What kind of restaurants are in Praterton?"

"Okay ones." Flustered, she reviewed the list of restaurants in her head. Several had good reputations; one had received national press and was the destination of weekly tour groups. But to take Halford . . .

"What's wrong? I don't embarrass you, do I?"

"God, no . . ." She stopped. "That's not true. You do embarrass me. Or rather, *we* embarrass me. Oh, hell. I don't want to take you to a restaurant in Praterton."

Halford's laugh was deep and genuinely joyful. She felt her own spirits lift. "Fine. Athens, then. Hell, let's drive to Atlanta. Just let me take you somewhere. You need a change of scenery. And I need to spend at least a small amount of time with you alone."

• • • •

The jar sat on a shelf in Grandma Ella's den. Katie Pru didn't like Grandma Ella's den—it was a scary room with long white curtains like ghosts and dried snakeskins tacked to the bookshelves as if during the night hunters emerged from the books and speared whatever they found slithering on the floor. There were other animals, too: crows in little vests and hats, squirrels in yellow boots. On a tiny desk, small enough for Katie Pru had she been inclined to sit at it, stood a gray field mouse with its ears pricked up as if she had startled him. Varmints, all furry and frozen with their little black-bright eyes staring at her. She couldn't understand why Grandma Ella had grasses and thickets to keep varmints from the yard but she let them live inside. And dressed them.

The den stood at the end of a skinny, dark hallway, which she padded down quickly, not liking it any more than her destination. When she reached the door, she opened it just an inch, half hoping to see Grandma Ella reading on the sofa, even if that meant asking if she could have the jar. But the den was empty. Silently, she slid inside and closed the door behind her.

It was like stepping into a jar herself. The den had six walls, all covered in bookshelves except for two huge doors with windows that opened onto the back yard. These were covered by the white curtains that, when the heat was on, fluttered and shook. But what made Katie Pru most feel as if she were in a jar was the circle of frosted windows that ran around the top of the room. They looked like the screw neck of a jar, and whenever she was in here, Katie Pru half expected the roof to fly off and fat giant-child fingers to lift her out and hold her up in its palm to study her.

The jar sat on a shelf partway up to the ceiling. Grandma Ella had put it there to keep it out of her reach.

"You can't get good wooden spools like that anymore, Katie Pru," she had said. "I won't have you going and messing them up." But what Katie Pru had in mind was not messing the spools up. She wanted to give her owls wings. She wanted to send them swooping in the air. Surely there was nothing "messing up" about that.

Beside the desk was a black chair, too small for the kitchen table but just right in here. With her eyes half closed so she wouldn't have to see the field mouse, she grabbed the chair and dragged it across the floor to the shelf.

The jar itself was beautiful. It didn't have a screw-on lid but a set-down kind with a fat red knob in the center. The knob made the jar look like a clown sleeping, and whenever Katie Pru played with it, she tweaked the knob like her mother tweaked her nose when they tickled each other. She did so, now. Then, carefully, she placed both hands on the jar, and clutching it to her chest, eased both body and prize to the floor.

There she froze. She hadn't thought about what would be the safest way to get the spools out of the den. Should she stuff them in her pockets (then she should have worn her coat and not this thin sweater and pants) or should she try to sneak the whole jar up to her room? She supposed she could just bring the owl heads into the den and do her work behind the sofa, but that would mean gathering all her supplies. . . . She stood in the middle of the floor, hands sweaty around the jar, feeling trapped. There was nothing else to do. She was going to have to get the jar down the hall, up the stairs, and into her room.

She hurried to the door and, hugging the jar with one arm, slowly turned the doorknob.

"I'm not going to listen to that, Reebe—I'm just not."

The voice was partly a whisper—Grandma Ella didn't want anyone to hear her—but there was no mistaking the anger. Katie Pru knew well enough what Grandma Ella sounded like when she was angry.

"I don't care what you heard. Now quit talking nonsense and act responsibly."

Katie Pru froze again. Grandma Ella had to be right next to the door.

"Darrell Murphy was as decent a person as they come. For you to suggest otherwise . . ."

The voice was suddenly closer. Still clutching the jar, Katie Pru darted behind the sofa, skidding on the wood floor and banging her knees.

She heard the door swing wide open then shut. But Grandma Ella's voice stayed a whisper.

"Let me tell you something, Reebe. I think it is reprehensible that you would repeat something like that about the dead. Never mind that you would say it to me, knowing how I liked and respected Darrell. . . . No, I'm not going to listen to you. You are talking about the mayor's *son*, for pity's sake. You are talking about a boy I've known since he was born. Don't you think I'd know if he got into those kinds of shenanigans? Do I look a fool? He was over here quite a bit, and I would have known if he was doing what you say. All I can say is shame on you."

Katie Pru heard the faint click of the portable phone being turned off. "Fool," Grandma Ella said. "Hysterical, hormone-deprived fool." Her great-grandmother's breaths came short and fast.

Katie Pru sucked in her own breath and cradled the jar tighter. She counted to twelve, hoping her great-grandmother would leave the room. But then she heard the furious clicks again.

"Alby? I want you to take me to brunch tomorrow. I know you're up to your eyeballs in this investigation, but that's why I want brunch. Alone. Without your partner there."

Quiet, then one word. "Ten." A final click, and Katie

Pru heard a creak and a puff of air as Grandma Ella sat down on the sofa.

"Old fool," her great-grandmother said. "However did I get to be an old fool? Like I don't know what foxes sound like."

The springs in the old sofa sighed; Katie Pru glanced up at the desk looming not far away and saw the bright eyes of the field mouse watching her. She scrunched up tighter behind the sofa. *Go away,* she thought. *Go away and leave me alone.*

The sofa huffed; she heard the rapid thud of Grandma Ella's heels upon the carpet. The breeze from her wool skirt ruffled Katie Pru's hair.

"I declare," Grandma Ella said. "What are you doing back there?"

Katie Pru looked up at her cautiously.

"What on earth . . . ?" Grandma Ella frowned at the jar. "What are you doing with my spools, Miss Katie Pru?"

Katie Pru said nothing. Maybe if Grandma Ella didn't know what she wanted the spools for, she'd forget Katie Pru had them.

"I asked you, little girl, what are you doing with my spools?"

"I need them for my owls," Katie Pru said, her voice thick. "My owls need bodies so they can fly."

Her great-grandmother was staring at her, her mouth pinched up in a tight circle. It was her stern look, the one she gave when she was about to send Katie Pru from the room. But as Katie Pru watched, the sternness left, and Katie Pru suddenly felt as if she were being studied, like she was a huge book and Grandma Ella was trying to make out the words and was having to mostly guess.

"Owls?" Grandma Ella asked. "Why are you making owls?"

Katie Pru shrugged. "I find them in the backyard. They live back there."

Her great-grandmother's mouth popped open. She stared at Katie Pru for a long time. Then, she took a step back. "You know, Katie Pru, it isn't polite to listen to people's phone conversations. You don't want to be a rude little girl, do you? Next time, either leave the room when someone is on the phone, or at least let them know you are there."

She turned and walked away. From over the sofa back, Katie Pru heard her great-grandmother's voice, quiet but firm.

"You may have my spools," Ella said. "Just leave the jar where you found it. But I think you should stop all this nonsense about owls. There are no owls on my property."

9

By seven P.M., the sky was at the edges of dark; a pewter wash covered the trees and obscured the dying color of the grass. From her living room window, Sally Robertson stared out over her yard, taking in the clouded glow of her brass porch lights, the damp pebbled stepping-stones and finally, beyond them all, the high hedges that blocked the view of anyone who might look in on her. When she and Mal had first moved into this small wreck of a house, she'd pronounced that as soon as the renovation was done, she was going to take a chainsaw to those hedges, cutting them back until they made nothing more than a quaint and natural fence around their house. But the renovation on the house had been completed, the renovation of the tearoom had started and ended, and still the hedges loomed on three sides of their property. Now she found she didn't want to cut them. The hedges reminded her that all her refinements, her trips to Atlanta to attend decorators' show-cases and restaurant trade shows, were nothing more than window dressings. This was Calwyn County, Georgia, by Gawd, and no amount of *Southern Living* gussying up would change that.

She turned from the window, crossing her arms against a chill and wishing Mal were home. He'd be gone for five days, taking the relief pilot slot on an Atlanta-Tokyo route. He'd call only once—tomorrow morning, roughly the midway point of his trip. This had been their system since their marriage four years ago: Any overnight trip warranted a call halfway through, no more unless there was an emergency. For a long time that had been fine with her. Their decision not to have children had given Mal's absences an air of freedom. But since she started the tearoom, she found herself longing for him more. She wasn't sure why; she certainly now had more friends than she had when they first moved to Statlers Cross. But the daily insertion into the world of business made her yearn for his steady presence at home, and she had to fight a growing resentment that he hadn't undergone a change as well.

"Mal, I want to talk to you!" she said aloud now. "Why can't you understand that I'd like to be able to talk to the man I married when I need to?"

Her words echoed through the house. Mal was fifteen years older than she, and he sometimes unintentionally made her feel childish, but he also had a way of grounding her. He would have the right thing to say about Le. He would tell her how to handle it.

She and Gale had both been silent on the way from the Nguyens' house. What was there to say? As Sally dropped Gale off at the Murphys', she had tried to apologize. "She's angry at me, Gale. That slap was meant for me."

"She's not angry with you, Sally. Look at what she's going through. She's just angry, period."

Yes, Sally knew it was egocentric to think that she was at the center of Le's rage, but she couldn't shake the fear away. Bosses are the root of all rage, aren't they? Isn't that what her own experience had taught her, that logical or not, it was the people who controlled the paycheck who received the enmity? When the school board voted to revoke her contract, it was they, not her own stupidity, that had been the focus of her fury.

Now, in retrospect, she could better understand what had happened. The school board had chosen to cut out the troublesome piece to save the viable whole. It would be the same between her and Le. In deference to Le's grief, she had closed the tearoom down for the day, but she couldn't keep it closed. She was going to have to find a replacement for Le. She couldn't stand around and wait for her to heal her wounds—or redirect her anger.

"That's the right decision, isn't it?" she said aloud. "I should set a time limit and then if she's not back, I should fire her." Outside a wind kicked up; the rattle of leaves blown against the windows sounded like fingernails rapping.

She sighed. Dead leaves were a poor substitute for Mal's confident voice. But she couldn't wait for his endorsement. She would have to reopen the tearoom as soon as possible. Until she could find a temp, she would have to do the cooking herself.

The leaves had been rattling against the door for several seconds before she realized they had gathered into a faint but persistent knocking. She glanced out the window to see a tiny, bundled figure on her porch.

Opening the door, her first reaction was that Le had disintegrated, her shoulders slack, her face melting off her skull. Then she realized that this bundled elderly woman had to be Le's mother. She reached out her hand and took the woman by the arm.

"Mrs. Nguyen," she said. "The wind is something awful out here. Please come in."

The old woman shook her head. "Le need job," she said.

Sally dropped her hand. "I know, Mrs. Nguyen. Really. I'm not going to let Le lose her job. I just need to know that she still wants it."

"Le need job."

"I'll keep the job open for her as long as I can," Sally told her. "I'm so sorry for your loss, Mrs. Nguyen. I wish there was something I could do."

The woman's bright eyes blinked. "Tuan good. Love America."

A wave of helplessness swept over Sally. "I know, I know, I'm sorry."

The woman's stare wouldn't let her go. "Understand? Tuan . . . love . . . America. Good boy."

"Yes, I understand. I'm sure he was a wonderful son and brother. I wish I had known him . . ."

"We not scared. Understand? We *not* scared. We stay."

Sally stared at her, astonished. "Of course you stay. I . . . We want you to stay."

"Le need job. Understand? We stay."

"Why wouldn't you stay? Of course I will see to it that Le has a job. Of course you can stay."

The old woman studied her as if she wasn't sure the American standing in front of her was sentient. A scowl crossed her face; then she turned and skittered down the steps.

Sally watched as she disappeared down the stepping-stones and darted between an opening in the hedges. There was a path, but it cut across uncultivated fields and didn't bisect a road for two miles. Sally ran into the yard and down to the roadside, looking to see if she could make out a car parked further away in the darkness. Nothing. The woman had walked here.

Slowly, Sally made her way back to the house. She wasn't sure what had happened. She wasn't sure what she had promised. But she couldn't dispel the thought that the Nguyens were very scared indeed.

.   .   .

In the end, Gale couldn't bring herself to take Halford to a restaurant in Praterton. It was illogical, she knew, but she imagined the raised eyebrows and the whispers. *Who is that man? He was the policeman who discovered her husband was a terrorist. My word. What is he doing with her now?*

She dabbed on lipstick and shook the whispers aside, reminding herself that she wasn't nearly as fascinating an object of gossip now that she was deemed a respected author by local standards. Wait until her memoirs were published. . . .

"You look beautiful."

Halford stood in the doorway to her bedroom. Gale felt herself blush even as she gave her reflection a last glance. If not beautiful, she had to admit that she looked unexpectedly good. She had discarded her usual skirts and cardigans for the fitted black silk pantsuit she had worn at the book-signing party; she'd pinned her hair up so that the silver streaks that framed her face fell forward in elegant wisps. As she looked in the mirror she was struck by the odd thought that whoever she had been the past several years, she didn't look like that person now.

She answered Halford: "Flatterer," then added, "Sorry. That's Ella's word."

"None of you Alden women know how to take a compliment. With the possible exception of Katie Pru. I think she still appreciates herself."

"It's because we set high standards for deserving compliments. And giving them." She grinned at him. "You don't look too bad yourself."

And he didn't. He leaned against the doorframe, dressed in a charcoal gray suit, looking, well, not too bad. He pushed himself upright and extended his arm.

"You can't possibly be any more ready. Let's go."

She found Katie Pru snuggled on Nadianna's bed,

child and caregiver engrossed in a chapter of *Charlotte's Web*. Michael was nestled between them, his smooth face flushed in sleep. After planting a huge kiss on Katie Pru's cheek, she followed Halford into the windy night.

The drive to Athens was only forty minutes, but to Gale it always seemed longer. The route took them past too many geographical features, through too many eras: out past the aging town center of Statlers Cross; into deeply pastured lands where cattle reposed under isolated trees; past burnt-red cotton and limp-leaved tobacco fields; past pecan groves and Christmas tree farms; and then the experimental agricultural properties belonging to the University of Georgia with their pristine buildings and uniform grasses; and finally the signs of industrialization—corporate chicken coops, low-slung factories, and the dots, then spurts, then long colorful lines of retail establishments.

"Statlers Cross seems so isolated," Halford commented, "but it's actually not."

"Places have to want not to be isolated. When we would stay there in the summer, Ella used to say Statlers Cross was a good fifteen years behind Atlanta. I would have put it at twenty-five."

"Yet there have been changes. That subdivision, for instance."

"Yes, but that was a county zoning decision—the people of Statlers Cross had little to do with it. More interesting to me is the reception Sally Robertson's tearoom has gotten. It used to be an old photo studio, opened up back in the 1920's. But like everything else it went out of business during the Depression and for decades it was mainly used for storage. Then Sally decides to start a business, one that would help spruce up the Main Street area. People seem to love it—Ella's commented a couple of times about people liking how cheery it makes the town. But whenever I've eaten there,

I never see any of the natives. It's mostly the people from Sag Harbor Estates, and a few folks from Praterton who figured it might be worth the drive to check it out."

"I notice you're not taking me there tonight. Are you not one of Sally's patrons?"

Gale smiled. "Not really. For starters, it's not open weeknights. And it's not exactly the kind of place one takes children. Besides, Ella loves to cook. I'd be insulting the head of the family to suggest we go eat 'Spoon Bread with Chives' or some of the other fancy treats Sally offers."

They were deep in the heart of Athens now, traveling up Lumpkin Street, the solid brick structures of the University of Georgia passing on their left. Gale swung the car onto Broad Street and began the difficult job of finding a parking space in the city's quaint, but limited, downtown. Her destination was a small Italian restaurant located in what used to be a corner drugstore in a long line of brick-front shops. But all the parking spaces on the one-way streets around the restaurant were taken, so she veered right and headed for a public parking lot located just off campus.

The easiest way to get back downtown was to hike through the university grounds, so Halford took Gale's arm as they weaved their way past clumps of students. Gale had been on campus several times, giving lectures to writing classes on the importance of research. She felt a familiar tug, but quickly pushed it aside. It was an old internal argument, one she would never resolve. This was the type of setting she had given up for Tom. This was the road she would never travel.

"I had an interesting conversation with Ron today." Halford interrupted her thoughts. "About the Keasts."

"Really? I have my own opinions about the Keasts, but I'd be interested in an outsider's opinion." She smiled as Halford paused to place his hand on his chest, feigning offense. "Seriously, I'm not putting Ron down, but he's been here, what, a couple of months? What on earth has he decided about the Keasts?"

"I think he used the word wild."

Gale laughed out loud. "With all due respect, that's the word people use to describe Southerners when they really mean they don't understand how we can eat squirrel."

"In his defense, he also used it to refer to a family in Cornwall. We were talking about Stuart. Ron said his impression was the Keasts played by their own rules."

"That's true enough. I said earlier that Statlers Cross is a pocket. The Keasts are something sewn inside the seam of that pocket. Very reclusive. Very independent. They refuse to be part of 'the system'. They are utterly self-sufficient."

"And yet Stuart obviously had ties with Darrell Murphy, the mayor's son. That's fairly well connected. And it was a strong enough connection that Stuart was willing to take Darrell's guidance and work with Ron—an outsider. Did you know the Keasts were helping Goddard?"

"Ron told me. He seemed quite excited about it. Rosen was evidently a 'find.' Lord, I wonder what effect Stuart's death will have on that poor woman. I wonder if she'll want to have anything to do with Ron's research project."

"I don't know. He also mentioned he thought Stuart was dangerous."

At this Gale frowned. "Dangerous. Well, we tend to think they are, don't we, people who refuse to conform? The people who say we don't need your welfare, your public schools, your health care, your largesse. Heck, the Keasts even built their own road. There's an implicit threat in that, don't you think?"

"Perhaps. But Ron said he felt physically threatened,

that Stuart would have killed him if he felt Ron crossed him."

"In that case, he should tell Alby."

"My advice exactly. I was just curious about your take on them."

"My take is that they are hyper-self-sufficient. Now, would I go so far as to say they were potentially violent? I don't know. I don't like folks butting into my business much, either."

Halford smiled. "Touché."

They had come to an intersection: Straight ahead would take them to Broad Street and the restaurant; right, down a tree-lined walk to the courtyard in front of the Fine Arts Building. It was chilly, and the warmth of the restaurant was enticing. But if the lack of parking places was an indication, the restaurant would also be crowded, and Gale wasn't sure she wanted a crowd just yet. Tightening her arm around Halford's, she steered him down the walk.

It wasn't exactly a courtyard, but the trimmed bushes and beautiful fresco that adorned the building's facade gave the space an intimate, relaxed air. They sat on the steps with their backs to the building. Halford took her hand in his and slid them both into his coat pocket.

"So, did you get any writing done today?"

"Some. Well, incubation, anyway. I'm closer to understanding the why behind what Tom did, but not the how." His fingers tightened around hers, and she felt her tongue thicken. "I still wake up in the middle of the night thinking, 'How could he? How could he leave knowing his child was about to be born? How could he choose an idea over this baby?' I've long since accepted that he chose 'the cause'—his ecoterrorism—as more important than me, but more important than his child? What's the good of protecting the earth if you betray your progeny? That's the part I can't get a handle on."

"I think I may see a bit of it," Halford said. "I've made a commitment to my job that entails agreeing to die if I have to. I don't want to, mind you, but the commitment is there. Law enforcement back home has changed—much more risky. American influence, I'm afraid. I know other men in the force who have the attitude that if it comes down to them or some stranger on the street, they'll make sure they're the ones going home to their families—even if it means killing someone else. I know there is always part of me prepared to die for my job. Perhaps Tom felt that way, too."

His face was close to hers; she could feel his warmth. Her eyes watered.

"Being prepared to die is different from being willing to die. Not only was Tom willing, he actively did it. He murdered someone knowing it would impact his unborn child. And he killed himself knowing it would leave us with an unspeakable burden. You wouldn't do that to someone you loved, Daniel."

"No. I would never do that."

Her tears spilled. Slowly, she lifted her mouth to his.

The kiss started slow, warm, then built in its passion. When they finally broke apart, she buried her head in his shoulder and wept. This was why she needed him. This was why she loved him.

I possess items that most survivors don't—hundreds of poems, some typed and ready for submission, others scratched on the backs of envelopes, on menus, on "honey-do" lists. I'll sit up late into the night poring over these, looking for the telltale clue. What does the word "sanguine" in this line mean? When he uses the verb "recuse" here, is he saying that he will not judge a wrongdoing . . . or that he will not obey the law? If nothing else, this adventure into the art of surviving has given me a finer sense of poetics. I have learned that poetry is a puzzle, not unlike a mystery novel. One has to match one's wits with the writer's to win the game.

— Introduction, pg. iii
A Missing Life: Memoirs of a Grass Widow
by GALE GRAYSON

10

Alby Truitt was in a good mood. He had given the sheriff department's receptionist, Blaire Stevens, permission to decorate the waiting area for Halloween; the first thing he saw upon entering the building was a life-size scarecrow stuffed with straw, wearing a crumpled fedora and a trench coat. It was better, Truitt supposed, than if Blaire had given her creation mirror sunglasses and a potbelly. He winked at her as he passed through the security doors, and in return she tossed him a bag of candy corn. It was a good omen—he loved candy corn.

But even better news was that the day before, one of his men had located a .22-caliber pistol in the woods surrounding the Kirby farm, about five hundred yards from where the bodies had been found. Neither Kirby— the timid little wife or the not-much-less-timid little husband—recognized the weapon, and the ATF was in the process of tracing it while the GBI lab tried to link it to any bullets found at the crime scene. With luck he would have the results from both within a few days. It would be sweet, he thought, if the owner of the pistol had conveniently murdered Tuan Nguyen. At least it would enable him to tick one part of this investigation off.

He stood at his desk, rifling through his mail. "Don't

suppose we've heard anything from the big guys?" he shouted through the wall to Haskell.

"Not a peep. I'll call GBI today and ride their butts."

"What about the rest?" Truitt sat down behind his desk as his deputy entered the room and shut the door.

"Nothing's turning up on the drug angle. I've had some men tossing Darrell Murphy and Stuart Keast's names around, but none of their informants'll make a connection. I've told them to keep trying. Could be there's nothing there, could be no one wants to be the first to talk."

"Hmmm. An ID on the .22's owner may help us with that."

Haskell ran his hand over his short, dark hair. "I have to tell you, Alby, I'm hoping this was some sort of messed-up domestic dispute. I hate to think where a drug link might take us."

Truitt tossed down the stack of letters. "I'm with you on that. But you know, I hate to say I think we've been lucky. Most of our dealing's been local stuff." He hesitated, wondering for the first time if Haskell knew about Truitt's own history, about his father's life and death as a small-time dealer. There was a good chance he did not. Haskell was a college-educated black man from Maryland—what local grapevine would trust him enough to provide him with the sordid details from the county sheriff's childhood? He realized with a shot of guilt that he had no idea how well his deputy had been accepted into Calwyn County's black community. "Small-timers," Truitt continued. "But all around us there are drug rings working. On my more pessimistic days I figure it's just a matter of time."

"I can tell you Geri's gonna want to pull my rear end out of here if we start tangoing with drug rings. Not what she signed on the dotted line for."

"Me, neither, Craig. So here's hoping this triple

homicide with two murder weapons was something nice and simple."

Haskell's laugh was bitter. "Right."

"Did you follow up with Siler?"

"Yes. He claims he was with his mother and brother at his parents' house from about eight Sunday night until four Monday afternoon when he left to check out the Kirby woods. Seems he had a sinus headache and was zonked out on prescription medication. We're following up with his family now, but mothers and brothers make iffy alibis. Doctor visits are more reliable."

"So the first thing he does after getting over a sinus infection is run and scout out a hunting site?"

"Southern boys are funny."

"All right, Craig. Good work."

As Haskell left the room, Truitt's phone rang. He listened for a second, then grabbed a pad and pencil and took down the message. When he hung up, his heart was pounding.

"Grab your coat, Craig!"

"What's up?"

"Got an ID on the gun owner. Sarah Gainer."

"Holy moly."

"That, my friend, is an understatement."

Ella Alden was about to give up on Truitt. She had arrived at the Butter-Me-Up Café at ten A.M. sharp, as she and Truitt had agreed, and here it was coming close to ten-twenty and the sheriff still had not arrived. She had other things to do, although, as even she would admit, probably not better. She knew that, like obstetricians, sheriffs sometimes had good reasons for being late. Nevertheless, she was irritated. She took the last sip of her hot tea and motioned to the waitress for another. She would give him ten more minutes.

The crackle of starch and red lipstick that abruptly

plunked itself down in front of her was not Alby Truitt; it took several seconds for Ella to recognize Reebe Vaughter's flashy eyeglasses and whispery voice. She began wishing the Butter-Me-Up served hot toddies.

"Ella. How are you doing? You looked so . . . drained yesterday at the Murphys. Are you feeling better?"

Ella dabbed at her mouth with her napkin. "Yes, Reebe. I'm feeling better. It was just such a shock. As you know, I thought a lot of Darrell."

To Ella's horror, Reebe signaled the waitress and asked for a cup of tea. "I'm expecting someone, Reebe," Ella said. "I haven't long . . ."

"Not to worry. I'll bow out when your friend comes. I just wanted to talk with you a bit. It's been a while since we've really chatted. We used to talk quite regularly."

This was true enough, Ella thought. When Reebe first got the job as society writer for the newspaper, she had sought out her fellow Statlers Cross native as "the oldest and wisest of the wise, old families." As city clerk, Reebe had her "in" with Calwyn County society, but she was perceptive enough to know that there was "barely in" and "truly in," and she needed a mentor to gain entrance into that more intimate circle. What she wasn't perceptive enough to know was that as society writer, she didn't need Ella to gain acceptance: The "in" circles, even the old, wise ones, craved their share of print. All Reebe had to do was spell the names right, and frequently, not even that mattered. If Reebe had possessed more subtlety of understanding, she would have realized that Ella was the last person she needed to contact. For Ella was part of that even rarer circle, the group of mostly wealthy, mostly elderly women who moved beyond the reach of publicity. Ella could have cared less if Reebe Vaughter mentioned her in her column. Ella Alden was, she was grateful to say, socially and culturally above it all.

She thanked the waitress who brought her second tea and carefully measured a spoonful of sugar. "I've been busy, Reebe, as I'm sure you have been. I find it harder and harder to keep in touch with people these days."

"Yes, I've heard you have quite a houseful. And now you have a guest. I'm right, aren't I? You are entertaining a guest from overseas?"

Ella dumped the sugar and gave her lemon slice a vicious twist. "Yes, that's right, we have an overseas guest. A friend of Gale's from England. But we don't need to announce it in the paper. He's only going to be here for a few more days, so there's no need to bring it to the attention of the public."

Reebe's laughter was silvery. "Ella, you've always been so acerbic in your humor. I truly appreciate you. No, I wasn't going to mention anything in my column. But I understand he's a Scotland Yard detective. Maybe our feature writer—"

"I'm sure your feature writer has plenty of local characters to write about. Truly, Reebe, Mr. Halford is here for a rest. He hasn't much time and there are so many things he wants to see and do." Ella knew this was a fib—as far as she could tell, the only things Daniel Halford wanted to do were play with Katie Pru and talk with Gale. "I hope you understand that asking him to be interviewed for a newspaper article would be intrusive."

"Oh, certainly. I understand. Pity we didn't know in advance. Maybe we could have done an article on him before he even got here. Anyway, that's not what I wanted to talk with you about. I've written a column about the murders—well, about the pathos of the families, an elegy, really. Since you know the Murphys so well, I'd like you to take a look at it before I turn it in."

She unfolded a typed sheet of paper and handed it to Ella. No cross-outs, no corrected punctuation. Word processor, Ella concluded. She had a hard time trusting writing done on a word processor.

She read as far as the second paragraph before her chest tightened. "You can't print this," she said.

Reebe looked at her in dismay. "I worked very hard on that. What's wrong with it?"

"For starters, the Keasts may be strange, and they may be reclusive, but you've made them sound like degenerates . . . 'their tar-paper home'? 'their bare-legged pain'? For God's sakes, Reebe, have you ever been to their house? Do you know anything about them? And then your description of the Vietnamese man: 'Whether or not he was here legally, he evidently had a good heart.' What are you talking about?"

"I'm talking about the house, for pity's sake, Ella. He looked after his family—you can tell that . . ."

"But look what you're implying here. You're practically claiming he's illegal. And it certainly isn't your place as the society writer to make such a leap."

"Our newswriter is checking on it. The sheriff's office hasn't confirmed one way or another. But be realistic, Ella, chances are—"

"Chances are nothing. If you want to write a sympathetic piece about the death of these three men and how we should reach out to their families, then I think that's fine. But you've crossed a line here, Reebe. You're not a news reporter. You shouldn't be making assertions you don't know are true. It's just like that garbage you tried to tell me yesterday over the phone."

Reebe's face reddened unattractively under her white hair. She reached across the table and snatched the article from Ella's hands.

"I wanted your opinion, Ella. Thank you for giving it to me. But I think you're being a bit sexist to suggest that because I do the society section I'm not capable of writing a more serious piece. I wrote this from the heart. I think it will reflect what a lot of my readers feel."

"That's fine, Reebe. Just make sure your facts are straight. Otherwise, you're nothing but a two-cent gossip, and you'll make trouble for us all."

Reebe pushed her chair back and left the restaurant, her tea untouched. The clock on the wall read 10:35. Ella paid the bill and walked out into the bustle of Praterton. Hell's bells. She was going to have to track Alby Truitt down.

Sarah Gainer lived three miles east of Statlers Cross, but Truitt knew enough to understand that neither she nor the locals considered her one of their own. Sarah's white trailer with its faded lime-green awnings occupied the end of a narrow dirt road. Two frayed lawn chairs, dirty and sagging, sat under a canvas overhang; an electric jack-o'-lantern face blinked from a window. Stacks of plastic flowerpots, some still wrapped in red and green Christmas foil, lined a makeshift walkway that led from a gravel patch to the front door. Leaving Haskell's blue Saturn parked on the patch, Truitt and Haskell scuffed their way to the trailer and knocked on the door.

Sarah Gainer answered immediately. It had been about six months since Truitt had seen her last, a little girl-woman about twenty-eight years old, with washed-out green eyes and lanky red hair that reached down her back. She was so thin it bothered Truitt to look at her—the first time he'd met her, he had quietly mentioned to the public defender assigned to her case that maybe she ought to be evaluated for anorexia, but he never heard anything more about it. At first blush, one would think that she was one of life's victims, maybe even an abused spouse, but the truth was much more chilling. Sarah Gainer was Calwyn County's premier racist. She was a woman filled with hate.

Truitt nodded at her and smiled.

"Good morning, Sarah. How's life treating you?"

She didn't answer.

"I sincerely hope that means it's been going well," Truitt continued. "I need to ask you a question, Sarah. About something you own. That little .22 Lorcin of yours. Have you seen it lately?"

Something shifted in her green eyes, and Truitt thought he detected a furrow of worry crease then pass from her brow. She shrugged and said nothing.

"Sarah, I need to ask you to go check on it. Will you do that for me? Just go see if it's where you left it?"

She studied him, mouth tightening, but she didn't move. "It's not there, is it?" she said.

"I don't know. Why don't you go look?"

" 'Cause you wouldn't be here if I still had it, would you, Sheriff Alby? Where did you find it?"

"So you know what gun I'm talking about? Do you only own one .22?" At her nod, Truitt pressed on. "When was the last time you saw it?"

Her gaze wandered away. "I dunno. Maybe this summer?"

"Was it this summer? I need you to think about it, Sarah. When did you see it last?"

"I cleaned it. August, probably."

"Where did you put it after you cleaned it?"

"In my kitchen drawer."

"You ever lend it to anyone?"

"Naw. It's my gun. I keep it for protection."

"Did anyone know you kept it in the kitchen?"

Again the shrug. "I dunno. It wasn't no secret."

"Do you have any idea who might have taken it?"

Her gaze wandered past his head, through him, and over to Haskell, where it then dropped to the ground. "No one would take my gun. Everyone knows I need it to be safe."

"Well, Sarah, if the last time you saw it it was in your kitchen drawer, then I can assure you that someone took it, because right now it's in state custody. Your gun was used to commit a crime. We need to know who had it last."

A flicker of fear sparked her eyes. "I don't know nothing about a crime. I haven't done nothing since I've been on parole, Sheriff. I swear to that."

"Just possessed a gun, that's all, Sarah," Truitt said quietly. "Hate crimes of the sort you committed are a felony. When you vandalized and set fire to the pews in that church, you committed and were convicted of a felony. Owning that gun was against the law."

The flicker disappeared; in its place grew a flinty stare. "I don't have to talk with you. If you need something more from me, you can talk with my lawyer."

She slammed the door, leaving Truitt and Haskell with the flowerpots and the jack-o'-lantern's pulsing face.

"Damn," said Haskell. "You know there's too much TV when someone like Sarah Gainer can deliver a line like that."

11

Nadianna Jesup fiddled with the lens on her Nikon camera, peering through the viewfinder, judging the light. The baby played on a quilt beneath the ancient pecan tree that dominated the Aldens' side yard. As a photographer, she knew the Georgia autumns were fickle. Some years the springs were too wet, the summers too dry, and the leaves dried up and turned brown before they even fell from the trees. Other years the southern Appalachians splintered into sprigs of color so intense they were the basis for a tourist industry. Here, in the rolling foothills, the colors rarely seemed as vibrant as those of their northern brothers. Distinct, they were nevertheless muted, as if God had splashed on the pigments and blotted them out before they could dry.

She held the camera up to her eye, settled her sight on the baby, and clicked. The pecan tree's yellow leaves were beginning to fall, creating a subtle aura around the baby's white quilt. In the background stood Ella's two red maples, which this year blazed a bright burgundy. Her baby kicked his feet up in the air, his blue shoes like two fallen scraps of sky. Click. She sat back on her heels, satisfied. It ought to be a nice shot.

She twisted around to study the house behind her. With its lance-shaped roof and bright red facade, Ella's

was a striking house, one she had gazed at often as a
child from her bedroom window in the little mill house
across the railroad tracks. Growing up, she knew by the
hushed tones of her parents that the Aldens were a
family to respect and to keep one's distance from. The
names of the women who lived there were always preceded by "Miss"—"Miss Nora," "Miss Ella." Nadianna had
thought the moniker was given to the women because
of their age, but during the time Gale helped her pre-
pare a grants proposal for the arts council, Nadianna
heard her father refer to "Miss Gale" and "Miss Katie
Pru." It was a sign of respect, but it was also a sign of division. Nadianna had figured out that in Statlers Cross,
if you named something, you put it in its place. In the
distant stirrings of her memory, she could also remember her father referring to "Niggra William" and "Niggra
Jackie," in tones not dissimilar to those used for the
Alden women. She had never sat down to figure out what
that meant, and she hadn't heard those uglier names
used for a long time now.

The baby stared up into the tree branches, kicking
his feet and burbling. Nadianna picked up a leaf and
placed it on his forehead. As he bubbled and laughed,
she straddled him and took a shot from above. His little
fists pummeled the air as he cooed.

She didn't hear Ron Goddard open the gate and
cross the yard; she gasped as he knelt down beside her,
smiling at the baby.

"What a terrific child," he said, holding his finger
out. The baby's fist swayed around it before finally un-
clenching and making a grab for it. "How old is he
now?"

"Seven months. Almost eight."

"Crawling, is he?"

"Absolutely. Gale tells me to enjoy this time. She says
as soon as he starts walking my life will change forever."

She watched the baby firmly grasp Goddard's finger. "You got kids?"

Goddard gave a soft laugh. "No. Always wanted them, though. Sons. Thought I'd make a good father of sons. But, no. I never married. Head too buried in my work, I suppose."

"You still have time. You can't be more than what, fifty? Men have longer for this than women."

Another laugh. "I'm forty-two, actually. And yes, I know there's time. But I really have been focused on my work. I figured it would be selfish to have children when I wasn't ready to scale back a bit on that."

Nadianna took the leaf from the baby's forehead and tickled his nose with it. His feet slapped the quilt. Nadianna's chest tightened: This was the grand debate, the one she and Gale had spent many late nights discussing, this idea of what place work—vocation, Gale called it—had in a house with children. Gale, the survivor of many solitary years of trying to focus on her work and raise a child alone, was almost militant about it. Women needed to band together to give each other the time and room to both parent and work. "We just can't let bright women continue to disappear into motherhood," Gale had told her, "any more than we can afford to have them not mother at all." Hence, The Arrangement. As Nadianna studied her child, she wondered if any of them understood exactly what they were doing.

Goddard cooed at the baby, but she caught his thoughtful glance at her.

"What?" she asked.

He nodded at her camera. "I've seen the book you and Gale did. Truly remarkable. I've been to that part of England, you know—not the village of Mayley specifically, but in West Yorkshire. I thought you captured it beautifully. You're very talented. As I was looking at your photos, it struck me that you see beneath the surface,

that you understand things as they really are. Then—
and I don't know how you do it, whether it's the light
or the lens or the developing process—you peel back
the surface and let us in on the true reality. That's a
gift."

"I don't know about a gift. It's just what I do, like
you listen to people talk, and Daniel solves crimes. You
do what you're good at."

"You're selling yourself short. You're good at
something that not many people are." He nodded back
at the house. "And yet you work here as a baby-sitter.
Don't you feel . . . thwarted?"

"Thwarted? Heck, no. I would feel thwarted if I *didn't*
work here. I would feel thwarted if I had gone with my
father and sister when they moved. They would've understood about the baby, but no way would they have
understood about my photography. That was just something crazy I did. Gale understands. And so does Ella. I
don't know what I would be doing if it hadn't been for
them. I'd be in a hot little house with baskets of diapers
to wash, that's where I'd be, and I'd be miserable and
hating my life. Thwarted. I can tell you about thwarted
and this ain't it."

The passion of her reply took them both by surprise, and Goddard looked away from her and traced
the white-on-white stitchery on the quilt.

"I see. Yes, that was presumptive of me. I didn't
understand. Of course, I know differently now. I'm
sorry."

"No need to be sorry."

He was silent a long time, running his finger up the
baby's chubby arm, lightly touching his snub nose. Finally he looked her straight in the face, his expression
serious.

"Nadianna, ever since I saw your book, I've had
this idea. I want to discuss it with you. It's a business

proposition. I'm working on grant money. Part of my proposal involves preserving the ethnographic data of my research—audiotape recordings, video. But I am wondering what it would be like to have a professional photographer, one with a very perceptive eye, come with me to my interviews and photograph my subjects. It's one thing to hear a person's voice and to watch their faces move as they speak, but it would be an entirely different aspect to catch their faces and freeze them right at the perfect moment to project their . . . well, their soul, if you will. I certainly don't have the talent for that, but you do. And better yet, you are from here, you are part of this culture. You would see things I don't."

She looked at him, struggling to control a budding excitement until she could judge his sincerity.

"I would need money," she said.

"Absolutely. That's what I'm talking about. I could pay you. You could accompany me, I would give you free rein to take the pictures as you saw fit—as long as they were authentic, I insist on my work being authentic, no staging beyond what would be technically necessary— and we would work up a payment schedule . . ."

"I would retain copyright."

"Um, yes, of course. I hadn't thought that far, but yes, you are the creator, you should retain copyright. I may have to talk with my university, but yes, I think that is something we can work out. What do you say, Nadianna? Should we at least give it a try?"

The baby's face was beginning to curdle—whatever fun there had been in the leaves and the sky was gone for now. He needed lunch and a nap.

"All right," Nadianna answered. "Let's give it a try."

Goddard literally rubbed his hands in pleasure. "Terrific. What do you say you come by my house tonight after dinner and we talk about it? And you can bring your little one."

"We could bring her in, you know. She's in violation of her parole."

"Yes, she is, and yes, we could, but I don't know how productive that would be right now."

"She knows more about this than she's letting on. She knows who had that gun last."

"She does. But the best way to clam her up is to bring her in."

"She might run off."

Truitt ran his hands through his hair and sighed. "She might, Craig. But I can't see her staying on the run. Sarah's a stubborn little thing who thinks it's her God-given right—probably her God-given obligation—to feel the way she does about things. Unless she's directly tied into these murders, I don't see her running off. And if she does, well, that makes her a fugitive and that's a whole 'nother ball game."

"I don't trust her."

"Nor should you. But the thing about the Sarah Gainers of the world is they have their own sense of integrity, and unless I'm reading her wrong, she's gonna go after whoever took her gun and she's gonna see that he pays."

"She gonna stay within the law to do it?"

"If she wants to stay out of jail she will. Something else about the Sarah Gainers of the world—they do not want to go to jail."

Haskell shot him a quizzical look, then stood. "You know these people better than me, Sheriff. I'd haul her skinny ass in."

"We might still have to. Let's give her a day. I bet you ten dimes I get a phone call from her by tomorrow morning."

"Ten dimes," Haskell muttered as he left Truitt's

office. "Ten damn dimes is what this man calls chicken feed."

Truitt waited until he heard Haskell exit the detective wing via the security doors. Then he stood, walked around his desk, and slammed his office door shut with a resounding *whump*.

He hoped to hell he was right. His gut told him . . . no, that was inaccurate; his years of experience, of reading body language and a person's tone told him that Sarah Gainer had fully believed her .22 pistol was safe in her kitchen drawer. Interesting that she kept it in her kitchen; he hated to think what was in her bedside table. And yes, he should call her parole officer and inform him that Miss Gainer was breaking the law. But he needed names, and Sarah Gainer had them.

He was making notes to himself when his desk phone rang, and Blaire informed him that Ella Alden was in the waiting area. Truitt looked at his watch—eleven-thirty. Damn. He had forgotten their meeting.

"Buzz her through, Blaire," he said. "Does she look pissed?"

"She looks sturdy," Blaire whispered. "I'll let you interpret."

He opened his door as Ella's stern form pressed into the hall. She smiled at him wryly as he motioned her into his office.

"Another man wouldn't get away with it, Alby," she said.

"Another man wouldn't have dared do it, Ella, and I wouldn't have either without good cause. I am sorry. I got called away."

"And you forgot."

"The two follow. I apologize."

"You're fine. This will probably work out better, anyway. I wanted to talk with you about the Nguyens."

"Nguyens? They doing all right?"

"To tell you the truth, I don't know. Gale had a run-in with Le yesterday. She went over to express her condolences and got slapped down. Literally."

"I'm sorry to hear that. Nothing worth pressing charges over, I hope."

"Of course not, but I think it indicates the kind of pressure that family's under."

Truitt reared back in his chair, sizing up the elderly woman before him. He supposed there were several Ellas in every county, community fixtures who recognized no rank above their own, who probably had the governor's phone number in their Rolodexes, along with those of both senators. Ella Alden could make heaven and earth move for her—he'd seen her do it.

"What you trying to tell me, Ella?"

"I think you ought to post a deputy outside their house."

"Why?"

"They're going to get hurt."

"Why do you say that?"

"I got a phone call yesterday from someone who wanted to warn me about the Nguyens. Specifically, they blamed the Nguyens for getting Darrell Murphy involved in something unsavory."

"Like what?"

Ella's gray eyes seemed almost white behind her silver-framed glasses. "Prostitution. Of Asian women."

"Who told you this?"

"It was gossip, Alby. I wouldn't even finish listening to it. But it was particularly mean-spirited gossip. And then just now, while I was waiting for you, I read a column Reebe Vaughter has written to run in the *Courier*. Nothing vicious, just the 'they're not our kind' type of stuff."

"Okay. I'll buy that you've heard some uncomfortable things about the Nguyens. But what makes you think someone's going to hurt them?"

She leaned forward, her leather purse planted on her lap. "Because no one's done it before. When the house was painted blue, there were all kinds of problems, Alby, all kinds of mutterings. But finally everyone gave up because they didn't know what to do. None of the actions they could have taken seemed to fit the crime—all the Nguyens did was paint their house. But now, the mayor's son is dead. And while people may not like the Keasts much, at least they're local." She paused. "And Caucasian."

"So what are you saying? That because people couldn't punish the Nguyens for painting their house a funny color, they're going to cause them harm now?"

"That's exactly what I'm saying. People didn't give themselves permission to take action over the house. But they're going to give themselves permission over this. The gossip's going to do it; the newspaper's going to do it. By the time word gets around about the prostitution angle, people will have all the reason they need."

Truitt let his chair legs slam to the floor. "Ella, there's no reason to believe there's a 'prostitution angle.' This is the first time the word's even come up."

"Like I said, gossip. But that's all it takes. You know that, Alby."

The elderly woman watched him carefully, her hands steady on her purse latch. Yes, he did know that was all it took. He'd seen it on a professional level—a neighborhood squall that erupted into violence because of what someone had said about someone else. He'd seen it on a personal level. And he knew the woman across his desk had seen it. One didn't achieve Ella's singular station in life without surviving a few viper tongues.

"Tell me who it was who called you. I need to check out the prostitution angle."

"It won't help you. There isn't one."

"I don't think so either, but I have to track down all leads. Now tell me who called."

Ella didn't hesitate, and Truitt suddenly knew she had decided to give up her source long before she entered his office.

"Reebe."

"Busy woman."

Ella nodded. "I want you to call Roy Dancer over at the paper. I want you to get him to agree not to run Reebe's column."

"I'll talk with him, Ella, but freedom of the press . . ." As he jotted down the notes, a thought occurred to Alby. "When you called, you specifically said you wanted to talk to me without my partner. I assumed you meant Sergeant Haskell. Any particular reason why?"

The gray eyes never wavered from his face. "I had a simple observation to make to you," Ella answered. "I figured it was in everyone's best interest to keep it . . . simple."

12

Statlers Cross was not like the small towns and villages to which Halford was accustomed. He had grown up in Nottingham, a sizable city in northern England, but his childhood had been punctuated by extended visits to the villages of the north where great-aunts and distant cousins puttered through lives that he could scarcely fathom as a teen. The villages there were compact with two-hundred-, three-hundred-, even four-hundred-year-old stone buildings stacked like blocks smack up against the streets. Houses sat atop shops, shops leaned against offices—an entire village, save for the church, which occupied its own green square, could stretch for half a mile with not more than a sliver of air separating the buildings.

Not so here, he mused as he crossed the abandoned railroad tracks and angled toward the Statlers Cross town center. On his first day in Atlanta, Gale had taken surface streets north through the city—out of the way, she admitted, but she wanted him to catch the flavor of the Old South's largest city. She had navigated first through downtown and then through what she called Midtown with its glistening city-on-the-hill art museum and bold architecture, then further out to Buckhead and the high-end malls and expensive car dealerships.

It had always struck him as odd how Americans didn't live among their activities, how they chose to seclude themselves in their suburbs, and he said so to Gale. She had given him a bemused look.

"You don't know what secluded is," she had said and turned the car onto I-85, I-285, and I-20 to make the long eastern trek to Statlers Cross.

Somewhere outside of Atlanta—he couldn't say where—the physical world had changed. The billboards boasted *No Roaming Charges* and the affluent subdivisions dwindled; the exit ramps spun off first to solitary gas stations and then to wilderness. Cars grew infrequent, trees fell rotting and uprooted from roadside forests. Finally he and Gale left the highway and snaked through the remote and peopleless expanse of north central Georgia. Every now and then they came across eerie mounds of vines that rose from the ravines like strangled giants, creating the uncomfortable sensation that they were reaching out and pleading with him.

"Kudzu," Gale had told him. "It's not indigenous and it's taking over everything. We Georgians pride ourselves on how green our countryside is; what we don't admit is that our countryside can't breathe."

They drove past gullies, trees, power poles, all covered thickly in the grasping leaves, withering from the onset of fall. When he recognized the sharp angle of a roofline beneath a blanket of vines, he had looked away. The damn stuff even ate houses.

Now, as he strode the cracked sidewalk through the town center, there were no signs of the creeping vines. The afternoon sun shone brightly on the clapboard storefronts, accenting the worn hardware on the doors and revealing the dust in the windows. Gale had once described the town as dying, but here and there Halford could see sparks of rejuvenation. A life-size witch perched on a haystack in front of a church consignment shop;

swags of gourds and dried corn looped from the overhang of the general store. At least some people were
trying, perhaps inspired by Sally Robertson's "cheery"
tearoom. This was the kind of Americana he thought
existed only in Norman Rockwell's quaint imagination;
it made him feel good that perhaps such a vision was
struggling to be reborn here.

He was thumping a gourd, listening to the rattle of
dried seeds inside, when a red Ford pulled up to the
sidewalk. The corpulent man who emerged stood several seconds beside his car, examining the contents of
his wallet before stuffing it into his rear pocket. Scowl-
ing, he looked around; his eyes lighted on Halford. The
man stared at him intently until his face broadened into
a grin and he hauled himself onto the sidewalk.

"You know, I found that when I was visiting Italy,
everyone could tell I was American. I didn't have to
open my mouth—there was just something about me
that said U.S.A. Well, sir, something about you says
England. And detective. You're Daniel Halford, aren't
you? Alby told me about you." The fat man stuck out his
hand and grasped Halford's. "Damn pleasure to meet
you. I'm John Bingham. County coroner." He stood back,
looking Halford up and down. "A Scotland Yard man.
Well, well, well."

"It's a pleasure to meet you, too, sir," Halford said. "I
was just admiring the view. Lovely little town."

Bingham stood with his hands on his hips, the grin
still big on his face. "Lovely little town—I suppose so. I
understand you're here visiting the Aldens. I've got
that gal's book sitting on my coffee table. Gorgeous
work."

"I'll pass on the compliment."

Bingham tilted his head toward the general store.
"Langley's," he said. "Best little store in the county. You
can get stuff here you can't get anywhere else. It's s

drive to get here, but it's worth it. I was running in to grab some clove gum for my staff—they eat it by the box and it's hard to find. But listen, how long are you here for?"

"I leave Sunday. Four more days."

"I'd like to get together and talk with you. Maybe we can grab Alby and go get some beers somewhere." He lowered his voice. "Course, Alby's got that damn case. The thing about living in a place like Calwyn County is that we have a murder maybe every other year. That's why I like my job. The problem with that is your local law enforcement don't get the experience they need to solve these things quickly. So much of it starts to depend on luck. That's one thing you can say about America, isn't it? You live in a big city, you're gonna have a thoroughly experienced homicide division. Not like the U.K., is it?"

"Oh, we're fairly well trained. But no, we thankfully don't quite have the volume you have here."

"That's what I want to talk with you about. What you say we get together? How about after dinner? You got an evening free?"

The man reminded Halford of a big happy dog, so infectious was his enthusiasm. Nevertheless, his heart sank. In light of the previous evening with Gale, the last thing he wanted was to spend a night drinking beer and talking shop. He really wanted nothing more than to curl up on a sofa with Katie Pru and her mother, reading E.B. White. Well, he admitted, maybe he wanted a tad more . . .

"My evenings are rather full—"

"What are you doing now? I was going to run over to the Keast place for a sec. A Keast was one of our murder victims. I wanted to pay my respects to the family. It's something I try to do when we've got particularly bad crimes. Want to ride with me? We'll talk on the way.

Besides, believe me, you'll see some things that I guarantee Gale's gonna leave out of any tour of the South she gives you."

Halford checked his watch. With Katie Pru intent on a craft project and Michael asleep, Gale had asked him to occupy himself for ninety minutes while she worked. "All right," he agreed. "I'm not due back for another hour. It'll be interesting."

Bingham rubbed his hands in pleasure. "Why don't you come on in the store with me a for sec. You met Coop? You ought to. Coop knows everything there is to know in these parts."

The sign outside may have said "Langley Drugs," but inside, as Bingham had stressed, the contents far outreached the typical apothecary. Halford walked through a maze of aisles with shelves that stretched almost up to the ceiling. The store smelled of brewing coffee and something sweet. The two men made their way past shelves of undergarments, waterproof boots, umbrellas, gardening tools, and over-the-counter medicines. The aroma grew stronger until they finally found themselves in a tiny snack area where coffee brewed in a pot and a sizable man in a plaid shirt stared intently at a small toaster oven. As the oven bell dinged, the man looked up.

"John," he said affably. "Toasted me up a Krispy Kreme here. How about yourself?"

"Trying to watch my weight, Coop, but thanks." He turned to Halford. "Gale bought you any Krispy Kreme doughnuts yet? You gotta try some. Baked fresh there's nothing like 'em. A day old and toasted up ain't bad, either. Coop, you know Detective Halford here? He's staying with Ella and Gale."

Langley slid the bubbling glazed doughnut onto a napkin and, licking his fingers, nodded at Halford. "We haven't met, but Ella's told me all about you, sir.

Pleasure to meet you. Let me fix you up one of these. No? Well, I suppose Ella's feeding you well enough. How you finding Georgia?"

"It's pretty much as I expected," Halford said. "Beautiful. Temperate. Friendly. I'm thoroughly enjoying myself."

"You caught us at a pretty time of year. You need to get Gale to carry you up to the mountains. The artwork of God."

"I'm fixing to take him out to the Keast place," Bingham said. "I want to go up there, check on 'em, make sure they're all right. They don't use a doctor, you know. Thought I might at least make myself available to them."

Langley shook his head. "God, what a pitiful family that is. What a horrible thing to have happen. Mind you, Stuart could be a handful—used to come in here drunk sometimes, wanting more beer. I wouldn't sell it to him when he got that way. Sometimes I'd have to call someone to drive him home." His face grew thoughtful. "Come to think of it, most of the time I'd call Darrell. He was close by and usually didn't mind dropping what he was doing to come help. I remember one time he said, 'What kind of man would I be if I didn't help my brother?' I said, 'Damn messed-up family you've got if Stuart's your brother.' But he laughed and said, 'Stuart's all right. You just got to understand him.' "

"And did you?" Halford asked.

"Understand him? Yeah. I think I did. Stuart just did the kind of living the rest of us would if we could. And sometimes that made him get drunk as a skunk. I used to tell Darrell drink was gonna kill Stuart Keast. There're forty-two different ways to drive up that road of his wrong, and being a drunken fool behind the wheel wasn't a smart thing for him to be."

"I can't swear by it," Bingham said, "but I don't think booze had anything to do with how he died."

Langley took a huge bite of his doughnut. "Wrong place at the wrong time, that's what they're saying."

"Who's they?"

"Folks. They're just saying that Darrell and Stuart were in the woods, probably thinking about hunting, when they came across the killer. Pure-tee bad luck."

"What about the third man in the car?" Halford asked. "Bad luck with him, too?"

The remaining bite of the doughnut disappeared in Langley's mouth. "The little Vietnamese guy? Double bad luck for him. Bad luck he was in that car, bad luck he was in the country to begin with." As soon as he said it, regret showed on Langley's face. "I'm sorry. That was out of line. I just had a conversation this morning with a man over in Middleton, about ten miles from here. He said a Vietnamese family has bought out their corner store. Just came in and bought the white owners out. Now the place has gone downhill—merchandise not as good. So the man said he'd decided he'd come here and do his shopping. Now, I'm as open-minded as the next guy, but I understand what that Middleton fellow was saying. They don't understand our ways. And worse, they don't want to."

Beside Halford, Bingham worked intently at rearranging a display of chewing gum. "I bet those owners didn't hand that store over. I bet they got money for it."

"Oh, I'm sure they got money. But it doesn't change the fact that their old customer is my new one, all because he doesn't feel those foreign people understand his needs."

Bingham picked up the entire box of gum. "That's what free enterprise is all about, Coop. Those new owners are going to have to figure out how to please their customers—either give them the standard merchandise they want or offer them things they've never seen before. That's how we all learn new things."

Langley took the money that Bingham held out to

him and, roughly wiping his hands on a napkin, punched in the sale on his cash register. "I'm with you there, John. I have no argument with foreigners, I really don't. I just wish once they come here, they knew to fit in quickly. Seems in the past, that was the case. But these immigrants now . . ." He shook his head. "Don't know why you'd want to come to a country and then act like you've never left your own."

"I think that's also a function of the marketplace," Halford said. "Two of the commodities the West has franchised out are self-awareness and cultural pride."

Langley shook his head again. "Maybe so. But it makes me uncomfortable. I have to admit I yearn for the days when I could pronounce everyone's last name. I'd be a liar if I didn't admit it scares me a little bit."

Backing out of the parking space, Bingham indicated Langley's store.

"You heard that in there? That is what I call genteel bigotry. Cooper Langley is the salt of the earth. I'd trust him with my sister. But then my sister's whiter than processed flour. I'd trust him with your sister because even though he'd say she talked funny, she'd still look right to him. The problem with people like Cooper—and I'm honest enough to admit even people like me sometimes—is they think their bigotry is refined enough to excuse it. And it's not."

"I see the same back home," Halford said.

Bingham made a grunting noise as he straightened the steering wheel and directed the car down Main Street. "I have a doctor friend from Vietnam—Ho Chi Minh City, in fact. He and his family came over in the late 1960's, true political refugees. They did just what people like Coop wanted them to do—after they worked a while building up some money, they settled in Atlanta, bought a respectable house in one of the better neighborhoods. Their daughter joined the Girl Scouts, learned to play soccer, became the star violinist in her middle-school orchestra. I go over to their house to visit and expect little My to speak with the same accented English as her parents, but her delightful voice is as Americanized as Oprah Winfrey's. They became Americans in the most predictable and recognizable way."

"Not like, say, the Nguyens."

"Exactly. I asked my friend Nhu once about it, was it my imagination or did the immigrants who came over right after the war assimilate more quickly, and he said it was absolutely not my imagination. Nhu explained it this way: That first wave was primarily made up of the professional class of Vietnamese society—college professors, lawyers, engineers. They came from money, and they adapted to American society as fast as they could. Perhaps they wanted the comforts. This most recent wave isn't like that. He said these were more economic refugees, people who had decided to stay in Vietnam after the war and found the country simply couldn't support them. So starting in the early nineties, they began immigrating. They weren't as well off as the first group, and they weren't as eager to blend into American society. So you have a larger language gap, a bigger cultural gap, and no real desire to close it anytime soon. Of course, that was just Nhu's explanation. I sense a bit of class snobbery in it, as well."

"Pity," was all Halford said.

Both men remained silent as they rounded the outskirts of town and turned onto a roughly paved road that made a serpentine route through a line of rolling hills. Here the signs of habitation grew more and more scarce—a farmhouse here, a barn there. By the time the road bumped from pavement to gravel to dirt, all indications of human activity had disappeared from the landscape, and Halford had to brace himself against the car's ramble.

"Jesus lives somewhere east of here," Bingham said cheerfully. "When you talk Keasts, you're talking the hintermost of the hinterland."

"I hear they're extremely reclusive."

"That depends on your definition of reclusive. They're rather legendary in these parts. Stuart Keast's great-great-granddaddy made the best moonshine in this part of the state, and he wasn't above shooting a man who claimed he didn't. So some folks still say the Keasts are mean as snakes. But my daddy called them independent and respected them for it—they didn't need nobody and just as soon nobody needed them."

"So I guess they've never been much of a part of the social fabric."

Bingham chuckled. "They were if your social fabric included a regular helping of white lightning. But, no, they don't go in for most of the social structures of the community. They used to go to the Baptist Church, then I heard they were going to the Pentecostal Church, and then I heard they gave up all together and turned one of their outbuildings into a chapel and just do the whole thing by themselves."

"So what do they do now that the moonshining is gone?"

Bingham gave him a hard glance. "What makes you think it is? I bet if someone really struck out in some of the woods around here, they'd come across a still or two."

"Is it possible that that's what happened? Did someone come across a still and three people ended up dead?"

"I've thought about it. And you can believe when Alby had his men canvasing the woods for the murder weapon, he had them keep their eyes open for other illegal contraptions as well. But to be honest, it doesn't feel right to me. I'm willing to bet there are stills around here, but I'm not so willing to believe they're important enough to kill for. These days, there are much more lucrative ways to break the law. And then there's the small problem that it was a Keast who ended up dead."

"You're right about more effective ways of making dirty money," Halford said. "I wonder if a family that has a history of illegal activity might not make the transition."

"You mean go into drugs or something? They might. Course, if you assumed every old family that kept 'shine transitioned into something more up-to-date, you'd be investigating a whole lot of bankers, schoolteachers, and preachers."

Halford lunged sideways as Bingham turned the steering wheel sharply to avoid a crumbling hole where the road was beginning to wash away. Once again they were in kudzu country; the vines looped over the tallest trees, slithered across the ground. Behind the mounds stretched dense woods. He could imagine that it would be very easy to hide a still in these hills. He could imagine that it would be very easy to hide a great deal.

"Why hasn't the kudzu taken over the road?"

"It's fierce stuff, but it ain't superhuman. The Keasts do enough driving back and forth to keep the damn stuff off the road. Of course, when they're all gone . . ."

"How many of them are there? Ron Goddard only mentioned Stuart and his grandmother."

"And Stuart's sister Bethy and her little Jud. Boy's about ten, I guess. I birthed him. Bethy wasn't about to go to the hospital, and she was having trouble. Stuart drove down to Coop's store and called me. Said they didn't use doctors much, but mine was the only name he could come up with at the spur of the moment. He helped me birth that baby right in their bathroom." Bingham let out a sigh and shook his head. "They all depended on Stuart to run the show. I don't know what they're going to do with him gone. That's one of the things I sort of want to check on."

"At least the child's in school. That ought to give them some outside support."

Again Bingham gave him a weird look. "You've got a family here who's decided to be their own church. Why on earth would you assume they send that child to school? Homeschooling, my friend. Bring him up in the family way."

The road took an upward slant, and Bingham shifted into second gear. On both sides trees leaned into the road, their roots barely clinging to the soil. It wasn't only kudzu that toyed with the entrance to the Keast homestead, Halford thought; it was as if Mother Nature herself couldn't decide whether to go or to stay.

Suddenly the ground flattened and Halford had his first glimpse of East of Jesus. He must have expected a tar-paper shack, because he found himself pleasantly surprised by the two-story clapboard house plunked in the middle of the small plateau. It was unpainted, and the wood had a weathered gray patina that matched the color of the autumn kudzu vines. A wooden porch stretched along the front, its roof held up by unplaned tree trunks. A variety of machines covered the porch—a quick glance identified an old wringer washing machine, a rusted refrigerator, and several partially dismantled vacuum cleaners. In the middle of the clutter was a simple wood-frame screen door, on which hung a construction paper cutout of a jack-o'-lantern.

"Halloween is everywhere," Halford commented.

"You have no idea," Bingham answered.

The coroner maneuvered the car to the side of the house where two vehicles were already parked—an aging black Chevy pickup truck and a newer tan-colored sedan that Halford had seen most recently on the other side of the barbed wire fence bordering the Alden house.

"Ron Goddard's here," Halford said. Bingham must have caught the surprise in his voice because he looked at his passenger expectantly. After his conversation with Goddard, Halford thought the linguist would have relished an excuse not to risk his neck visiting the Keasts again. But then, not being an academic, Halford had no idea what kind of motivation accompanied the passion of loving an idea. Shrugging without comment, Halford climbed from the car.

They mounted sagging plank steps to the porch. Halford took in the busted appliances and the nests— bird? squirrel?—that hung from the rafters as Bingham rapped on the door.

A stout young woman answered, her cheeks apple red. Odd that her skin looked so healthy given the deep shadows under her brown eyes, Halford thought. She didn't look much older than Nadianna, which would have placed her in her mid-twenties. Terribly young to have a ten-year-old son.

"Bethy," the coroner said gently. "You remember ol' Dr. Bingham, don't you? I've come to pay my respects to your grandmama and see how y'all are doing." When the woman's gaze moved to Halford, Bingham reached out and patted the detective on the shoulder. "This here is a friend of mine. He's a policeman. From Scotland Yard, like on TV. He's not working on Stuart's case, now—I want you to understand that—but he knows all about what it's like to lose someone in such an awful way. I thought Jud might like to meet him. Do you mind if he comes in, too?"

Bethy's eyes roamed up and down Halford, then she nodded. Bingham held the door open and motioned Halford into the house.

Once inside, Halford knew immediately why Bethy's cheeks were so red. The furnace burred full blast, filling the cramped room with a stultifying heat. Seated tall and upright in an armchair in the center of the room was a thin woman with long white hair. As his eyes adjusted to the dim light, Halford realized that she was wearing shorts. On one side of her stood a stocky, towheaded boy. On the other side, seated in a vinyl-covered recliner, was Ron Goddard.

"Dr. Bingham," the woman said as the coroner came into the room.

Bingham walked up to her and took her hand. "Rosen, I am so sorry. This shouldn't have happened. It just shouldn't have."

" 'S all right," Rosen replied. "Lord's ways. 'S not ours to question."

Her vowels were broad, and her mouth moved widely when she spoke. The peculiarity of her sounds made Halford struggle to understand her words. While he certainly couldn't attest to the significance of her dialect, it was singular enough that he could see why Goddard had been excited.

She looked at Halford. "In'r'duce your friend, please."

Both Bingham and Goddard rushed to provide the introduction. At the mention of Ella Alden's name, Rosen lifted her chin and spoke.

"Ella's been by. Harsh woman, but a good'un."

That, Halford thought, was probably as accurate a description of Ella that he had heard. He wondered briefly at the idea of Ella making the journey over rutted roads in her Buick, but then he dismissed the thought. Of course Ella would have come. It was the proper thing to do.

"Rosen," Bingham said, "I just wanted you to know that this county is going to do everything it can to find out who did this to Stuart. And if you need anything . . . anything a doctor might provide you—"

"Don't need doct'rin'," Rosen said. "Lord's will. He'll give me stren'th."

"You're right about that. He does provide. What

about anything else? Is there anything else I can get you? Or Bethy and Jud?"

Beside her, Goddard fidgeted. He opened his mouth, then slumped back in his chair.

"You want to say something?" Bingham asked.

Goddard looked from Bingham to Halford to Rosen. Then his confused gaze swept over Jud and his mother. He leaned forward again in his seat.

"Rosen," he said urgently. "I think you should tell Dr. Bingham. He'll get in touch with the sheriff. Someone needs to know."

"Know what?" Halford asked.

Goddard kept his stare on Rosen. She studied his face, her jaw muscles working, before she shifted her eyes to Bingham.

"Sarah Gainer was by. Said our boy took her gun. Our boy ne'er took nothin'."

"You mean Stuart? Sarah said Stuart took a gun that belonged to her?" Bingham asked.

Rosen shook her head and glanced at Jud, who stood next to her, his grimy fingernails digging into the wooden chair arm. "Naw. Jud here. Sarah come over, mad as a pint of a woman can get, yelling like I don't know what. Cussin' in a house in mournin'. Started to drag Jud out into the yard. Bethy and I had to beat up on 'er to get 'er to let him go. Our boy never took nothin'. Y'all make sure she don't bo'er us no more. If she does, I may hafta kill 'er."

13

"Grandma Ella is mad at me."

Gale looked up from her laptop at Katie Pru, who sat spread-legged not three feet away from her. For the past thirty minutes, as the porch screen filtered late afternoon sunlight over her skin, the child had worked in silence, diligently gluing dried corn kernels to the side of a wooden spool. It had been a companionable mother-daughter silence, one that had allowed Gale to slip into a quiet remembrance of the final days of Tom's courtship of her—the intense, impassioned meeting behind the Colonial-style house that served as William and Mary graduate housing, where he had convinced her to forget her studies and leave with him for England. Those had been heady days, and as she typed the words, unedited and uncensored, into her laptop, she felt the tinge of that distant excitement and possibility. She really had believed him when he promised to support her academic pursuits once they were abroad, really had believed that her potential was as important to him as his own. And perhaps at one time both had been true. But ideological demons had eventually erased those domestic commitments from his mind. The more she focused on her memoirs, the more she marveled at the path she had taken since agreeing to be Tom Grayson's wife. Gone were her plans for a Ph.D., for a career writing accessible historical nonfiction, her later years spent in a comfortable position at a respectable university. Instead, her decision to marry had plunged her into a decade of confusion, betrayal, and pain— and a makeshift career that at best could be called mediocre.

At Katie Pru's words, she stopped her furious typing.

"What did you say?"

"Grandma Ella is mad at me."

"How do you know?"

"She looks at me funny. Like she doesn't know what to do with me."

That was a typical Ella statement—Gale remembered hearing it from her own childhood, and she had heard it several times directed at Katie Pru—*Child, I just don't know what I'm gonna do with you.* It was usually said more in exasperation than in anger. Ella didn't usually vent her anger verbally on children. When Gale had been a child, a switch had been swifter. In the post–corporal punishment era of Katie Pru's childhood, Ella tended to retreat and leave the discipline up to Gale.

"What did you do to make her look at you funny?"

At this Katie Pru let out a big sigh. "I don't know," she said, shaking her head. "I think I was in the wrong place at the wrong time."

Gale stifled a laugh. Katie Pru had obviously heard someone use that phrase. Then she realized with a sobering jolt that she very well could have heard it in reference to the murders.

"Now, why do you say that, baby?" she asked gently. "Why would you think you were in the wrong place at the wrong time?"

A corn kernel had become glued to Katie Pru's

fingers, and she tried to shake it loose. When that didn't work, she plucked it off and flicked it away. "I don't know. I think I'm not making her very happy."

Behind them the screen door opened. "Of course you make me happy," Ella said, her voice gruff. "You're my great-granddaughter." She held out a colander. "I need you to see if you can find any more muscadines out there."

Gale looked at Ella, frowning. "It's awful late in the season. I doubt she'll find many unless she goes deep into the thickets, and I don't want her to do that."

Ella continued to address Katie Pru. "I know it's late in the season, but you might find some. Could you take this colander and go look, please?"

Glancing at her mother, Katie Pru stood and took the colander. "Stay on this side of the thickets, K.P.," Gale said. "Stay where I can see you. Don't go down the path. I'll have my eye on you."

Ella said nothing until Katie Pru was out of the screen porch and walking toward the overgrowth at the edge of the yard. "You'll make her timid telling her not to go out there alone."

"Perhaps if we kept the path cut back, 'out there' wouldn't be so dangerous. But you know good and well there are foxes and wild dogs and snakes in those lower acres—not to mention a hunter now and again. She doesn't need to be going back there alone. I thought we'd already agreed on that."

"When I was a child, Nora and I used to roam all over this place. Three hundred acres and I knew every inch."

Gale felt her irritation flare—*Katie Pru isn't you and this isn't 1928*—but she squelched it, seeing the exhaustion on Ella's face. Perhaps she hadn't understood just how deeply her grandmother was feeling

Darrell Murphy's death. Gale had viewed these murders as yet another local tragedy, the instigator of a round of mournful rituals, but not personally affecting. Even given the fact that Darrell had helped around the house, she found Ella's deep response unsettling. She closed down her laptop and leaned toward Ella, concerned.

"Do you want to talk about Darrell? I should have asked you before. I'm sorry. I didn't realize you were as close as you must have been."

Ella turned to her sharply. "Close? That's nonsense. Darrell was just a good young man who took time out to help me keep this house up. What are you trying to say?"

"You look tired. I don't think you're sleeping well."

"How well am I supposed to sleep? A year-and-a-half ago I had a house all to myself. Now I share it with two grown women, a preschooler, and a baby. The baby was fussy last night—didn't you hear him? I wonder how you can sleep. I forget—you're probably used to it. Women don't sleep once they become mothers. But the secret is we finally do. We might be seventy, but at last we're able to sleep again. And then what happens? I open my house up to a bunch of children. What makes you suppose I'm ever going to sleep?"

Gale threw up her hands. "Ella, I'm sorry, but I don't buy it. I've been living here for almost two years, and you've been fine. Nadianna has been here for four months. I've only seen you look this bad since the murders. What's going on?"

"Hell's bells, Gale. Nothing's going on. Two of the town's young men—"

"Three."

"Oh, crap. I've voted Democrat all my life, which passes for liberal around here, but I am not going to count that Nguyen boy as part of this town. Maybe if he'd lived here like his mother and sister, but as far as I'm concerned he was just an outsider who got caught in some bad mess and ended up dead. People get unlucky sometimes and sometimes the price is very high."

"What kind of bad mess?"

"So what, you're a detective now, too?" Ella's voice grew shrill and loud enough so that out in the yard, Katie Pru turned to stare at them. "I don't know what kind of bad mess. But it was bad enough to get them all killed, wasn't it?" She stopped, her face red, her breathing strained.

Gale stood and tried to guide her grandmother to a chair, but Ella shook her off. Gale took her arm and held it tightly. "Ella, there's something you're not telling me. I want you to tell me right now. What is bothering you?"

Ella's mouth was a tight line; she stared hard at her granddaughter, trying to straighten a spine that had long since started the curve to old age. "You don't talk to me that way . . ."

"Ella, if it's affecting your health—"

"No. You listen to me." Her voice dropped to a whisper. "Darrell and Stuart are dead. I can count on one hand how many murders we've had since I've been alive. You think this was a random act? You think some box dropped around those boys and separated them out for death? No, ma'am. This was not an accident, it wasn't an act of domestic violence. And it damn sure wasn't because they were in the wrong place at the wrong time. They were in the middle of a patch of woods so remote that no one ever goes there, and they got shot. That was *planned,* Gale. And in a town this small, that means we're all in danger."

Gale shook her head in disbelief, but she felt the hairs on her neck rise. "I don't buy it."

"Listen, little girl, you better 'buy it.' In a town this size, nothing happens to one person that doesn't affect us all. And if those two boys—all right, *three*—got shot, it was for a reason." Tears welled in her eyes. "Other people are going to die, Gale. You better buy it."

"Ella . . ."

"Leave me alone." She started toward the door, but stopped and turned. "I forgot what I wanted to tell you. About Katie Pru. That child is listening too much. You need to teach her to mind her own business."

The Statlers Cross City Hall was no more a hall than the town was a city. It took up the front half of a corner store on the south side of Main Street; the back half, accessible only from the parking lot behind the shops, was a video rental business, new since the last time Truitt visited. A brass bell jingled as he entered the city hall, and the fragrance of pine and something flowery hit him strong enough to make a point. As he walked across a dark green carpet and past peach-colored walls bordered in wallpaper magnolias, he knew what that point was—more women than men spent time here.

Reebe Vaughter sat behind an oak desk situated catty-corner in the back of the room, typing on a computer. A vase of dried blue hydrangeas provided the sole color counterpoint to what he could only describe as Southern overkill. He wondered if he hung around long enough a possum would appear from behind the file cabinet.

He smiled at her as she looked up from her work. "So I see you're sharing quarters with a video magnate now."

She rolled her eyes. "This month. Last month it was a fingernail salon. Like there're enough women around to get weekly silk wraps. People get these ideas for businesses, think it's gonna make them rich. Ends up eating all their savings and saddling them with a huge debt."

"Welcome to America," Truitt said. "It's what we came here for."

"Lord, and I thought we came here because we were ornery cusses." She smiled a lovely Southern-belle smile at Truitt, her green eyes crinkling behind her oversize red glasses. "What can I do for you, Sheriff?" As Truitt pulled a chair up to her desk, her eyes grew serious. "It's about the murders, isn't it? Whatever I can do, whatever the city can do, you know we'll do it."

Truitt eased himself into the chair. "That's fine, Reebe. I do have a couple of questions I need to ask you. You must have known Darrell Murphy pretty well."

"I would think so. I've worked with his father for about fifteen years—seven out at the plastics plant and eight here as city clerk. I belong to some of the same clubs as Myra—well, we attend the United Methodist Women together, and I'm supposed to be in the reading club she goes to in Praterton, but what with my newspaper work and all, I haven't had time. So I've known Darrell since he was a boy."

"How would you describe him?"

"Oh, well, just the best kind of young man. He was his father through and through. Conscientious, hard-working. Had a mischievous streak in him that gave him sort of a twinkle in his eye, but that was just him. He went out of his way to help people. He just about laid the new roof on the Methodist Church by himself. Got everybody lined up, gave them a pep talk, and they all went to work. He was a leader. Someday he could have been . . ."

She stopped, and her fingers nervously tapped the desktop.

"Mayor?" Truitt finished for her.

"He could have been anything he wanted. His parents brought him up to be responsible. People around here respected him. Yes, I could see Darrell running for mayor at some point—after his father stepped down."

"So you wouldn't naturally expect him to be involved with a prostitution ring."

Reebe's mouth contracted and her face turned a blotched pink. "Whoever repeated that to you shouldn't have."

"Can I get you to guess who it might have been?"

The fingernails had stopped their tapping; now they worked the curled edge of the blotter. *She's trying to think of all the people she's talked to about this,* Truitt thought. Judging by the length of her silence, there must have been many.

He reared back in his seat and brushed imaginary lint from his trouser knee. "Aw, listen, Reebe, I'm not getting on to you. It was good that this piece of gossip got back to me. I need to check it out. I believe you when you say Darrell was a terrific guy, but even terrific guys sometimes get into stuff they shouldn't, and if that's what got him killed . . ."

"I don't think it was gossip, Alby." Reebe had collected herself. Her coloring had returned, and she had placed her hands in her lap. "Gossip makes it sound like it wasn't true. There are people around here who think that the Nguyens were into something bad, and that Darrell got caught up in it."

"I'm not making judgments, Reebe. I just want to find out what happened to those three men so their families can stop wondering. It might not be the answer they want, but at least it will be an answer. So where did you get the idea that we might be dealing with prostitution?"

"I—I can't remember who told me first . . ."

"Then who told you second? I just need a place to start, Reebe. Help me out here."

She turned away from him and typed for several seconds on her computer. When she turned back, he could tell she had made a decision.

"Ilene Parker," she said. "She told me first . . . and second."

"Meaning?"

"Meaning she called me twice. She wanted to make sure I understood exactly what she was saying. She trusted me because she knows I'm a newspaperwoman. That's why I don't believe it was gossip. I take it as fact."

Ilene Parker's white clapboard house sat on a neat parcel of land banded by camellia bushes and forsythia. Both were beginning to take on the look of winter, but even in dormancy the yard kept its swept and trimmed appearance. Ilene Parker must be a proper woman. Truitt had learned over the years that while you might not be able to judge a book by its cover, you could tell a helluva lot about a person by her yard.

As he approached the front walk, he studied the Nguyen house, separated from Ilene's property by an expanse of blank ground about fifty feet wide. An equal amount of space separated the Nguyens from a brown bungalow on the other side. No doubt about it, he thought, that house was blue. Not a normal shade of blue, either, and he mentally kicked himself before revising his assessment: It wasn't a shade of blue typically chosen by Americans for their houses, not even their shutters. It was closer to a neon blue, a blue a marketer would choose when he wanted his bag of chips to grab buyers from the grocery store shelves. It was a blue to draw attention.

But drawing attention was not something he associated with the taciturn Nguyen women. He had interviewed them around the cramped table in their kitchen—Tuan's mother Phoung and his sister Le, with the glossy-headed child Chau running in and out—but after an hour he had given up. If Tuan had been dependent on the females in his family to give him his identity, he must have been a disappointed man. The two women had been mum, murmuring that they knew nothing about Tuan's life in Atlanta. And when, on a whim as he left, Truitt knelt on the floor and asked the little girl what was her favorite thing about her uncle, she had turned on her heels and run from the room.

Well, the late Tuan Nguyen had a story, whether his family would tell it or not.

He knocked on Ilene Parker's door and gave her a smile as she peeked out the front window at him. She opened the door cautiously.

"Good afternoon, Miz Parker. I'm Sheriff Truitt. Have you got a minute you can spare me?"

She opened the door wider, her small gray eyes frightened. "You need me for something?"

"Nothing to worry about, ma'am. I just need to ask you a few questions. I'm trying to figure out what happened to your neighbor's brother, and I'm hoping you could help."

"I don't know anything about them. We've never talked."

"That's fine. What I need to know might not have required talking. Can I come in for just a second?"

She stood aside, her hand pressing against the buttons on the chest of her green sweater. As she closed the door, she motioned him to her sofa and hurried to turn on the overhead light.

"I forget how dark it gets in here. I'm not used to having much company."

"You've lived here quite a while, haven't you?"

"Yes, sir. About forty years. My husband and I moved here right after we got married. He passed a few years ago."

"A good house for a good family. I bet you've been happy here."

"Yes, I have."

"So you say you haven't had much contact with your neighbors, the Nguyens?"

"No. Not that I haven't wanted to. But I never could figure out the right thing to say. And then we had the problem with their paint, and there just didn't seem to be anything to say."

"We?"

"Pardon?"

"When you say 'we' had a problem with their paint, do you mean you and the neighbors on the other side, or someone else?"

"I mean everyone. No one liked it. I mean, it's such a small town. Something like that affects everyone. I think people thought it was just a little rude on their part. A little, well, arrogant."

"I see."

"It is arrogant, I think, not to look around good when you get to a place. They should have seen what our houses looked like. If I moved to their country, I would have been polite enough to do that."

"What country is their country?" Truitt asked.

"Well, I don't know exactly. I believe it's Vietnam, but I suppose it could be Cambodia. Or Laos. It's hard to tell sometimes. If I'd ever been able to talk to them . . . I wanted to. Really."

"I believe you, Miz Parker. Now, I need to ask you something. I just came from talking with Reebe Vaughter down at City Hall. You know Reebe?"

"Of course. I know everyone in town."

"Reebe told me that I needed to check up on some information she had heard. Information she had gotten from you. You know what I'm talking about, Miz Parker? She told me you thought there might have been some prostitution involved in the murder of those three men out in the woods."

At this Ilene Parker squared her shoulders. "Saying it like that, they sound so . . . anonymous. I knew Darrell Murphy. And while I can't say I knew Stuart Keast as well . . ."

"Had you ever seen the third man, Tuan Nguyen?"

"I might have. There were a bunch of men who were over there sometimes"—she pointed in the direction of the blue house—"Vietnamese-type men. He might have been one of them."

"I see. Were they over there often?"

"Yes. Quite often."

She sat stiffly, giving him strange signals. *She's being both vague and defensive,* he thought.

"Were they always in a group?"

"Yes."

"Is this why you think there was prostitution involved?"

She hesitated and began rubbing her knuckles. "Yes," she said finally, "and because I just suspected it. My son was in Vietnam. In the army. He wouldn't tell me about what went on over there, but he told his father. A lot of the women were prostitutes. That was just a fact."

"I see. So when was the last time you saw the men over at the Nguyens'?"

Her knuckles shone white under her skin. "I don't know. Several months ago."

"What do you think they were doing there?"

"Well, it was ostensibly to paint the house. But we all know what they were painting the house for. Why else would they have chosen that awful color?"

"I don't know, Miz Parker. Why do you think?"

She leaned forward, her eyes suddenly hard. "It's a bad house, Sheriff. Bad things happen inside. And they painted it that color so they wouldn't have to hang out a sign."

A year after my daughter's birth, I started keeping a journal. More of a list, really—I wasn't ready for strung-out thoughts. I once heard the writing process described as "collect and connect." That's what my journal was, columns of collections, phrases that Tom had said, odd looks at odd times (or more commonly, looks that at the time hadn't seemed odd at all, or ones he had glossed over when I pressed). It's through this peculiar collection of words and glances that I sift for connections. Surely, when he said this, he was sending me a message. Of course, when he said that, he meant it as a sign. He was pleading with me, wasn't he, that I not be so obtuse, that given enough indications I should put it all together and understand his life? That list is now four years old, and still I pore over it, adding to it, waiting for the connections, like a sudden highway system, to link word to word and lead me to an explanation. Otherwise, I have to accept the fact that he decided that I was to have no life. Everything I was was to be subsumed to his cause. What a shitty realization that would be.

— Introduction, pg. iv
A Missing Life: Memoirs of a Grass Widow
by GALE GRAYSON

14

The tearoom had been closed for only two days, but it carried the forlorn emptiness of a longer shuttering. Most of the chairs were still pushed under the tables; Sally had closed suddenly, as soon as Le had left with Truitt and Haskell to identify her brother's body, so none of the chairs had been stacked for the floor to be cleaned. The only exception was the table where the Monday Morning Militant Moms had been brunching. Those chairs were pushed back at odd angles, as if news of the murders had left the furniture itself aghast.

Sally let the glow of the street lamps through the front windows guide her along the dining room and to the door that led to the kitchen. Here it was much darker. One of the aspects she had loved most about this space before she started renovation was the impressive bank of windows that spanned the rear of the building. They covered the expanse of the back wall— in the building's previous incarnation as a photo studio, it had been these windows that bathed the room in natural light. Initially, she had thought to have the tearoom open to the rear to take advantage of this evocative quirk, but Mal and her loan officer convinced her that a tearoom in a place like Statlers Cross was risky enough without ignoring the pointed benefit of a Main Street front. So, regretfully, she had shuttered the magnificent windows, protecting the expensive cooking equipment from prying eyes. The result was she and Le had worked in the uninspired grayness of burnished stainless steel and plastered granite walls.

Tonight she didn't care about protecting what she owned. She walked to the windows, and with determined tugs, pulled up the shades to let the full light of the moon inside. She looked around, hoping for a transformation. There wasn't one. The gray took on the faintest of lusters, so that the countertops and appliances looked vaguely pearlized. But it wasn't enough. There didn't seem to be any magic here.

She pulled a stool over to the metal island in the middle of the room and perched on it. It was Wednesday night. She was going to have to reopen—she couldn't afford to stay shut any longer. Tomorrow she would start searching for a temporary replacement for Le. It wouldn't be easy. She knew now that her employee situation was the weak link in her business plan. The payroll of the Rose Cross Tearoom consisted of herself as management, hostess, waitress, and cleanup crew and Le as cook. On Friday evenings, she paid a teenager from the church to help serve. Given the volume of business so far, the setup had been challenging but adequate. But she hadn't considered what would happen if Le couldn't work. The woman had always been so dependable. Sally had been lulled into a false security.

She stood up abruptly, the scrape of the stool doing damage to the old wooden floor. How ridiculous of her. She hadn't been lulled. She had damn well pushed the idea of a contingency plan to the side of her mind, focusing her attention on the more immediate concerns of opening a new business. It was her fault she was in this fix. She hadn't anticipated.

Mal had said as much when he called that morning.

He had listened in silence to her rush of explanation—the murders, Truitt's request that she help Le, Le's brush-off, the stunning slap at Gale, and then the evening visit by Le's mother. She had faltered as she told him she had closed down the tearoom. "I don't know what to do, Mal. What should I do?"

There had been a long pause. Then in that steady voice of his: "You're going to have to figure something out. As sad as all this is, you can't wait on Le forever. If you can take her back without a problem, then you should do so. But if you have to hire someone to take her place, and that person is doing a good job, it would be wrong to fire her just because Le's ready to return to work."

"But I promised her mother, Mal. I told her that I would make sure Le had a job. She made it sound as if they would have to leave if Le couldn't work here. She sounded *scared*."

Another pause, then a deep sigh. "Sally, listen to me. That is not your responsibility. You have a responsibility to yourself, to me, and to be quite frank, to the bank. Your job is to keep that business afloat. You've got to stop thinking like a teacher and start thinking like a businessman. If giving Le back her job will help your business, then everybody wins. But if giving it back to her will hurt someone else who is doing an equally good or better job, then that is not a good business decision. Le needs time to adjust to her brother's death, no question. But honestly, Sally, your first concern has to be the welfare of your business. Le can take care of herself. That's the thing about immigrants—they have support systems out there you wouldn't believe. They look after each other. It was true when our ancestors came over and it's true with the immigrants of today. You don't worry about Le. Worry about your business and in the long run that will be better for everyone."

The words had stung, and even now she felt a hot

burn in her throat. *Stop thinking like a teacher and start thinking like a businessman.* What he had really meant was that she should stop being an emotional woman and start being a practical man. And part of her knew he was right. But only part.

She entered her office and dialed Le's number. After seven rings a little girl's voice came on the phone.

"Chàu, sweetheart, this is Miss Sally." Sally had met the child only once, when she had delivered Le's work clothes, but she and Chau had hit it off—hell, she always hit it off with children. She had immediately told the little girl to call her Miss Sally, as her students used to do, but now it sounded phony and ridiculous. That wasn't the name for a boss. "Is your mother there?"

"She's with my grandmother."

Not for the first time, Sally noted that Chau spoke English with almost no accent, a statement that could not be made about her mother or grandmother. Sally had noticed the same phenomenon among her foreign-born students in Atlanta—the children would be the best English speakers in the household, sometimes the only English speakers. But she had chalked that up to the influence of school and *Sesame Street.* As far as she knew, five-year-old Chau didn't yet attend school, instead remaining in her grandmother's care while Le worked. So either the child spent a whole lot of time in front of the television, or she had some fairly frequent contact with native speakers.

"Can you get her for me?" She paused, then added gently, "You doing okay, Chau? You feeling all right?"

"I'm fine," the little girl said. Sally heard the clunk of the phone being laid down and in the distance Chau hollering for her mother.

A rustle, and Le picked up the phone. "Yes, Sally?"

The voice sounded imperious. Sally's chest tightened as her nerves began to fail.

"Listen, Le, I need to ask you something. But first, how are you doing? Is your mother okay?"

"We're fine. She told me she went to you last night. She was wrong to do that."

"No, really, that was fine. She should have come to me. I need to know when you need something, and she—"

"We don't need anything."

"But your job—"

"I told you I don't want the job."

"Your mother—"

"My mother is old. Tuan's murder frightened her. She thinks we will be sent back to Vietnam. But we won't be. We are legal. I don't want your job."

"But Le, for pity's sake, think about it for a minute. This is not Atlanta. It's not like there's a job on every corner. Do you think you can just up and find another place to work?"

"That's not your business."

Sally sank down onto her desk, not caring about the papers she crushed as she sat. "What is it, Le? Were you not happy working for me? I'm trying my best to reach out to you. Are you telling me that even if I kept the position open for you, you wouldn't want it?"

The silence was so long that Sally began to wonder if Le had left the phone off the hook and gone back to her mother. Then she heard steady breathing, and the muffled consonants of Le's words. With a shock, she realized the other woman was crying.

"So much meanness," Le said, "from such nice-looking people. I hear it, all the time. They say such bad things. About me. About you. About other people. Where I come from, there are mean people—my mother can tell you about mean people. They do horrible things. But we say the war did it, the war made them mean. But here . . . I don't understand why. Tuan told me you all were scared. Scared of what, I said. Scared of food? Scared of cars? Scared of all you have? He just nodded. Scared of all that. And now he's dead. I'm not like that, Sally. I will not be scared."

The phone clicked dead. Sally sat on the desk, staring at the handset in her palm. She had tried. Anyone would agree that she had tried. *God, let Mal be right,* she thought. *Let them take care of their own.*

Halford had grown accustomed to Ella's elaborate dinners. On his first day, Gale had confided that the freezer and pantry were full, that Ella had been cooking for weeks in preparation for his arrival—corn soup; sweet potato biscuits; muscadine jellies, pies, and wines; tomato gravy, sawmill gravy, and a gravy made of rabbit; butter beans; field peas; and Cherokee bean cakes. And those were just the delectables that could be made in advance. At four P.M. every day Ella retreated to the kitchen, as she said, "to fix a bite of something." Three hours later she emerged with dishes full of chicken, roast beef, or catfish, and a heavenly food called "spoon bread," which was a cross between a dumpling and a custard.

Gale had taken him aside that first night. "It isn't always like this. Usually we eat pasta and a salad. But this is your indoctrination. This is so when you go back home you can say you understand what being Southern is. It's having the memory of eating more than any human being in his right mind would eat. It's so you can sit back and say, 'Nobody makes better butter beans than Ella Alden. That woman's corn bread can melt in your mouth.' "

"This is important?" he had asked.

"Oh, my word, yes. You don't experience the south, Daniel. You *eat* it. There are two ways to get to know this part of the country, and they both have to do with our mouths. You figure out our food and our dialect and you've just about got us down." She had patted him lightly on the chest. "It's our way. Get used to it."

Despite the odd taste now and then (grits hadn't been much to his liking), he had gotten used to it quickly. Breakfasts were fairly light affairs consisting of fruit and biscuits, and lunches were negligible, but the dinners were grand undertakings that lasted more than an hour. Through her vegetables and breads Ella Alden communicated with him, and he, the congenial guest, responded by digging into his food.

Wednesday night's dinner, however, was a lesson in another form of communication. Ella sat at the head of the dining room table, overseeing the passing of the dishes, the casualness of her conversation belying the fact that she looked no one in the eye. Gale kept glancing at her, chewing the side of her mouth the way she did when she was bothered. Nadianna repeatedly checked her wristwatch and shoveled spoonfuls of mashed potatoes into Michael's mouth so quickly that the pale mush dripped from his chin and onto his high-chair tray. Even Katie Pru, who usually had to be reminded that it was someone else's turn to talk, looked from her mother to her grandmother mutely, her huge brown eyes watchful, and, Halford wagered, comprehending.

At seven, Nadianna scooted back her chair abruptly and wiped Michael's face. "I gotta go," she said. "I'm due next door."

Ella looked at her in astonishment. "Next door? What do you have to do next door?"

Nadianna unbuckled Michael from his high chair and began the awkward process of freeing his legs from beneath the tray. "I don't have time to go into it, Ella. Gale, would you tell her? I told Ron I'd be there as close to seven as I could make it, and I got to change the baby's diaper." The child freed, she pulled loose his bib and tossed it on the table. "If y'all want to leave the dishes, I can do them later. But I gotta run."

Nadianna's footsteps thudded up the bare stairs; they could hear the creak of the hall floorboards over their heads. Ella turned to Gale, thinly veiling her irritation.

"What is she up to? Why is she so hell-bent on going to see Ron?"

"Ron's making her a business proposition."

"What for?"

"He saw her photography and was impressed and wants her to take photographs of the people he interviews for his study. I think it's a great idea."

"Will it pay?"

"That's what she's going over to discuss."

"What's she going to do with the baby?"

Gale broke open a cornbread muffin and slipped a pat of butter between the halves. "Tonight she's taking Michael with her. As far as what she'll do with him if she decides to take the assignment, we'll have to talk about it."

"*You'll* have to talk about it. You two are the ones with the children. You'll have to work it out yourselves."

Katie Pru stuffed a forkful of green beans in her mouth. Gale glanced at her, winked, and twisted sideways in her chair so that her daughter couldn't see her face. But Halford could. Her mouth was tense as she spoke.

"Ella, Nadianna and I will find a way to work this out. If you don't want to be a part of the arrangement, that's fine. But this is a good opportunity for her, and if it's valid, she needs to do it. The book on the mills is doing well; she's gotten the attention of not only the local arts council, but some of the arts people in Atlanta, too. She needs a follow-up project that is respectable and allows her to stretch her talents. She's shown that she's good with structures. This would be a chance for her to demonstrate how she handles portraits. You've seen some of her shots of people—they're very good. If this project with Ron can give her some more exposure, it will benefit all of us."

Gale's words were clipped and filled with an undercurrent Halford wasn't sure he understood. Ella laid her napkin on the table and sat back in her chair.

"Exposure isn't exactly what this house needs more of, is it, Gale Lynn? While you're pursuing your 'creative nonfiction' and Nadianna goes off to 'stretch her talents,' perhaps you two young women need to keep in mind that this family has to be taken care of." She stood. "Starting with the dinner dishes would be nice."

Gale smiled weakly at Halford as Ella exited the room.

"I'll help," he said and started gathering plates.

"I'm finished, Mama," Katie Pru said. "I want to go with Nadianna and Michael."

"No, Nadianna is going to do work. And you have not finished. Two more bites of beans."

Gale looked weary as she followed Halford into the kitchen, a load of plates in her arms. "Sometimes," she said, "my grandmother is an old goat."

"So is mine," Halford said. "As my mother says, that generation earned it. But that doesn't excuse what she said to you. It was hurtful."

"Nah. Believe me, on the hurtful scale, it could have been worse. These murders are bothering her more than I would have expected."

Halford started collecting the sterling silver flatware from among the plates. "She seems to have had a fondness for Darrell."

"Hmm. More than I realized. But I think she's more frightened than grief-stricken, and I can't figure out why."

"Has she said anything in particular?"

"She got real upset earlier today—told me that in a town this small, other people were going to end up being hurt by these murders. In anyone else, I would shrug it off as fear reaction. But that just isn't like Ella. Give her a crisis, and she's the rock, regardless of how much being stoic eventually costs her."

Halford chose his words carefully. "Is it possible that she knows something about Darrell that she's afraid to tell you?"

Gale looked at him in surprise. "Something to do with the murders?"

"Just anything at all. She seems to have spent more time with him than you realized."

She turned on the water faucet and set the dishes in the sink. "Surely she would go to Alby. On the other hand, she is acting strangely. Tense. I was beginning to think it really was the pressure of having a sudden family foisted upon her, but maybe it's more than that. Would you mind talking to her?"

A butter knife had been hidden between two saucers; Halford retrieved it and slid it into the sink. As he did, his hand brushed Gale's. Grasping her fingers, he lifted her hand to his lips and kissed it.

"Me mind talking to an Alden woman? It will never happen."

15

Nadianna had been in the Greenes' old house only once as a child, when her mother had taken over some food. She couldn't remember now what the food was for—a death? a birth?—but she had been young enough to sit under a table next to the sofa where she had watched the shoes and hems of women move past. The Greenes had a red-and-brown braided rug that covered the living room floor, and she remembered running her fingers along the braids, trying to find the stitches so she could unloop it. Her mother had removed her before she could do damage, but she had never forgotten Mrs. Greene's eyes on her as her mother tugged her out the door. Serious and considering eyes.

Mrs. Greene had been a widow when she died more than a year before, and the house had stood empty until Ron Goddard rented it. The grass had grown up in dry bunches, and the runoff from the overflowing gutters had streaked the light blue paint with dirt. Her photographer's eye had always been intrigued by the house, juxtaposed next to the vivid red of the Alden place. She had taken several photos, huddled in a sniper's position behind the railroad tracks that ran in front of the two houses, peeking out over the abandoned rails like a soldier not wanting to get shot. At the time, she had been attracted to the contrast between the houses—large, small; bold, demure. To her the houses were the two extremes of Statlers Cross. This was before the Nguyens moved to town. Her artistic perception had been forced to undergo a shift.

She pressed the baby's carrier to her chest as she strained to hike up the front porch steps without dropping her portfolio. The outside light was off, and she was beginning to wonder if she had been wrong about Goddard's invitation when the door swung open.

"Gracious, Nadianna, I forgot to turn on the light. Here, let me help you with the baby. He looks awfully heavy."

Nadianna turned sideways, away from Goddard's outstretched hands. "I've got him. He's just about asleep. Let me set him down inside and I'll bet he'll drift right off. Here, you take this," and she handed him the portfolio.

Stepping into the house, she was immediately greeted with the warm smell of cinnamon. The baby rubbed his nose as she gently lowered him to the floor and tucked his blanket around his chin.

"Smells nice," she said. "Have you finished supper?"

"Oh, yes. I'm making up a spot of spiced tea for us. You do drink tea, don't you? I could make you something else if you prefer."

Nadianna shrugged, not wanting to admit that to her tea came in one style—plain with sugar. She had no idea what someone would spice tea with. "Tea's fine. Not much, though. Just a taste would be good."

He smiled and motioned her to the sofa as he left the room. The place was not at all as she remembered: no rug covered the wooden floors, and the side tables had disappeared in favor of a long sofa table piled with papers and books. A metal desk, also mounded with materials, dominated the left side of the room. In the right-hand corner was a dining room table with four chairs, and across the sofa table from her was a worn upholstered rocking chair. None of it seemed familiar to her, and she wondered if when he moved in, the English Dr. Goddard had scoured American garage sales trying to furnish his new residence.

The cinnamon aroma grew stronger and she looked up as Goddard entered the room with a mug in each hand.

"This isn't the instant stuff," he said, setting the mugs on the table and taking a seat beside her. "My grandmother would have strictly disapproved of the instant stuff. She used to make this every autumn, would just keep a big pot of it on the stove for us to ladle out. Oranges, lemons, cinnamon sticks, nutmeg, and a whole lot of sugar. And tea, of course. There, try it. Tell me what you think."

She brought the mug to her lips and sipped the steaming liquid. The tea was sweet and rich on her tongue. "This is yummy. I mean it. This tastes delicious. I've never had it before."

"Like it? Tell you what, I'll keep a pot of it going and you can come over whenever you want and fix yourself a cuppa."

"Yeah. I'd come lugging over here with the baby exactly two times and you wouldn't think that was such a good idea."

"I bet I would. All right then, a compromise. You stick your head in the back door and if you smell the tea on the stove, you know I'm open to company. If you don't smell it, then I'm in a difficult mood and you're better off turning tail and running."

His whole body was open as he said it, his hands uplifted, his face wide with friendliness. Nadianna relaxed into the sofa.

"You're on. I'm good at hightailing it when I need to."

He took a sip of tea, his blue eyes amused behind his glasses. "So did you run my proposal by Gale? What did she think?"

This question irritated her a bit—why would he assume she would go to Gale?—but since she had, and since the tea was filling her with a comforting warmth, she brushed the irritation away. "She thinks it's a wonderful idea as long as we agree on working conditions and I get satisfactory compensation." He nodded solemnly. "*I* think it's a wonderful idea because it will give me a chance to practice a different type of photography. For the past year or so, I've focused mainly on buildings—houses, factories, the old mills. I would like to see what I can do with people's faces. Here, I thought you might like to see what I've done in the past."

She unzipped her portfolio and quickly flipped through the first several sheets, bypassing her architectural photos. When she neared the end, she turned the portfolio toward him so he could see the contents.

"These are several years old," she said. "They're not bad, but I could do better now. I understand light better. And it may sound funny but I think studying the lines and planes of buildings may help me see the human face in a different way. More effectively." She pointed to a close-up photo of an elderly woman, her mouth open to reveal bare gums, a spoonful of black-eyed peas inches from her face. "See, I would shoot this differently now. The light is all wrong. The emphasis is on her eyes, and I think the emphasis should be on her mouth. See this little bit of shine right on the corner of her mouth? That's saliva. And see how the liquid from the peas drips right here from the spoon? I shot this in a homeless shelter. I thought what I was doing by focusing on her eyes was to show her humanity. But to show her humanity I should have played up that speck of saliva, mirrored by that drop from the peas.

That was the picture. I let my preconceptions ruin the shot."

Goddard pushed his glasses back up his nose. "I see. Well, actually, I don't. You're way ahead of me here, Nadianna. I know precious little about photography or what makes a good or bad picture. I will have to trust your judgment on that. What I do know is that your stills, your close-ups can evoke an image that my poor video camera cannot. And certainly my audiotapes can't. I talked with the head of my department today and he thought it was a jolly good idea. We'll have to work out the details of copyright because we will need to have the right to publish for academic purposes, but neither he nor I think that is an insurmountable issue. This is what we came up with: We'll pay your expenses— film and processing—and then we'll pay you fifty dollars per selected shot. I can't tell you how many photos that would be at this time, but I am thinking several per subject. My entire research project is scheduled for a year, and right now I have ten subjects whom I'm interviewing. So I think you could safely say we're looking at about three to four thousand dollars for the project, excluding costs. Not great money, but as you say, an opportunity. And it might open up doors later on."

"There might be a book."

"I don't know how my text would adapt . . ."

"We could work on the text. If the photos were good enough . . . Gale could always help with the text."

"Well, that's your department, not mine. My first concern is how the photos will augment my research. But it's not something to rule out."

"I think this could be wonderful, Ron. I really do. When do I start?"

"Any time. I was up at the Keasts' today, and of course Rosen is in no shape to be interviewed, poor thing. But you could come over here and watch the videos I've made, listen to the tapes. It might give you some background on the woman. What do you think?"

At Nadianna's feet the baby plumped his mouth in his sleep. Goddard quickly added, "Bring the baby. He looks like a good sort. I know it's too soon for you to have worked out child-care arrangements. So please, don't worry about bringing him. I can put you in the bedroom with the VCR and I'll never know you're there."

"You don't have children, Ron," she said. "You always know they're there."

"I insist. It will be fine. Just come over after breakfast tomorrow and we can get started."

She looked from the man to the baby, her confidence plummeting. It was all right for Goddard to act open-minded now, but the first time she had to cancel an appointment because the baby was sick or no one could look after him, Goddard would chalk her up as uncommitted, or worse, unmotivated. She felt a familiar knot in her stomach. The baby was getting in her way.

Goddard's hand was suddenly on hers, warm. "Nadianna," he said softly. "I don't know anything about your past. I don't know really why you're living with the Aldens, or who the baby's father is. I don't need to know. But I do know that you're a talented young woman. I want to help you. Can you let me?"

The knot grew heavier until it was a physical pain. "There's nothing you can do," she whispered. "This is my problem."

Goddard was silent for a long moment, his hand kneading hers. She didn't pull away. She wanted to hear him tell her that he would help. She realized, with both shame and excitement, that she wanted to feel his arms around her.

But he didn't give her that. Instead, he stood and

walked around the table. Kneeling, he rested his finger against the baby's closed fist. The baby didn't move. Goddard looked up at her, his eyes kind.

"Do you know you never use his name, Nadianna? Not once in the two months I've been here. You call him 'the baby.' I had to ask Gale his name. Michael. She said it had some significance to you, but she wouldn't say what. Is it his father's name?"

"No." Her voice sounded hoarse. She had never told anyone why she had chosen the name but now, hearing the soft care in Goddard's words, she wanted him to know. This man who had so much faith in her, she wanted him to know.

"It was just a man I read about. He made a mistake that ruined his life." Her words caught in her throat.

"So you view Michael as a mistake?"

"People told me I shouldn't have him. Then they told me I shouldn't keep him. But I didn't listen."

"And now you think you should have?"

"Sometimes."

She couldn't believe she had said it. She couldn't believe she had trusted him enough. But then he was on the sofa next to her, her face in his hands. The kiss he gave her was full on the lips but gentle. It wasn't amorous; when she pulled away, she had the overwhelming sense of being comforted.

"You're a brave and talented woman, Nadianna Jesup," Goddard said, his fingers still on her cheeks. "You will be fine. The people who care about you will make sure you are fine." He paused, dropping his hands. "About your Michael who made the mistake—I find that many people who make mistakes are actually quite brave. They do great things. I'll wager your Michael was a brave man, for all his mistakes. You should think about that when you look at your son. You should see how mistakes make men stronger."

"You're right," she said quietly. "I need to look at a whole lot of things differently."

He smiled and stood. "I think we've just agreed to a new partnership. I say we drink our tea to celebrate. Let me freshen yours up."

He retreated into the kitchen with their mugs, leaving Nadianna alone with the sleeping baby. She closed her portfolio, zipping it up and propping it against the side of the sofa. Idly, she walked to the front door, and feeling warm from the tea and excitement, went out onto the porch.

The night air was crisp, the stars brilliant. Nadianna glided down the porch steps and into the grass. She remembered the weekend the grass had finally been cut following Mrs. Greene's death. It was after Goddard's arrival. Three men had shown up with tractors and mown the two-feet-high grass. Goddard himself had hooked up a hose and washed down the house's neglected walls. A couple of days later a teenager had scrambled onto the roof and cleaned out the gutters. From her room in Ella's house, Nadianna had watched the transformation with a mixture of sadness and relief. The house deserved better than the weatherworn look it had acquired; on the other hand, it was now a respectable house on a respectable plot of land. It didn't have a story to tell. It was as if the upkeep had scoured away its melancholy words.

She crossed her arms against the chill and glanced over at the Alden house, lit up like a huge, sculpted lantern. A figure paused in front of the window in the dining room. She recognized Gale's petite form. No doubt cleaning up the supper dishes. Then, as she watched, Halford came up behind Gale and, placing his hands on her shoulders, turned her around to face him. Nadianna smiled. After more than a year of aridity, intimacy seemed to be in abundance.

The squeal of tires jerked her attention to the road in time to see a dark-colored pickup truck speed past the house. It peeled toward the center of town, making a sharp left-hand turn down Baxter Street. Five seconds later she heard the shattering of glass, the barking of a dog, and then a horrific, shuddering explosion.

She began running back to the Greene house, her first thought illogically on the baby—Was he safe? Had the broken glass flown this far? She was vaguely aware of people running from the Alden house, confused shouts from further off. Stumbling up the porch steps, she ran into Goddard's arms.

"Are you all right?" he cried. "What was that?"

Across the fence a car engine started, and Gale's car spun around in the yard and started down the road.

"It was an explosion," Nadianna stammered. "A truck went by. I saw it. It turned down the street—and then—"

From the direction of the explosion, she could hear a gathering of cries in the night. "Come inside, Nadianna," Goddard said. "We need to call the police."

Fire could be seen through the front window of the Nguyen house as Gale slammed to a stop by the curb. Halford scrambled from the passenger side and, finding the gate latched tightly, leaped over the fence and dashed up the porch steps.

"Get to a phone!" he yelled to Gale. "Get some help."

The door was locked. From inside he could hear cries, first of astonishment, then of fear. A screaming of words, shrill, piercing. Frantically, he tried to climb in through the broken window, but the flames beat him back.

He ran around the back of the house, searching for another entrance. The blue house was shuttered tightly. At the back, a screen door rose from a short flight of stairs, but when he opened it, he met with another door of solid wood. He slammed his shoulder against its face, but the door wouldn't budge.

The cries from inside continued, accompanied by a thudding sound. He looked around, trying to find a stone large enough to hurl through a window. But the ground seemed to have been swept clean. He ran further from the house, into the dark spread of lawn, searching the ground. Nothing. Not a goddamned twig.

He'd have to use his fist. Ripping off his coat, he wrapped it around his arm. As he turned to race back to the house, he caught sight of something about fifteen feet away.

It was a figure, standing stock-still behind a growth of brush. In the dark, he couldn't make out the gender, but there was no mistaking the outline of a shoulder, and the outer curve of a face.

"Hey! You! Help me!"

The figure turned and ran, long hair flapping with each footfall. He could tell by the curve of the hips, the way the figure's legs moved as it ran that it was a woman.

"Come here! You've got to help!"

But the woman disappeared into the shadows, the sound of her feet, the intake of her breath outlasting her image. Halford turned and barreled toward the house.

He mounted the front porch again and prepared to drive his fist through the window opposite the burning room. He lifted his spare arm over his eyes and braced himself for the shattering glass.

Silence. No more cries. No more thuds. He opened his eyes and realized that flames no longer covered the curtains.

He hammered on the door. "Miss Nguyen! Are you all right? Is the fire out?"

He heard a scrambling sound. Then the door

opened a crack. A frightened, elderly face peered out at him.

"Fine. Go."

"Can I help? I'm a police officer. Is anyone hurt?"

"Fine. Go."

And the door shut in his face.

16

Two things struck Truitt as he stepped from his truck in front of the house—the distinct smell of kerosene in the air and the number of people milling around on the opposite side of the road. None of them broke from their clusters as he made his way down the driveway. They watched him in silence, their faces grim and strained under the streetlights.

Haskell waited for him by the front door. "It happened about forty-five minutes ago, at about seven-thirty. Molotov cocktail. You can still see the glass."

Truitt nodded toward to people outside. "Anybody see anything?"

"Not that they're admitting."

"Have one of our guys get their names and addresses. I wouldn't expect anyone to say anything out loud, not with a crime like this. They might be more likely to admit seeing something in the comfort of their own homes."

Haskell nodded, understanding. Truitt left him to carry out his instructions and entered the house. It was a house like a hundred turn-of-the-century houses in Calwyn County—long central hallway that ran from the front door to a back room, a room opening from the hallway on each side. The ceilings were low, and Truitt, not overly tall himself, had to duck to avoid hitting an old hanging light. In the room to his left, he could see the fire marshal, an affable fellow nicknamed Job, bent over and sifting through some soot.

"What you got for me, Job?"

Job stood, and looking down at the burnt debris at his feet, pushed his hair back from his face and gave a wry grin.

"You want the technical version? The device entered the house through the left front window here, shattering a pane and catching the curtain on fire as it passed. It exploded when it hit the floor and, courtesy of the fact that the room has no furniture, burnt a nice, circular scar into the wooden floor before the women beat it out." He pointed to a heavy woven rug heaped in a pile in the middle of the floor. "Lucky it was an empty room. Kerosene and flames love upholstery. They'd have eaten this place up if it had been furnished."

"Don't suppose you can say anything about the materials used to make the bomb," Truitt said.

The fire marshal indicated a jagged piece of glass. "Looks like a Ball jar to me."

"Typical. So we've got an arsonist who likes canning."

"That or a bit of 'shine. My daddy always liked his 'shine in a Ball jar."

"My mama used Ball jars to decorate the bathroom," Haskell offered from the hall.

"There you go, Sheriff. You just go find yourself a nice little arsonist drunk off his ass and dressing like Martha Stewart."

Truitt slapped the fire marshal on the back. "A sound plan, Job. Let me know what else you come up with."

He left him to join Haskell in the hallway. "Where are the Nguyens now?"

"Outside. I offered to let them sit in the kitchen, but they won't come back in."

"Don't know that I blame them. I would imagine you wouldn't know which was better—sitting inside where someone could try and burn you out again or outside with a bunch of people you're not sure you can trust."

"They did say one person tried to help them put out the fire, but they don't know who it was."

"Who called it in?"

Haskell checked his notes. "Nadianna Jesup."

"Nadianna? You remember her, don't you, Craig? She's living with the Aldens now. Why don't you run over and see what she can tell you?"

Truitt stepped into the night, trying to see through the glow of the porch light which of the clustered people outside were the Nguyens. He finally spied the three of them inside the fence, huddled side by side like a piece of welded sculpture.

"Miz Nguyen," he said to the elderly woman as he headed toward them. "I'm so sorry about this. Can you tell me what happened?"

Her daughter broke free from the huddle and stepped forward. "You said we were safe. You said when my brother was killed that we were still safe."

He studied her for a second, trying to remember what he had said to her that she had interpreted as a promise of protection. "I'm real sorry about what happened here, Le. Anyway you look at it it shouldn't have happened. But now I need you to help me find out who did it. Did you see anything?"

Le looked over her shoulder at her mother and daughter. None of them spoke. All appeared frail, their hair loose around their faces, thin robes covering their small frames. Even the face of the child looked drawn as she clutched her grandmother's hand. When he caught her eyes, she buried her head in her grandmother's robe.

He was aware of the other groups of people behind

him, eerie oblong figures in the night. None of them uttered a sound, so intent were they to hear what the Nguyens were saying.

He knelt beside the little girl. "Chau," he said gently. "Where were you when this happened?" She pushed her head so hard into her grandmother's stomach that the elderly woman tottered off balance; Truitt reached up and steadied her. "Chau," he repeated. "You need to tell me. What did you see?"

"She was with me in the kitchen." Le said it sharply. "We were all in the kitchen. We couldn't see. We heard the crash, the noise."

He ignored her. "Chau. Bad people did this. Only bad people would want to hurt your home like this. I need to know who they are so I can put them in jail. You know that a person shouldn't be allowed to do something bad without being punished. Someone did something bad to your family tonight. Please tell me what you saw."

He reached up to stroke the little girl's hair, but the grandmother said something harshly in Vietnamese and knocked his hand away. She gathered the child closer to her.

"She didn't see anything," said Le. "You said we would be safe, but we're not. She didn't see. You leave her alone."

Truitt sighed and stood up. "Le, I am doing all I can to find out who killed your brother. It's going to take some time. But a case like this, happening in the evening before people were in bed, well, if we have cooperation, we can have this cleared up before tomorrow. If your daughter saw something, you need to convince her to tell us. We don't want these guys coming back. Maybe next time y'all won't be back in the kitchen out of harm's way."

She literally sniffed at him. "Chau didn't see. You

leave her." She waved expansively at the people behind him. "What about them? What did they see? Have you asked them?"

"I will certainly do that again, Le. But the grim little secret about law enforcement is that it's the victim who cares the most about the crime. If you want me to find out who did this, it's in your best interest to help me."

His speech did nothing to alter the angry set of her face. He shook his head. "Fine. I'll go speak with your neighbors."

He made his way to the clusters on the other side of the road. "Ladies and gentlemen," he said. "I need your help in this. If any of you saw anything unusual tonight, whether you think it was related to this crime or not, will you please let me know?" No one spoke. "According to my notes, this crime happened around seven-thirty. None of you out taking a walk, sitting on the porch? No? Well, I'll be in my office all day tomorrow. If any of you remember seeing anything, give me a call, okay?"

He saw some heads nod, but mostly everyone stared at him, cautious. He walked back to the Nguyens.

"I've done my best, ladies. Like I just told all them, I'll be in my office all day tomorrow. If any of you remember seeing anything, give me a call."

He had started to walk to the house when a figure separated itself from a group of people and walked in the dark toward him. It took him a few seconds for the height and the gait to register. He stuck out his hand to Daniel Halford.

"Couldn't stay away from the commotion, Chief Inspector?"

"Gale and I came as soon as we heard the explosion. I tried to get into the house to help put the fire out, but the front door was locked. By the time I had tried all the doors, the fire was pretty much extinguished."

"That was brave of you, Daniel. I appreciate it."

Halford frowned. "You would have done the same if you had been here. But that's not what I wanted to tell you. I saw a woman standing about twenty-five yards from the back of the house, behind some bushes. I shouted to her to help, but she turned and ran."

"Twenty-five yards. Pretty good distance in the dark. You sure it was a woman?"

"I was closer than that, about fifteen feet. She was slight and had long hair. She was wearing pants. But my impression was that it was a woman."

"Maybe heard the noise and came out to see what was going on? Ran when you asked her to get involved?"

"Except there aren't any houses behind here. From what I gather, a few yards past where she was and you run into three hundred acres of Alden land. That's uninhabited except for Ella's place. The only house even close to here from this direction is the place where Ron Goddard is staying. All the other houses front the street. The most logical action for the people living in them to take would be to run along the road. There's really no logical reason for someone to be back here."

Truitt looked across the open lot that separated the Nguyens from Ilene Parker's white house. "You say this woman ran away? So by your estimation she was pretty young."

"She didn't need any help running, if that's what you mean."

Truitt nodded slowly, imagining in his mind the layout of the fields and rolling hills that spread out from this side of Statlers Cross. Halford was right—it was all Alden land. And beyond that, the pastureland of cattle farmers and the Kirbys' woods. If there was a logical reason for someone to be waiting in the bushes behind the Nguyen house while someone else was firebombing the front of it, she was going to have to explain it to him.

"Thanks, Daniel," he said. "Let me chew on that one a while."

17

Nadianna was edgy. She hadn't slept well the night before—the excitement that had started with Ron Goddard's embrace reached a crescendo with the fire-bomb, and she had spent much of the night downstairs in the kitchen with Gale and Halford, going over the events of the evening. But when they retired around midnight, she had stayed up, pacing the floor, playing over in her mind first the sight of the truck wheeling down the road, then the image of herself setting up her camera equipment in the Keasts' gloomy house, at work again at last. At three A.M. she had climbed the stairs to her room, but the first tinge of light at six-thirty had roused her, and she was up again, pacing the room, like a cat aching to be put out.

At six-forty-five, the baby lay asleep in his crib, his relaxed lips forming a wet arch over the visible tip of his tongue. During the night he had kicked his blanket off, and Nadianna drew it over his curled body and tucked it around his shoulders. He should sleep for at least another forty-five minutes, enough time for her to shake off her excess energy by taking a walk.

The house was silent as she made her way downstairs. Gale was usually an early riser, but the late night had probably taken its toll even on her. Nadianna encountered no one as she hurried through the house, pausing at the back door to pull on her jacket. The air held enough of a nip that she shoved her hands into her pockets. Nudging the screen porch door open, she padded down the steps and headed across the dew-tipped grass for the gate.

The barbed wire fence that separated the Aldens from the old Greene place had been there as long as Nadianna could remember. She had no idea how far the fence stretched—it disappeared into a clog of vines about fifty yards from the house. It was possible that it bounded the entire three-hundred-acre plot of land, but if so, it was no doubt in disrepair in the outer regions. She couldn't see Ella hiking the whole fence line, armed with pliers and nails to patch the holes. Whether it was critters or strangers that the fence had originally been meant to keep out, it no longer provided that function. The border around the Alden property was definitely porous.

She worked the rusted nail that served as the latch and swung open the gate. It let out a long whine. She glanced at Goddard's house to see if the noise had attracted his attention, but the curtains remained still. Then, straining one last time to hear if the baby was crying, she shut the gate behind her and struck out across open land toward the Nguyen place.

She didn't know what she was looking for. Maybe it was just gawker's curiosity—Halford had described the house on fire so vividly—or maybe she just wanted to validate what it was she had been witness to. After Goddard helped her place an emergency call from his house, they had wrapped up the baby and gone back over to the Aldens. In the distance, they could still hear noises, and in retrospect she wondered if the masculine cries she had heard were Halford's. But the timing must not have been right. Halford had told them about the mysterious woman, but no figure had run past her and Goddard as they made their way through the barbed wire fence to the Alden house. And surely there would have been no other way for the woman to have run than over the open ground between the two yards.

It was all speculation, and she brushed it aside as she tromped through the grasses behind Goddard's house. She had given Deputy Haskell her statement: A dark pickup truck had sped past her sometime between seven-fifteen and seven-forty-five and turned down Baxter Street, after which she heard an explosion. Could she be more exact in the description of the truck? No, she couldn't. Could be she more exact in the time? No. Could she see how many people were in the truck? Well, she could say that there wasn't anybody visible in the truck's bed. Could she tell them anything else at all? She had thought hard, going over the brief five seconds in her mind. The taillights. The taillights had been odd. In what way? Haskell had asked. I'll draw them, she had answered.

Goddard sat by her on the sofa while she sketched. She started over three times before she got a sketch she felt was close to accurate and handed it to Haskell.

"That's, well, that's bizarre," Haskell told her.

She shrugged. "That's what I remember seeing. Maybe my memory is just bizarre."

The drawing she had made was of a two-headed serpent. It appeared to have been painted over the lights, so that the red glowed through where the snake's body would have been.

"You saw this while in Mr. Goddard's yard, some fifty feet away from the road?" Haskell asked.

"No," she had said, her irritation growing. "That's what I remember seeing. That's a different thing altogether."

Now, twelve hours later, she wasn't sure what she saw or remembered. The truck had been dark; she thought there was a strange design on the taillights. That would be all she would swear to.

It took her a little under ten minutes to angle around brush and fences to reach the back of the Nguyen house. There was no mistaking it—its blue signaled itself as boldly as a flag. But in the morning light the bright intensity seemed to have softened. Another few months, she thought, and this house will have aged into a mildly flamboyant respectability.

A white picket fence started at the side of the house and wrapped around the front. Nadianna followed it, keeping an eye out for fire damage. It wasn't until she reached the front that she saw the broken window and detected the scent of scorched wood in the air.

She started past the house, intending to walk the long way home via Baxter Street and then Main, when her eye caught the flicker of something pale in the Nguyens' yard. Looking over the fence, she at first thought a bag of garbage slumped against the corner pickets, waiting for the sanitation truck. But there was no curbside pickup in Statlers Cross and as Nadianna looked, a child's face appeared from under a yellow piece of cloth. With horror she realized that the mound of debris was three small females, huddled together, a bright yellow quilt wrapped around them, their faces pressed against each other's bodies like sleeping birds.

The child was awake. Her brown eyes stared at Nadianna.

"My word," Nadianna said. "Have you been there all night?"

The girl didn't answer. "Honey," Nadianna said more softly. "Did you stay outside all night?"

One of the women stirred. When she opened her eyes and saw Nadianna, she drew her arm protectively around the child and pressed herself deeper against the fence.

"What do you want?"

"Are you Le Nguyen? Have you been out here all night?"

The woman's nose was red from cold. "Go away," she said.

"No, ma'am," Nadianna said, a mixture of dismay and anger rising in her. "It's too cold for you to be out here."

"The house caught on fire. Somebody wanted to hurt us in that house."

"Well, you're going to get sick out here." She motioned at the little girl. "What about her? She's going to really get sick. Don't you have anyone to call? If you're scared, isn't there someone you can stay with?"

As soon as she said it, she realized what a futile question it was. The woman's brother was dead. The family itself wasn't exactly part of the community. Where would they go? Why would she assume there was anyone within eight thousand miles they trusted?

She walked around to where the gate opened onto a walkway and went into the yard. The three females—now all awake—didn't move as they watched her approach. About six feet from them, she sat down upon the wet ground.

"What are we going to do?" she asked. "You can't stay like this. We have to figure something out." She paused, trying to decide the right thing to say. "I'm Nadianna. I don't live too far from here." Another pause. "I have a baby at home. Your little girl here—I take care of a little girl about her age." The Nguyens looked at her, blinking. What on earth should she say? "Katie Pru. The little girl I take care of is named Katie Pru." She focused on the girl. "What's your name?"

The girl's fingers emerged from the blanket. She pulled down an edge that covered her mouth. "Chau," she answered.

"Chau," Nadianna repeated. "I'm glad to meet you.

You know, my little Katie Pru has brown eyes like you, and brown hair, too. She sings a lot and makes things with her fingers. There's glue everywhere. Sometimes her grandmother gets mad at all the glue and goes thundering through the house, 'Katie Pru! I swear if we cleaned up all this glue the whole house would fall apart!' "

Chau giggled. "My grandmother gets mad, too."

Nadianna expected one of the women to tell Chau to hush, but neither of them did. They simply watched her.

"You know what I think? I think Katie Pru would like to meet you. I think you two could be great friends. There aren't many girls around here y'all's age. I bet she would like to have a friend."

Chau nodded, her tired eyes suddenly bright. Nadianna looked up at Le.

"Listen, I know you don't know me. If it helps at all, I saw the truck that did this to you. I called the police. A friend of mine tried to help you put out the fire, but it turned out you didn't need him. We would love to help you. You can't stay out here."

"Safer outside than in," stated Le.

"Maybe, but it won't be safe anywhere if you get sick. Why don't you come with me to our house? Chau can play with Katie Pru and we can all think about what to do next. I live with the Aldens. You know the Alden house? The big red one at the edge of town. I bet when the leaves are all gone you can see it from your upstairs windows."

Le looked at her strangely, like she half expected Nadianna to sprout wings and fly. But her fatigue was obvious as she leaned her head against the pickets.

She spoke so softly Nadianna had to lean forward to hear her. "American sluts," she said. A pause, and Le broke into a weary laugh.

· · ·

Serpents on the taillights. Truitt turned the drawing
Nadianna Jesup had given Haskell on its side, trying to
force his vision into free association. The likelihood of
Nadianna nailing the image from fifty feet away was slim,
but there was a good chance that the taillights were indeed unusual.

Haskell placed a mug of steaming coffee on Truitt's
desk. "No cream around," he said. "Today is shopping
day."

"I keep telling Blaire to make it Wednesday," Truitt
said absently. "You'd think I didn't carry any weight
around here. What do you know about taillights? You
ever heard of one having a decorative covering of some
sort?"

"Nope, but I'm not a truck person. Want me to
check?"

"Yeah. Call Mike Spivey over at the Chevy dealership. See if he knows where you can get something like
that. Have we heard anything from the state yet?"

"The preliminary autopsy results will be ready this
afternoon. That was a promise. The ballistics will take a
week. But the autopsy should tell us a lot about the
guns."

"I want to be buzzed as soon as they come in."

"Yes, sir. I'll get the word out."

After Haskell left, Truitt sat at his desk, sipping coffee, staring at Nadianna's two-headed serpent. Ella had
warned him. Ella had told him that tensions in Statlers
Cross were running high, and he had confirmed it during his interview with Ilene Parker. But he now admitted that he had dismissed it as the extenuated emotions
of women—elderly women at that. It hadn't been prime
sheriffing, but the truth was until the tensions boiled
over, there had been very little he could have done. He
frowned. That wasn't accurate. There was one thing he
could have done, and he hadn't even bothered.

He rifled through his Rolodex until he came up

with the phone number of Gwinnett Tech. He punched
the buttons and asked for Dr. Wiley Dawkins.

Gwinnett was a monster suburban county northeast
of Atlanta. For twenty years it had claimed the title of
one of the fastest-growing counties in the country, and
the reality was only a portion of its acreage was developed. This meant that the growth continued unabated
in constant explosions—growth in this pocket, in this
corner, along this stretch of I-85. What had twenty years
ago been a quiet rural area of 125,000 was now a high-
tech industrial area of 500,000 with the largest and
some said best school system in the state. And no public
transportation. Not so much as a bus or a hansom cab.

He hadn't known or much cared about the im-
plication of this until he met Wiley Dawkins at a civic
development conference last year. Dawkins was a native Georgian of Asian and Western European descent;
Truitt, cringing at his own penchant for stereotypes,
was always disconcerted to hear this well-dressed man
with Asian features lapse into what he called his "Wiley
schtick," a monologue of exaggerated cornpone humor
and overdone Southern accent. An economics professor,
Dawkins was fluent in three languages—Spanish, Japa-
nese, and English—and that was one of the reasons he
served as a cultural conflict consultant for Gwinnett
County.

It was the issue of no public transportation that created the need for his expertise, Dawkins had explained.
By consistently voting down public transportation, the
good citizens of Gwinnett had created a tight, densely
populated band of immigrants along its western border
with the more urban county of DeKalb. DeKalb had public transportation, and families of immigrants, not yet affluent but wanting the lower crime and better schools
of Gwinnett, moved as close as possible to DeKalb so they
could walk across the border to use the bus and rapid
rail services for work.

"Like our own little Mexican border," Truitt had commented at the conference.

"Almost. Except there's nothing illegal about it. Which makes some of the natives pissed as hell."

Hence the need for a cultural conflict expert, whose function was to mediate disputes rising from cultural misunderstandings. Dawkins had his share of war stories, which he had shared amid repeated beers. His depth of knowledge of Asian and Hispanic cultures had been astounding. Truitt should have called him as soon as he found Nguyen's body.

Dawkins's voice sounded surprised and genuinely pleased. When he heard Truitt's story, he grew more somber.

"This is the kind of thing we've been seeing for years now. I don't care what century it is, what nationality you're talking about, immigrants have it hard. I'm glad my mama went through it and saved me at least a little bit of the trouble."

"So what's going on here, Wiley? My coroner tells me it's an education thing—that the Vietnamese refugees who came immediately following the war were highly educated, more Westernized, and more willing to assimilate. Does he have something?"

"Yeah, I think so. What we're seeing now are more so-called economic immigrants, people coming over not for ideological or even safety as much as economic imperatives. They stay in communities with others from their homeland, give each other jobs. They've formed networks to help each other with healthcare, with INS, even with things like finding housing or getting a building permit. Just like my mother's family did in the 1950's. And just like your family did probably back in eighteen-aught-aught."

"So do you find it surprising that these women would be living in Statlers Cross?"

"A little, maybe. But we've noticed more and more

immigrant families moving further out, primarily for jobs. A lot of the more rural counties have poultry, egg, or other industries that provide attractive opportunities. It can make things more difficult for a family because they lose the huge support base that's available in the urban areas. But like every other population, there are always pioneers. Those two women are brave, I'll tell you that. Of course, you go through a situation like Vietnam of the past forty years and you're talking about some character-building experiences."

"So it wouldn't be unbelievable that these women would be living out here legitimately and relying on their male relative in Atlanta—Chamblee to be exact—to provide the support base."

"Wouldn't be unbelievable at all. But I'm curious about your word 'legitimately.' That has a loaded connotation. Or am I reading something into it?"

Truitt paused, trying to finesse his response. Finally, he decided he trusted Dawkins enough to forge ahead.

"They bought this house, Wiley, a big old house that used to belong to one of the more affluent residents of Statlers Cross. That's not to suggest it's a grand old place—Statlers Cross is not a wealthy community. But it was a fairly prominent part of the town. As far as I can tell, the reaction to them was minimal. But then they painted the house blue—this brilliant, electric blue. Quite a few of the townspeople took offense at that. One nice old lady told me very seriously that they chose that color because they were establishing a whorehouse."

Dawkins chuckled, but the chuckle held a bitter edge. "The whore business is a stereotype and a pitiful one. But I will tell you about that blue. We see a lot of it around here. If not a whole house, then the shutters or the mailbox or even the outside air-conditioning units. We had one house with only the roof painted. That color has special significance in Vietnam. It's the color of prosperity, of wealth. It's a royal color."

"So they wouldn't have chosen that to be deliberately provocative."

"Provocative? I wouldn't think so, no. Operatic? Yes."

"Operatic?"

"You bet. I would say that anyone who painted a whole house that color would be demonstrating the highest level of optimism. They would be positively singing out their hope."

18

Sally had made the phone call to Honey Johnson the night before: The Rose Cross Tearoom, closed because of the tragedy in the cook's family, would reopen Thursday morning at ten. Not that the MMMM's usually met on Thursday, Sally had said, her courage fleeing, and this certainly wasn't a call to beg them to come, but she just wanted to let them know that she would be open for business, even if the menu would be a bit limited until she could find a replacement for Le.

"Has she left town?" Honey had asked.

"Well, no, she hasn't. It's just that I had offered to hold her job for her, but she was downright hostile. I shouldn't tell you this, but when Gale Grayson and I went over to pay our condolences, Le struck Gale. Right on the porch steps. I'm sure it's all the grief—I can only imagine what I would be like in those circumstances—but I have a business to run. I'm placing an ad tomorrow. In the meantime, I'll do the cooking."

"You're a good cook, shug," Honey had said. "I've tasted your cooking. Don't you worry—you'll do just fine."

Sally had hung up, her stomach in knots. She wanted nothing more than to bury herself in a deep hole. Why had she said all that to Honey? She had meant to make a friendly, semiprofessional phone call to let her friends know that she was back on track. Why had she let herself slip into gossip?

She arrived at the tearoom at seven A.M. to start baking the sweet potatoes for the muffins. But the sight of all that barren metal glowing in the morning light, the absence of warm aromas, the stark silence of the place panicked her. To squelch it, she had plucked several metal cooking spoons from their magnetic strip and dropped them clanking onto the counter. The sound seemed to shock the kitchen to life, and within minutes she had the potatoes washed and roasting, the butter softening, and a hot pot of coffee brewing.

At ten A.M. she steeled herself and reversed the "Closed" sign on the door. Not that she expected hordes—Thursday was never a busy day—but she nonetheless felt . . . successful. She hadn't backed down. She had opened up. And if no customers came today because they expected her to be closed, well, that was just the nature of business.

She wiped her hands on her cornflower-colored apron and pulled a small black chalkboard from behind the cash register. The smell of sweetness and nuts filled the room. In a flowing hand, she wrote out the day's specials—Virginia peanut soup, sweet potato muffins, raisin scones, and dandelion salad. No one needed to know until they were inside and hungry that for the time being these offerings comprised the entire menu.

She was hauling outside a large ceramic goose on which to hang the chalkboard when she heard the drum of shoes on the sidewalk. Turning around, she was greeted by two of the MMMM's, each holding a pot of hothouse pansies.

"I got on the horn as soon as you called last night," Honey said, "and me-oh-my we all decided we had a hankering for some scones this morning."

"Donna's coming in a minute," added Sue Matthew-

son. "She had to drop something off at 'City Hall.' "
Even with her hands full of pansy, she managed to put
the quotation marks around the word. She held her
flowerpot aloft. "And we decided that those tables of
yours could probably use some sprucing up after a couple of days of neglect. Never say we don't care about
you."

Sally felt a surge of gratitude. These truly were her
sister soldiers far from home. She was stupid for getting
mired in depression and self-doubt. So what if Mal wasn't
here? So what if Le was difficult? She had a community.

She took the flowers from Sue and motioned them
into the tearoom. They cooed favorably as she placed
the pots on the tables.

"Something smells good, Sal," Honey said as they
claimed their seats. "Maybe you don't need to hire another cook. Maybe you should just get a waitress and do
all the cooking yourself."

"Do you need us to fetch our own plates?" Sue offered. "We wouldn't mind, really, if you're too busy in
the kitchen."

"I smell raisins. Whatever it is you've cooked with
raisins, that's what I'll have."

Sally beamed. God, it was great to have friends. It
was great to . . . well, just to belong.

She left them nattering while she went to fetch their
orders from the kitchen. The scones and muffins still
warmed in the oven—these she put in a cloth-covered
clay basket. The dandelion salad, sprinkled with vinai-
grette, went into a large crystal bowl. She carefully ladled
the creamy pale peanut soup into four pewter porrid-
gers. Not bad, she thought as she placed the dishes on
a tray. Not bad for hired help.

As soon as she entered the dining room, she could
tell something was wrong. Donna Crow stood beside
the MMMM's table, her coat still on, her hand on her
hip. All the women turned to look at Sally.

"What's going on?" Sally asked.

"Why didn't you mention what happened to Le last night?" Sue asked.

"What happened to Le?"

"Her house was firebombed," said Donna.

Sally's throat constricted. "No," she whispered.

"I was just over at City Hall, talking to the clerk. It was early in the evening, too. Someone just drove by the house and threw a Molotov cocktail through the window. She called it 'molly-tov,' but, oh well."

"A Molotov cocktail?" Sally forced her thoughts to focus as she set the tray on the table. "Was anybody hurt?"

"No. Evidently Le and her mother put the fire out themselves. But it made a tremendous explosion. I didn't hear it out in the subdivision but the clerk said everyone in town heard it."

"I didn't hear anything," Sally said. "About what time?"

"About seven-thirty. You should have heard it, Sally. From the way the clerk described it, it was something else. I would have thought you'd have heard something that loud."

Sally placed their bowls one by one in front of them. "I wasn't home at seven-thirty."

"All I can say is what a horrible thing. Evidently, the sheriff's treating it as a hate crime."

Honey shook her head in disbelief. "A *hate* crime? Really? I agree it was awful . . . and dangerous, but I don't see how he can just jump to the conclusion that it was a hate crime. I mean, how can he claim it's a hate crime when he hasn't caught who did it? I bet if it happened to you or me he'd just say it was vandalism."

"I don't know, Honey," said Donna. "A Molotov cocktail . . ."

"Heck, that's what college students used back in the sixties. You going to tell me all that protest was nothing but a hate crime? No, I feel sorry for Le and her family, but I'm just not going along with that. I'm tired of every single crime being called a hate crime. A church is burned, it's not arson, it's a hate crime. A house has graffiti on it, it's not vandalism, it's a hate crime."

"Well, Miss Honey, since you're not sheriff . . ."

"Maybe I'll just run for office. Get me a big ol' ten-gallon hat . . ."

The women burst into laughter as Honey stood up to do her impersonation of a Southern sheriff. She slipped her thumbs in the belt loops of her jeans and talked out of the side of her mouth as if she chewed a piece of straw.

"Hate crimes," she said, her natural Southern accent cast deeper and slower. "Why, I ain't gonna have me none of them hate crimes. You gonna commit a crime in my territory, son, you make sure you do it up right. Give me some old-fashioned crimes, like cow-tippin'. Yep, now cow-tippin's a bon' fide crime. Get your ass over to the jailhouse, boy."

The women were bent over in peels as Honey high-stepped around the room. Sally felt suddenly light-headed. Picking up the empty tray, she rushed back into the kitchen.

She grabbed the phone and punched in Le's number.

She stopped counting at fifteen rings, but still held on to the handset, praying for someone to answer. "I'm sorry," she whispered, over and over. "I'm sorry, I'm sorry, I'm sorry . . ."

The three Vietnamese females sat side by side in Ella's peach-colored parlor like children at a recital. Their hands were folded on their knees, their eyes shifting nervously from ceiling to wall to floor. There really wasn't much difference that Ella could see between mother, daughter, and granddaughter except for age. As she examined them, she could see the one in the others. *Lordy,* she thought. *If I were plopped on a sofa with Gale and Katie Pru, would someone think they could roll us all together into one?*

From her seat across the coffee table from them, she cleared her throat. "Can I get any of you more hot tea?" she asked loudly. "How about the baby—is she thirsty?"

At the word "baby" the little girl glanced at her, then looked quickly over to where Katie Pru sat by the door, playing with two spool-owls and watching. The little girl scooted deeper into the sofa and wrapped her hand around her mother's arm.

"Her name is Chau," the mother said. Ella suspected she meant to say it defensively, but the words came out cracked and vulnerable. "We call her Chau."

"Chau," Ella repeated. Nadianna had told her the girl's name when they first arrived, but it hadn't stuck with her. All she could remember was that it reminded her of a dog and how odd it was to name a child after a dog. "Well, then, Chau, would you like to go play with my great-granddaughter over there? You two look like you would get along just grandly."

The little girl again shot a look at Katie Pru but didn't move. Ella sighed.

She didn't know where the other grown-ups were. When Nadianna had shown up at the door with the Nguyens in tow, there had been a great fanfare of welcomes and solicitousness. They had stood on the porch in an odd assortment of clothes—Ella learned later that Nadianna had to go into their house alone to look for things for them to wear—shivering, the little girl's lips an alarming shade of lavender. Then everyone had filed into the parlor, where the three females had clustered on the sofa as if seeking a safe haven within a stranger's house. More stilted conversation, a kettle of hot tea and bowls of oatmeal, and when she looked around Gale, Nadianna, and Halford had left, leaving her to play hostess and ambassador.

The silence was driving her nuts. She tried again, believing that children were as good as pets when it came to fostering small talk.

"What about Halloween? What's little Chau going to dress up as for Halloween?"

The mother—Le, she had to remember the name, Le—gave her a scowl. "No Halloween. We don't have Halloween."

"Oh well, you must," Ella said in surprise. "I know some people object to it because of the witches and devils and such, but I've always thought it was such a healthy holiday for children. Lets them use their imagination. And if it gets a bit of the devil out of them, all the better."

The two women said something to each other in a foreign language, which irritated Ella, in her own house. "We don't let Katie Pru go trick-or-treating—there's just not a good place around here. But still, dressing up is fun. Last year—what were you last year, Katie Pru? A cat, was it?"

"A jaguar," Katie Pru said, not looking up from her owls. "I had big claws."

"See, some sort of cat. And what about this year? What are you going to be?"

Katie Pru shrugged. "I don't know. A muscadine critter, maybe."

"A muscadine critter. Well, all right. The point is," Ella said, turning to the Nguyens, "you let them dress up as anything they like. If they want to be something scary, that's just fine."

The women spoke together again. Le shook her head. "No," she said to Ella. "That sounds bad. We won't let Chau do that."

"Suit yourself," said Ella. She let her voice grow

distant. "Pity that baby doesn't get to join in childish fun . . ."

This was really getting awkward, and Ella grew increasingly irritated with Gale and Nadianna. Where the hell were they? And since when was she the one to be left in the dark while they plotted?

She heard footfalls on the stepping-stones outside and was out of her seat before the doorbell rang. Ron Goddard stood on the stoop, clutching some papers.

"I'm sorry, Ella. I've come to see Nadianna. I should have called . . ."

Ella grabbed him by the arm. "Don't mention it, Ron. You come right on in. You know you're always welcome here. Come on in and join our other company in the parlor."

Goddard looked from Ella to the Vietnamese women as he stammered a hello. Ella directed him to the chair she had just occupied.

"Ron here is a professor from England," she said, patting his shoulder as he sat. "So y'all have something in common. You talk a minute while I go see what Nadianna is up to."

In the foyer she encountered the others. She eyed Gale suspiciously.

"You've decided something. I can see it in your face."

"Ella, this has to be with your permission, of course, but the three of us have come to an arrangement that we think might work. The Nguyens are terrified to go to their house. I'm going to see if there is anywhere for them to go, but if not, I think we should ask them to stay here, at least until we can find them someplace through DFACS."

"Here?" Ella looked at her blankly. "Three more people? Where do you propose we put them?"

Halford spoke. "They can have my room. I'll stay in

a hotel in Praterton. As Gale said, it would just be for a couple of days."

Ella fought a flare of anger. What on earth made them think they could make a decision like this without her input? Since when did she become the housekeeper who didn't need to be consulted? "A couple of days and you're leaving for England, Daniel. Are you going to tell me that you would rather spend that time thirty minutes from here in some hotel?"

"No, of course I'd rather be here. But they are obviously scared. And until they can find a place—"

"Daniel Halford. That is the most ridiculous thing I've ever heard. It may be chivalric, but it's plain crazy. You came here to spend time with this family, and that's what you're going to do. My heart goes out to those people in there, but this is none of our doing. Gale, if you want to get on the phone and call Alby and see what he suggests in the way of finding them a place to stay, that's fine. But you are not going to run this man out of here because of your bleeding heart. I'm not going to have—"

"Ron," Nadianna interrupted.

Ella didn't intend to stamp her foot as she turned to Nadianna, but the sound filled the foyer. "What?"

"Why can't Daniel stay with Ron? He's got the whole Greene house to himself. Surely if we ask him he'll let Daniel stay there for a couple of days. You'll be over here most of the time anyway, won't you, Daniel? I'll ask Ron. I can't imagine he'll say no."

"Say no to what?"

Goddard had come up behind them, his face pleasant but curious. "I suspect I was abandoned in there on purpose, Ella. I'm not a very good conversationalist in situations like that. We spent a good deal of time staring at each other's feet. But what do you want to ask me?"

"The Nguyens may have to stay here, Ron," Ella said. "Which means Daniel will have to give up his room. Now, he's offered to go to a hotel in Praterton, but that's far from here, and since it's only for a couple of days, we were wondering if we could impose on your hospitality and ask if he could stay with you. Just till Sunday. That's when he's going home."

Goddard was nodding in agreement before she finished. "I think that would be fine. I've got one room that I'm not using. I'm afraid the other's littered with tapes and papers, but the one, no, I haven't even gone in it much. No sheets on the bed . . ."

"We'll get you sheets. So will that be okay with you?"

"Yes, yes, that will be fine. I'll have to work long hours—"

Halford held up his hand. "I promise I'll only be there to sleep. I won't bother you."

"Well, then, yes. I say we do it."

"Terrific. That's settled." Ella felt her old power surge through her veins. If she could get those women to let that child dress up for Halloween, she'd be a full woman again.

19

Blue roofs. Blue air-conditioners. Alby Truitt drove his truck down Highway 441, looking right then left at the white houses, black mailboxes, and gray roofs that sped past him. Occasionally the loden color of a pressure-treated wooden fence flickered by, and a yellow farmhouse or newly painted red barn would reveal itself beside a stand of trees, but the cultural tastes of this part of Georgia ran to the earth. The colors of granite were the colors of home. The only blue around here was the cloud-wisped roll of the sky.

Three miles before Statlers Cross he came upon a fifteen-foot lighthouse, paint still glossy. This was the entranceway to Sag Harbor Estates, the ritzy development that had lured all manner of former suburbanites to this rambling rural county. If it wasn't a gated community, it might as well have been. The sternness of its lighthouse, the intimidation of its real estate signpost— *Houses from the 250's to 400's*—pretty much guaranteed that only invited guests would enter. Hell, he thought as he turned into the subdivision, one of the nice things about being sheriff is that you learn real quick you're not quite accepted anywhere.

He drove slowly down the street, huge brick houses rising on both sides. He had grown up in a five-room house with peeling siding and a ceiling with brown water stains in every room. While he never wanted to go back to that, he wasn't sure he ever wanted this, either. How does one exist in a house where the living room echoes? What does it do to you when you can't hold the sounds of your own words close to you?

He turned onto a cul-de-sac and let it direct him back to the primary road and on out to Highway 441 again. No blue there, either. Even the shutters reflected the ground.

From 441, he decided to take a backroad route into Statlers Cross and swung onto a dusty road that would eventually lead him to town. He passed an old dogtrot house, spruced up and painted beige. Mal and Sally Robertson's place. No question that Sally had done an excellent job on refurbishing the house, but it irritated him whenever he passed. A dogtrot house deserved the respect of what it was—low-country, functional. With the dogtrot enclosed and the exterior doused in legitimate Williamsburg colors (Sally had informed him of this), it reminded him of something unnatural, like a yard dog in a poodle's frilly coat.

Seven minutes and he found himself on Baxter Street, at the opposite end from where the firebombers would have entered. He stopped in front of the Nguyen house. God, it was *blue*. Someone had taped butcher paper over the broken window. That's not going to last, he thought as he climbed from his truck. They're gonna need to get someone out here to fix the glass or else board the space up.

He first knocked on the door, then pounded when there was no answer.

"Nobody's home," came a warbling holler from across the empty lot next door. "I think they've left."

He looked over at the crooked figure of Ilene

Parker. She sat in a chair at the side of her house. Her hands were busy doing something, but from this distance Truitt couldn't tell what.

"They've gone?" he asked as he walked toward her. "Know where they've gone?"

She waited until he was in front of her. In her lap was a pile of white crocheted yarn. "I can't say. Although it was the Jesup girl that got them."

"Really? What did she do, just come and pick them up?"

The crochet needle drove into a loop of yarn and pulled another strand out. "She walked away with them. That's all I know."

"Huh." There was something she wanted to tell him, he could sense that, but her small gray head stayed bent over her work. "So they all walked off? No car?"

"No car. They walked through the back. It's shorter that way. But harder. I don't walk through the back anymore. Barry Greene used to keep the brambles cut down, but when he died they just grew back. I can't go out there without worrying about scratching my arms or turning my ankle."

"I don't blame you. Did anything else happen last night after we left?"

The needle went in, came out with a loop. "Nothing happened. It was quiet."

"Must have been hard getting to sleep."

"A bit, yes."

"Stayed up by the window, did you, to make sure nothing else happened?"

At this she glanced up at him. "Nothing happened," she said.

"Listen, Miz Parker. Did you see a woman anytime in the back last night?"

"A woman? I don't think so."

"I've got a fella said he saw someone in the bushes behind the Nguyens' house. You can see those bushes from your kitchen window, I bet."

"Probably. But I wasn't looking out my kitchen window last night."

"So you didn't see anything suspicious, even before the house was firebombed?"

Her hands stopped, the needle poised in the air.

"Now, wait a minute. I did see someone. I didn't get a good look, but I remember thinking there was something odd about him . . ."

"Odd?"

"I don't know . . . just something off . . . About the clothes, maybe?" She sighed and sank her hands into the yarn, fluffing it. "I don't remember now. But I do know I saw *someone*."

"About what time?"

"Oh, earlier than what you're talking about. Around four."

"Could you sorta point to where you saw him?"

"Back there." She gestured toward the rear of the Nguyen house. "Where you're talking about."

"Thank you, Miz Parker. Now, is there anything else you want to tell me?"

She began crocheting again. "I don't think the Nguyens are going to be coming home anytime soon."

"Why not?"

"They left with their suitcases. With the Jesup girl."

"I can't say I blame them for that. For starters, that house is going to be cold until they get the window fixed. If they think that butcher paper's gonna keep out the chill, they're gonna realize how wrong they are."

"Oh, they didn't put that up. I did. After they left."

"Really? That was considerate of you."

Her face flushed slightly. "I thought it was something

I could do for them. I really do want to do something. I always have. They're just so . . ."

"Unapproachable?" Truitt asked gently. "Listen, Miz Parker. I want to tell you something I found out. That color blue—it doesn't have anything to do with prostitution. It's considered a very dignified and important color in Vietnam. So you can put your mind at ease. There's nothing going on over there like you thought."

He was surprised to see tears in her eyes. "I figured that. I knew I was wrong last night."

"How so?"

The tears spilled onto her veined hands, and she hid them under the pile of yarn. "They didn't go back into the house. All night long, they slept in the corner of the fence. Even the child. They looked so cold. I saw them and knew they couldn't have been bad people. Bad people wouldn't have been afraid of anything. Bad people are fearless, don't you think? Those three were too afraid to go inside."

Truitt tried to keep his face neutral. "They were outside all night? Did you go out and talk to them? Why didn't you call me?"

Her face was streaked now, her mouth trembling. "How could I apologize? I did take some quilts out to them. Quilts my sister made. I set them inside the fence. But how could I talk with them now, after so much time when I never said anything? I feel like I've done something bad to them. Why would they talk to me?"

Truitt knelt beside her and rested his hands on her cold fingers. "Miz Parker," he said, "I'm going to give you an order. When they move back into that house, it's your job to go talk with them. Le, the mother of the little girl, speaks English very well. Now, I'm not saying she's going to welcome you with open arms. She might slam the door in your face. But maybe she's earned the right to do that. And once she does, maybe y'all can start on equal footing and be neighbors."

She was silent a moment, her hands under his worrying the yarn. "Those are fine words, Mr. Truitt. But it's not like that. I pray that it could be. But I don't know if I believe it."

Truitt left her and trudged over the yellow weeds of the empty lot to the rear of the Nguyen house. A figure with something odd about him—clothes—had been seen here a few hours before the house was firebombed and a woman was later spied in the same location. Mentally, he went through the houses on the street, trying to decide if any of the male residents fell in place as potentially "odd." No one immediately came to mind. He'd have Haskell check it out.

The brambles certainly earned their names—they towered and drooped over him, cascading in a tumble of gray vines and withered leaves. They looked to him like a combination of muscadine and honeysuckle, although he thought he detected thorns in their tangled insides. He walked around them, trying to fix in his mind where they broke and then closed again. They stretched far past the Nguyen property, out to the Greenes' yard and the Alden land. He examined the ground where Halford had said the woman stood. He couldn't see anything, not even an imprint, although it would have had to be a heavy woman to leave a mark in this hard clay earth.

The buzzer in his pocket sounded. Checking the number, he sprinted back to his truck and called Haskell at the department.

"Preliminary's in," Haskell said.

"Sum it for me."

"Stuart Keast received three wounds from a twelve-gauge shotgun—slug that entered his right hand also penetrated his chest above the second rib—"

"Maybe a defensive wound . . ."

"—and the fatal shot that severed the pulmonary vein in his neck. Darrell Murphy received two wounds from the same gauge shotgun—one to the front of his face which shattered his skull above the jaw, and one to his chest."

"Any other sign of trauma?"

"Not on them."

Truitt's chest tightened. "Go on."

"Tuan Nguyen received one bullet wound from a twenty-two-caliber pistol square in the right temple. This was the fatal wound. But there was evidence that the bruising around the eye area was not exclusively the result of the bullet. He had been struck with some force prior to the gunshot. And the state pathologist found something else interesting: In addition to the duct tape that bound his hands and ankles, the back of his knees showed severe bruising, like with a ligature. And the inside of his mouth—tongue, roof, and gums—was covered in small puncture marks."

"Weird," said Truitt.

"I'll say. I got a quote from the pathologist: 'This is not inconsistent with a man being hung upside down by his knees and something thorny, maybe a small pine-cone or even a vine, crammed into his mouth.' "

"Jesus."

"My exact word. But the interesting thing was that his mouth seemed to have been washed out. So the pathologist's doing more tests on the soft tissue in the mouth and the stomach contents to see if he can pinpoint what it was in the man's mouth."

"Does he have an estimate on how long that will take?"

"He said maybe a couple of days. I told him about the firebomb and asked him to make it a priority."

"What about the times of death?"

"He was iffy, but he said that Keast and Murphy were probably shot between noon and four P.M. Nguyen, on the other hand, was killed several hours earlier, as early as two or three A.M. Monday morning."

"So chances are he was put in the truck after he was killed."

"The lividity confirms that. He was on his back for awhile after death."

"What about Siler's alibis?"

"His doctor says he called in a prescription for sinus medication Sunday night, and the twenty-four-hour pharmacy shows that his brother picked it up around ten. The doctor says that if he took the medicine, he'd be sleeping like a baby for eight to ten hours, which would take us to around nine A.M. And his mother swears he didn't leave her house until four Monday afternoon."

"A pretty solid alibi, but not perfect. Good job, Craig."

"That's not all, Alby. I talked with Mike Spivey at the Chevy dealership. I showed him the drawing, and he suggested that maybe instead of a snake it might be a ram—you know, the two horns. He also said that Dodge has taillights like that for some of its Ram trucks."

"Interesting. So we need to go to the nearest Dodge dealership—"

"Which I will do. But Mike said something else. He said he saw a Ram truck in Praterton last week with those taillights. He noticed 'cause it was a monster of a truck with lots of custom features. And he recognized the driver. Sarah Gainer."

Truitt whistled. "Now where did Miss Gainer get herself a honking big truck like that?"

"I don't know," Haskell replied. "I took the liberty to call her parole officer. He didn't know either."

"When did you place the call?"

"About thirty minutes ago, why?"

"Meet me at Sarah's place, Craig. And let's hope her parole officer was smart enough not to contact her."

20

After the baby-filled, child-filled—all right, he'd admit it—*woman*-filled bustle of the Alden house, Halford found his new accommodations serene and depressingly familiar. This was a place where a solitary man lived. The clutter was the clutter of academic maleness: a discarded sweater next to a heap of books, a half-empty cup of coffee atop a scatter of papers, loafers—tasseled, no less—blocking the doorway. The whole house had the closed smell of someone sitting on a sofa too long, the musty fragrance of cologned sedentariness.

"Lord, I had no idea how messy the place was," Goddard apologized as he preceded Halford into the house. "The activity of last night, everything that's been going on . . . I'm afraid I've become a lackluster housekeeper."

"No apologies. As I said, I'm only going to sleep here. I'll be out of your hair during the day and won't care a whit about what the place looks like."

Goddard smiled, a tad wearily. "Ah. You say that. But there are now three—count 'em, *three*—children in that house over there. Three anxious mothers, two strong-willed grandmothers. Consider this your home while you're here."

"Thank you. But I really think I'm not going to mind the sixteen-aunts-and-forty-two-cousins bit. I can be alone all I want once I get back to London. This has been a vacation on several levels."

"Hmmm. I felt like that when I first got here, too. Now I could use a brisk walk by the River Aire." Goddard motioned him down a short hallway. "The second door on the right is your room. Across the hall's the loo. Make yourself at home."

Halford made his way down the hall, glancing into a bedroom stacked with makeshift shelves neatly lined with videotapes. The man seemed to have as many tapes as other men had books, Halford decided as he hauled his luggage into the adjacent room. This room was exactly as Goddard described it— not "gone into much." The single twin bed featured a wagon-wheel headboard and the thin mattress was folded in a yogalike curl. The springs gave a metallic whine as he opened the mattress and sat down. Besides a small dresser with wagon-wheel pulls and a mirror topped with a wagon-wheel adornment, the room was bare. Whoever the Greenes were, they must have had a son. The room had the feel of a twelve-year-old.

Halford shoved his suitcase into the corner and began making the bed. Ella's sheets were fresh and flowered, the coverlet she had given him a bright quilted yellow with purple appliquéd roses. When he finished, he stood back and winced at the effect. Now the room smacked of adolescent sexual confusion and old-lady preciousness. He had no doubt he'd be spending the bulk of his time over with Gale.

He found Goddard in the kitchen fixing coffee. "Instant," he told Halford. "Would you like some? I rarely make a whole pot unless I'm on deadline. But something about being in America, I find myself wanting the damn stuff all the time."

Halford took the cup Goddard offered. "Nadianna said something about you making a brilliant spiced tea."

Goddard grinned. "Special effects, I'm afraid. Not the tea itself—that was genuine, straight from my grandmother—but I was practicing a little of the art of persuasion on Nadianna. I need her to help me. She's fantastically talented. You've seen her work."

"Of course. And yes, she's talented."

Goddard blew steam from his cup. "I really need her. Do you know what my job is here? I listen. That's all I do, all day long. I listen to aspirates, vowels, consonants, diphthongs. I focus in so closely I can hear the tongue move. It makes its own sounds, like being in the forest at night and hearing insects that you would never hear during the day. My worry is that I am so busy listening, so busy watching the muscles of the mouth, I'm missing something the face can tell me. Nadianna's going to take this project to a whole new level."

"So you're using her a bit."

Goddard looked at him in surprise, then relaxed into a chuckle. "As if anyone could use Nadianna Jesup. You know better than that, Daniel. That young woman's tough as nails. What is she—twenty-one, twenty-two? God, she has more presence about her than I ever did at that age. Or any of my students, for that matter. I would say it's more of a case of us using one another. Mutual benefit. The way of a sane world, eh?"

"As long as you both see eye to eye."

"You think I'm not being fair with her?"

Halford sipped the hot, black coffee. "I don't know. I do know that you have an entire university behind you, a grant, a committee, presumably a publisher. She has nothing. That lessens the 'mutual' to some degree."

"Don't sell her short. She knows how to look after herself."

"Remember that she's only twenty-two, and we're all subject to mistakes at that age."

Goddard ran his finger around the rim of his cup, not looking Halford in the eye. "I got the feeling you were interested in Gale," he said slowly. "This sounds as though I may have been wrong."

"No. But I think Gale's come to look upon Nadianna as a protégée, maybe even a younger sister. I know she feels responsible for her."

"In that light, it sounds like you're giving me the father talk—make sure there's plenty of petrol in the car and have her back by ten."

Halford smiled. "If you wish."

"You don't have to worry, Daniel. I think Nadianna is an intriguing young woman. She's even beautiful, in a rather exotic way. But what I'm interested in is her ability with her camera. Besides . . ."

"Besides?" Halford prodded.

Goddard set his cup on the table and ran his fingers through his hair. "Besides. Let's face it. We're not exactly each other's type. I mean, I can see enjoying Nadianna's company here . . ."

"But not back in Leeds?"

"Not back in Leeds. That makes me a snob. But I dare say she would admit to the same thing."

"Ah."

"You disagree?"

"Yes."

"Really?" Goddard pulled out a chair and sat down, folding his arms across his chest. He looked at Halford curiously, and, Halford noted, with a touch of sadness. "So you believe that you could settle down here, perhaps marry Gale, be a father to Katie Pru? That you could become a part of this town, go to the church, spend your money in the shops, the sheriff slapping you on the back and tossing back beers with you? I think you're deluding yourself, Daniel. I think if you were to stay here, you would always be the odd man out. People would stop drinking their beers when you entered a room. They would count your money twice when you came into their shops. And Gale? Well, Gale would make excuses for you because she would know that you'd never fit in. Of course, the truly sad part for you is that since she's already an outcast, you would make her more like part of the group. She would stand in contrast to you. You would be more alien than she, and that would be very beneficial to her, wouldn't it?"

"That's an incredibly cold thing to say, Ron," Halford said evenly.

Goddard slumped forward and rested his forehead in the palms of his hands. "Not cold, Daniel. Academic. I am, at heart, an extremely dispassionate observer."

No Dodge Ram truck with fancy taillights sat in front of Sarah Gainer's trailer. The jack-o'-lantern in the window had either been turned off or had run out of batteries—it stared at them, its plastic eyes blank and yellow. Slowly, Truitt mounted the flimsy metal steps and knocked on the door. Behind him he heard Haskell unlatch his holster.

"Sarah? Sarah, it's Sheriff Truitt. You need to come on out so I can talk to you."

No sound. The canvas overhang waved in the breeze, its rivets clanking against the poles. Truitt knocked again and hollered.

"Sarah! You need to talk to me. I have a warrant."

A low wind skittered through the dried plants in their Christmas pots, but still no human sound. Drawing his own weapon, Truitt tried the doorknob. It turned effortlessly.

He went in with Haskell at his back. Quickly, they divided, Truitt taking the kitchen and living room, Haskell the two bedrooms and the bathroom. Nothing. The trailer was empty.

"Search it?" Haskell asked.

Truitt nodded. "Anything that suggests she's been making Molotov cocktails or likes to drive a Dodge."

Pulling on gloves, Truitt took the living room. The last time he had been in Sarah Gainer's trailer was the night he arrested her for setting fire to the church pews. He had been shocked at what he had seen. Nazi flags, racist propaganda materials—only one weapon, though, a hunting rifle that had belonged to her father. He had had to face one of his own prejudices at that moment, that women could not be involved in such things. It just hadn't seemed right to him. Sarah was such a thin girl, almost childlike, her red hair long and sensual. He had almost been drawn to her, admitting at some point during the trial that she might, under different circumstances, have been his type—gutsy, sinewy, outspoken. It was the content of her character, as the great man said, that made her so repulsive to him. The ignorance that came out of her mouth was the ignorance of poverty and a bad education. He should have had pity on her, but he had found that he did not.

Haskell spoke from the back bedroom. "At least Albert Speer's no longer her decorator. If her parole agent couldn't persuade her not to use a gun as self-protection, at least he convinced her to improve her color scheme. Red and black is out, man."

"Don't let a UGA fan hear you say that," Truitt said as he lifted the sofa cushions. "If it hadn't been for the swastika, she'd have been right in style."

He heard Haskell grunt. "No comment."

With the offensive elements out, there wasn't much to Sarah Gainer's style. A stained mustard-colored sofa, a television, two mismatched chairs. Truitt shone a penlight under the television, checked a pile of yellowed newspapers beside the front door. In the kitchen, he found what he assumed was Sarah's gun cabinet, a long narrow drawer built into the counter where he figured she had stored her Lorcin. He opened the drawer and drew out a keychain. From it dangled a key with the distinctive stamp of the Dodge Corporation.

"One down, Craig. I may have found our key."

"Maybe two," Haskell said, coming into the kitchen. In his gloved hand he carried a can of kerosene. "Now you give me one good reason why a sensible person living in a trailer would keep this next to a box of rags."

Katie Pru had six owls. She had worked hard on them, first getting Grandma Ella to agree to let her have the spools, then gluing the dried corn kernels to the body. She looked into their walnut-shell faces, each one of them hers and hers alone. She handed Chau one.

"You can play with this," she said. "If you want more you'll have to make them."

"It's beautiful," Chau said. "I don't want to make more. I could never make mine as beautiful as this. Maybe I'll be an owl for Halloween."

That made Katie Pru feel good, and they played for a long time, whispering in the den so the grown-ups would not hear them. The grown-ups were not in a good mood, that had been clear to Katie Pru all morning. Lots of loud voices, lots of rushing about, but not a lot of good mood. Something big was happening.

Chau's owl came swooping out of the sky and pecked at the floor. "Katie Pru is a funny name," Chau said.

"I know." Katie Pru tucked her owl in its nest made of pillows. "I want my name to be Caroline, but my mother keeps forgetting."

"I like Caroline. I want to be Anh, but I haven't told my mom."

Chau's owl hooted and flew back into the air. Katie Pru looked at her nest with its five sleeping owls and felt guilty.

"You know what, Anh, we could make you an owl together. It could be practice for making your costume. I know where to find owl heads."

Chau's eyes widened. "You know where to find their heads?"

Katie Pru nodded. "But we have to be careful, Anh." She said the name loudly. "It's on the other side of the thickets. We have to walk on the path. But we can do it. I've done it lots of times. Want to go?"

Chau tucked her owl in her pocket. "Yes, Caroline. Let's go."

Grandma Ella kept the key to the den doors hidden, but Katie Pru knew where it was. She dragged the chair away from the desk, climbed on it, and, gathering her courage, reached under the field mouse to pull out the black iron key. "We have to be very quiet," she cautioned, "or all the owls will fly away."

Quietly, she turned the key in the lock, and quietly they stole from the house. Katie Pru put her finger to her lips and took Chau's hand as they high-stepped through the grass. Once they were a good distance from the house, Katie Pru dropped Chau's hand and they both ran to the thickets.

They didn't stop as they reached the path, their feet hammering the hard dirt. It wasn't until the thickets closed in around them and they could no longer see the house that they stopped, and Katie Pru held up her hand.

"Listen, Anh," she whispered. "If you listen you can hear the owls calling each other."

Chau stood very still, scrunching her eyes closed. "I think I hear them, Caroline. Far away."

"We . . . must . . . be . . . very . . . quiet. We . . . mustn't . . . scare . . . them. . . ."

Hand in hand, they tiptoed further down the path. Katie Pru knew owls were scaredy-birds. They would fly away at the drop of a pin. Sometimes they flew so fast their faces couldn't keep up and fell behind crying in the dirt. She'd heard them crying in the night, mournful for their lost bodies. She squeezed Chau's hand. She'd have to remember to tell her that story when they got back safe to the house.

From behind a huge thicket, they heard a snap. They stopped and stared at each other.

"Owls?" asked Chau.

Snap. Rustle. Katie Pru's throat dried up. Another snap. Closer. Then with a roar of breaking twigs and ripping vines the thickets opened up like a giant mouth and standing in front of them was a witch, her skin smeared black and her hair hanging like red teeth over her face.

"Arrrrrrraaarrrrrr!!!!!" the witch screamed.

"Arrrrrrraaarrrrrr!!!!!" screamed Katie Pru and Chau.

All three broke into a scramble. The witch grabbed both girls by the shoulders and vaulted over them. Her red-teeth hair flapped as she pounded down the path and vanished from sight.

Katie Pru and Chau didn't stop screaming until they reached the house and were in their mothers' arms. They didn't stop screaming until their mothers had cuddled and rocked them and their breath came out in rasping gulps. As she rested her head against her mother's shoulder, Katie Pru felt like screaming some more. It occurred to her as her mother listened with worried eyes to her story, that screaming was the only thing to do.

21

Sarah Gainer was found running in a ditch along Highway 441. The interesting thing to Truitt was that she ran toward him, actually stumbling to turn around in the eroded baked clay. Her hands had come up to him, outstretched, and he had reached down to help her climb. Afterward, she wouldn't let go of his wrist, even as he read her rights, even as Haskell struggled to handcuff her. She was breathing hard and was filthy. *How long have you been out there, Sarah?* he had asked. *How long since you've had anything to eat?* But she didn't say anything, just stared at him, blood dried on her cracked lips, as Haskell guided her into the backseat of a patrol car.

Now Truitt faced her in the interview room of the Calwyn County Sheriff's Department. Haskell sat in a chair in the corner of the room, arms crossed. Truitt could tell by reading his deputy's body language that if they were to play good-cop-bad-cop, he would have to take the role of the good cop himself. He opened up a white paper sack and pulled out a foil-wrapped biscuit.

"I think this one is egg and bacon, Sarah." He rummaged around in the bag. "Got an egg and cheese. A country ham. Then just a sausage. You've got your pick. What about you, Deputy? You got a preference?"

"Nah," said Haskell. "I'm not hungry."

"How you can smell this and not be hungry is beyond me. What about you, Sarah? Which would you like?"

She hesitated, her eyes on the bag, then reached up and grabbed the biscuit Truitt held. Like having a wild animal eat from your hand, he thought, as she slumped back in her chair and hungrily unwrapped the biscuit.

"Egg and bacon. Good choice. Think I'll have me the country ham. It's too salty and not good for me, but there's nothing on heaven and earth I love better."

Behind Sarah, Haskell made a give-me-a-break face. Truitt ignored him and pushed a paper cup of coffee toward Sarah.

"Not as hot as you'd probably like, but still pretty fresh. Sorry that you'll have to take it black." He watched her gulp her biscuit as he bit into his own. "How long were you out there, Sarah?" he said as he chewed. "It's a chilly time of year to be out in someone's fields all night."

She didn't look at him, just concentrated on her biscuit. Her hands were grimy and her face streaked with mud. He chuckled. "I tell you, you must have given those two little girls a fright. I'll give you a chance to wash up in a bit. You put that dirt on your face to hide, Sarah, or was it just a messy night?"

This time she glanced at him, and for a second Truitt wondered if he had hurt her feelings. But then she was back at the biscuit again, the bread crumbling around her lips and falling onto the table. She shoved the final bite into her mouth.

He pushed another biscuit toward her. "Eat up, Sarah," he said softly. "Then I want you to tell me what on earth you've gotten yourself into."

She watched him as she ate the second biscuit, chewing slower this time. When she finished, he passed her a napkin.

"I ain't gotten myself into anything," she said. "I ain't done nothing."

"Then why were you hiding in the Aldens' fields? Why didn't you want to sleep in your own bed last night?"

She shrugged and reached for the coffee. When she set the cup down, Truitt leaned over and took it away from her.

"I'll get you some fresh in a minute. I need you to tell me why you were hiding in the Aldens' fields."

"I need my lawyer."

Truitt nodded at Haskell. "Deputy, you want to take this young woman out to call her lawyer?"

"I already left a message on his answering machine," Haskell answered. "But she's welcome to try."

Truitt waited while Haskell escorted Sarah from the room. In less than five minutes they were back.

"Well?"

Sarah looked pouty—and, Truitt thought, a little scared. "He wasn't there. I left a message."

Haskell shrugged as he sank back into his chair by the wall. "I tried to tell her I'd been trying to do her a favor. Now she's used up her phone call and still hasn't talked to her lawyer."

Truitt leaned over the table to Sarah. "I will give you another phone call—don't worry about that. But honestly, Sarah, you are in some trouble. If you want to halt this interview and wait for your lawyer to get here, that's fine. I will have to detain you, though. If you can explain all this stuff away, I would surely appreciate it. I wish you would talk with me."

Her face seemed to pale under the grime. "I haven't done nothing," she said. "Honest, Sheriff."

Truitt sighed. He opened up the folder lying beside him. "Okay, then, let's go over some stuff." He pushed a piece of paper across to her. "Here's a copy of the warrant we used to search your home. Inside we found the key to a Dodge vehicle, which we've taken to the dealer to see if he can match it to a particular automobile. Just so happens we have a witness who says he saw you driving a Dodge Ram through Praterton last week. In your home we also found a can of kerosene and some rags. Last night, about seven-thirty, a Dodge Ram drove past the Nguyen house in Statlers Cross and someone inside tossed a Molotov cocktail through that family's front window. Nobody was hurt, Sarah, but someone sure as hell could have been. Did you know a child lived there—a five-year-old girl? You did? Just checking. It always amazes me when people do things that will hurt children."

Her eyes were wide with alarm. "But I didn't—"

"Sarah, where were you last night around seven-thirty?"

"I was home . . ."

"Really? Can you verify that? Because I have two eyewitnesses who say they saw a woman hiding in the bushes behind the Nguyen home last night during the firebombing." He paused, letting that sink in. He didn't mention that one of the witnesses was five-year-old Chau Nguyen who, in the aftermath of the "witch in the thickets," confessed to Truitt that she had seen the witch outside her house the night of the firebombings. Truitt continued. "I don't mind saying that a jury will find one of the witnesses very convincing. He tried to save the Nguyens. When he saw the woman hiding in the bushes, he cried out to her to get some help, but she ran off. I think that woman was you, Sarah. What were you doing behind the Nguyens' house? What do you know about the firebombing?"

Her head bobbed; she shivered hard. Tears filled her eyes.

"I didn't hurt no one."

"Make me believe that, Sarah. Explain to me what is going on. Because you have one helluva a case going against you. And the final nail in your coffin is the fact that the twenty-two-caliber Lorcin you possessed illegally and you claimed you last saw in your kitchen drawer was used to kill a man. Whoever is behind all this is doing a damn good job of framing you, darlin'. If I were you I'd find me some new friends to trust."

"Jud Keast. He took my gun."

"A child? You gonna tell me that ten-year-old boy broke into your house and stole your gun? How did Jud even know you had a gun?"

A soft knock sounded on the door; Truitt kept his eyes trained on Sarah as Haskell answered it.

"Sarah," he said softly. "You are in so much trouble. Tell me what is going on."

She was crying openly now, the tears washing away the dirt. "Jud knew I had a gun. Stuart told him."

"How did Stuart know?"

"He helped me get it. He knew a gun dealer who would sell me a gun legit, even with my record."

"Give me the gun dealer's name."

"I never knew it."

"Where was he located?"

"Out over in Marietta," she said, referring to an Atlanta suburb seventy miles northwest. "I couldn't tell you where. I'd never been there before."

"Didn't you know it was illegal to own that gun?"

"He said it was no big deal. It's not like the church burnt down—it was just a pew. He said he'd register it and I'd be legal. I wanted to be legal. I didn't want to do nothin' wrong."

Truitt ran his hand through his hair again. "Sarah, what you did *was* 'a big deal.' You painted swastikas on a church. You wrote 'Burn Niggers' on a church. You hung nooses from the rafters of an African-American church, and then balled up a bunch of choir robes, put them on a pew, and lit them. You don't consider that a big deal?"

She was silent. Truitt sighed and, pushing his chair back, stood. Haskell leaned over and handed him a note.

Truitt read it, then passed it to Sarah. "You want to explain this to me?"

Her eyes scanned the paper, but he could tell she couldn't comprehend it. Sarah Gainer, in addition to being an unrepentant racist, was barely literate. Truitt took the paper from her.

"It says that when my men searched the Alden property they came across what looked like a camp— a pile of blankets, some clothes, a box of food, even signs of a campfire. They say it looked fairly recent. How many nights were you planning to be out there, Sarah?"

"I don't know," she whispered. She wouldn't look at him. "As long as it took."

"As long as what took?"

"For you to catch the murderer. Whoever killed Stuart and Darrell is surely going to kill me. And you, dammit, have my gun."

The *Calwyn County Courier* was delivered around 4:30 every afternoon, flung by a genderless arm out the window of a rusty red Valiant. Today Ella sat on the back porch, ostensibly keeping an eye on the dozing baby but in reality listening for the scattered *plunk* of the paper hitting her driveway gravel.

At 4:36 she heard it, and she was out the porch door, striding down the side lawn. When she reached the paper, she grabbed it up and started shuffling through the pages.

"I'll be damned," she whispered. The heat of anger hit her face. "I'll just be hogdamned."

She marched back to the house and through the front door to where Gale, Nadianna, and Halford sat in the parlor.

"Where's Le and Phoung?" she demanded. "Where's Chau?"

"They're all in the den," Gale answered. "Why?"

Ella rattled the paper as she held the opinion page out to Gale. "They printed it. They printed Reebe's ridiculous article on the murders. I told Alby he had to stop it. I told him it was trouble. And that was *before* last night. What do you think's going to happen now?"

Gale frowned and read aloud: " 'Time was when Statlers Cross was a typical Georgia town. Its Main Street shops and country churches were the relics of a bygone era, the types of buildings found in thousands of small towns across the south. Drive by there now, and you'll see a visible sign that change has come—a vibrant sign that alters the very colors of the place. Some say change is good, and this reporter will not disagree with them. But the dark possibility exists that change brought on the death of three young men Monday night, and for good or ill, this county will be left with the painful chore of rebuilding and repair.' "

Gale stopped there and scanned the rest of the article. "Yuck. Doesn't show a whole lot of sensitivity, does it?" She passed the article to Halford. "But you can't blame Alby, Ella. He certainly doesn't have any control over the newspaper."

"Hell's bells, he doesn't! He's the damn county sheriff. He's a good ol' boy. He's a politician. He knows how to play the game. I bet he and that editor Roy Dancer play poker together. They sure as hell go out for breakfast once in a while. That's how things get done in this county, and you know it, Gale. Alby could have stopped this if he had wanted to. He just didn't think it was important enough. And you know why he didn't? Because I told him about it. Because I'm a silly old woman and he's the elected sheriff and which one of us do you think has more sense?"

Ella could see the alarm in Gale's eyes. Halford had stood up from the sofa and was walking to her.

"Ella," he said, taking her arm. "Why don't you sit down?" His eyes met Gale's and they exchanged some message, but Ella was too furious to read it. She shook off his hand.

"Don't you go treating me like I'm infirm. I'm telling you, this is trouble. Those people were bombed out of their house last night. That article comes out and says they are troublemakers, that they don't understand our ways. And who does Alby have locked up right this minute? Sarah Gainer, that's who."

Gale shook her head. "I admit this article is in bad taste, Ella. It paints the Keasts as white trash and the Nguyens as, well, outsiders, but I don't understand why it's getting you so upset. You need to sit down. You look pale."

How could she look pale when she was so blasted *hot?* She turned to Nadianna. "You know what I'm talking about, don't you? Word's already gotten out that Alby's holding Sarah Gainer for questioning in the murders. You know what that's going to mean, don't you?"

Gale still looked perplexed. "Sarah Gainer is an avowed, despicable racist. She was convicted of a hate crime. Everyone in town at one time or another has seen her passing out neo-Nazi flyers. Why are you so worried about Sarah Gainer? Who do you think gives two hoots about her? My only concern was what the heck was she doing out in our field."

Ella tried to focus on Nadianna. "You understand. You know what I'm talking about." Nadianna's face appeared wavy, and Ella blinked, trying to get the spots out of her vision.

"I think I know, Ella. You're saying that people know Sarah Gainer but they don't know the Nguyens. And for some people, that's enough for them to choose sides."

"That's what I'm saying. And they're in our house. You've brought them to *my* house."

Ella was swaying now; another second and she'd be on the floor. Halford drew his arm around her waist and for a moment it felt as though he lifted her off the ground. The next thing she felt was the cool fabric of the sofa pillows, and her body sinking into the upholstery.

Far off, she heard a bustle, and then a cold cloth was on her forehead and Gale was urging her mouth toward a glass. Someone was talking on a phone. Dammit. She waved the glass away and struggled to sit up.

"I am not having a stroke," she said loudly. "Put that phone down. I am not going to the hospital and if you try to get that old fool Bingham over here I'll throw things at him." She grabbed Gale's hand and pulled herself into a sitting position. "Where's Katie Pru?"

"Playing with Chau in the den."

"Good. Go watch her. You oughta be with her anyway after what happened this afternoon. And Nadianna, go check the baby. I left him asleep on the porch. Wolves could have gotten him by now. You girls leave me alone. I want to talk with Daniel."

Halford closed the door behind Gale and Nadianna before easing down beside her on the cushions.

"God, that girl." Ella wasn't sure if she spoke aloud,

so she raised her voice. "All this back and forth between here and England—it's almost like she's built her own ivory tower. Nadianna sees it. Nadianna hasn't been gone so much."

"Is that what you wanted to tell me?"

The room still swam, but her stomach was settling and the sweat on her face felt cool as it dried. "I saw Darrell Murphy's car parked on the back of my property Monday morning."

"Pardon?"

"Darrell's car. The one they were murdered in. It was parked far out in my fields. I wouldn't have noticed it except—you're going to think I'm as silly as Katie Pru seeing animals in clouds—but I had been watching this mound of kudzu way back of the house. It had started out looking like a bear, but as the fall came on and the leaves died, it took on the shape of a fox. I had been having some fun with it, wondering if it was going to end up looking like a rabbit. You know, Br'er Bear, Br'er Fox, Br'er Rabbit. No, you probably don't. Anyway, I had gotten into the habit of looking at it through my bedroom window every morning when I got up. You can't see it from downstairs. It's far off. So far off, I've let kudzu have the ground."

"So what makes you think you saw Darrell's car?"

"Because I did. The leaves had pretty much turned brown and were beginning to fall off. That's what was turning it from a bear to a fox. But Monday morning I looked out and I saw something glinting behind it. It wasn't there Sunday morning, I was sure. So after breakfast I went out for a walk and had a look. It was Darrell's car. I've seen it a hundred times."

"So did you call Darrell to ask him why it was there?"

"I meant to, I really did. But there was something about it that bothered me. It was hidden, Daniel. There are a couple of roads that cut through those back acres, and he must have come down one of them. But he wasn't parked near one of those roads and he wasn't parked where you could see the car from the house. Or at least it would be reasonable to conclude that you couldn't see the car from the house. How was he to know that a silly old woman was playing games with her imagination?"

"Did you think there was something suspicious at the time, or is this in hindsight?"

"No, at the time. I remember thinking, well, whatever it is, he must have a good reason. But I didn't go up to it. I was afraid to do that. He had no business being there, Daniel. If it had been anyone else, I'd have called them in on trespassing. He parked there because he knew he could trust me. He knew I would take his word on anything."

"So why haven't you told Alby this?"

The dots returned, but fewer this time. "It would be admitting I was a fool. Darrell was killed because of something he was doing. And now, in retrospect, I wonder if he'd been using my land as a hideout all along, if all those favors he did for me, all those compliments, those little *generosities,* were to keep me on his side. I'm right here on the edge of town, Daniel. You can go miles west of here and never hit another house, another person. What if he was using me? What if all this time he was laughing behind my back?"

Halford laid a dry hand over her moist one. The dots disappeared. "Ella, there may be nothing to this at all. Darrell may have had a perfectly valid reason for leaving his car out there Monday. But even if that's not the case, even if he was involved with something illegal, it doesn't mean you were a fool. Sometimes people blind us. If we operate with a conscience and with integrity, we don't always see the deceit. It isn't an ignoble thing. As Gale would say, it just means you're good people."

The sofa fabric held a sharp smell, like skin after a mosquito bite. "As Gale would say. Yes, I imagine she would."

22

*After the pain—or more accurately, during it, since
there was no moment when the sky cleared and hope
returned—the idea that I struggled with the most,
the one that kept me inside my house, kept me from
answering my family's letters, from returning home,
was the notion that Tom had made a fool of me. I
had been betrayed in a way that was deeper than
sexual. An affair would have been easier; there are
personal and societal scripts for dealing with an
affair. But what script could I, as a terrorist's
widow, pick up and follow? I was a political
cuckold. If there is a body of women who have
experienced that, they have been silent, hiding their
wisdom from us younger arrivals . . .*

Gale leaned back in her desk chair and took a sip of
coffee. Of course, there was a body of women who had
been through what she had, or versions of it. Perhaps
every political wife had. And perhaps that's all she had
been—one more sacrificed political wife. Maybe the
difference between Tom and every other self-destructive
politician was that in the end, the poet had turned out
to be the most literal. . . . She put the mug down and ran
her hands over her forehead, hard. She was exhausted.

It was only eight P.M., but the events of the day had been numbing, and she was grateful for the hush that filled the house. Katie Pru and Chau were asleep in Katie Pru's bed; she had left Le and Phoung speaking in Vietnamese whispers in the den; and Halford—she stretched sideways to look out the window at the lights in Goddard's kitchen—was probably enjoying a cup of tea with the linguist. He was planning to come back over at nine-thirty, after Katie Pru was soundly asleep and she'd had a chance to get some work done. She strained to see into the kitchen, trying to discern a figure through the white cotton curtain. She wanted Halford with her now. She wanted him on the bed, reading to Katie Pru while she worked, breaking every now and then to rub her shoulders. . . .

God, she *was* tired. She glanced over to her dresser where Michael's baby monitor sat, its red light indicating it was on. But the receiver wasn't by Michael's crib. It was on Ella's bedside table, and over the static, she could hear her grandmother's even breathing. John Bingham had come by despite Ella's protests, greeting her with a jovial, *Why, Ella, you're lucky. I usually only make house calls when the caller can assure me the person is actually dead.* Ella had been strong enough to call him a coot and lead him to her bedroom. Bingham's verdict had been fatigue and stress, although he had arranged for Ella to undergo a series of tests next week.

"She's strong as an Ella Alden," Bingham had told Gale as he left. "God help us, she's going to outlive us all."

"Including Katie Pru?" Gale had asked in a weak attempt at humor.

"Not Katie Pru. Katie Pru gets to be her own generation's Ella."

That truth hurt. Gale stood and moved to the window. Outside, the pecan tree shivered, sending a shudder of leaves to the ground. Katie Pru had all the elements of an Ella—strong-willed, bright, and female. What else did it take? A couple of disappointing men? A couple of forsaken opportunities? A couple of hard choices that made one hard, made one have to chose between callousness and regret—and God knows, the Ellas of the world never chose regret. Gale rested her forehead against the coolness of a windowpane. She wanted more for Katie Pru. She didn't want her, sixty years from now, committed to this house and the dwindling power her family name exerted over the neighbors. If everyone had to have boundaries, she wanted her daughter at least to have different ones. Katie Pru would have no choice but to live with the legacy of her parents. But Gale didn't have to sit by and watch that legacy deform her.

Across the fence, the door to the Greene house opened, and instinctively Gale moved back, out of sight. Ron Goddard, his slight figure recognizable in the moonlight, hurried to his car. Gale watched as the engine started and he pulled out of his driveway, the red taillights disappearing over the hump of the railroad. Eight o'clock was awful late to start an outing by Statlers Cross standards. Perhaps an evening with a Scotland Yard detective wasn't all that great an experience.

Smiling, she picked up her mug and headed for the stairs. If she was going to get any more work done tonight, it was going to have to be with a fresh dose of caffeine.

At the bottom of the stairs she encountered the warm smell of bread baking. Bread and raisins. Scones, she thought as she entered the kitchen. Someone in Ella's house was actually making scones.

"You did say that sedative Dr. Bingham gave Ella would put her out for the night, didn't you, Gale?" Nadianna asked as she lifted the baking sheet from the oven. "I know Ella prides herself on her cooking, and she is good, but I have been missing the taste of scones."

"Just up the street, at the tearoom," Le said. She slid a spatula under the rounded circle of bread and loosened it from the sheet. "You could have had them for three months. Sally even has Devonshire cream."

Gale opened the cabinet. "That looks wonderful, Le. Do we need three plates or four? Where's Phoung?"

"Asleep," Le said as she sliced the scone into sixths. "She couldn't stay awake anymore. She was awake all night."

"As you must have been."

Le shrugged. "I don't need much sleep. I stay awake a lot."

Gale decided not to pursue it. As she set the plates on the table, she could feel Le's eyes on her, but when she glanced up, Le looked away.

"Nadianna, you want to get the jam and butter from the fridge?" Gale asked.

When Nadianna's head disappeared behind the refrigerator door, Le leaned forward. Gale set herself to accept the apology: *I'm so sorry I slapped you; I was upset, and you've been so kind.* But the woman's dark eyes grew hesitant and she dropped her gaze. "Cream," she mumbled. "It would taste better with the cream."

Gale didn't answer, and the three of them pulled out chairs and sat down to eat. "Le, this is so good," Gale said. "No wonder the tearoom is doing well."

Again Le shrugged. "Sally taught me. English-Southern, she said. That was all she wanted. I knew nothing of Southern. But I was a good cook in Vietnam. A hotel chef. I had many European customers. I learned some things English. Scones. Teas. Crumpets. How the English want their eggs. Sally taught me about biscuits and how Southerners want their eggs."

"A chef." Gale took another bite of scone. Le's face

was noncommittal, seemingly concentrated on the task of lathering butter on her bread. "This must have been a huge decision for you, coming to the U.S." She paused, waiting for Le to take the bait and answer. Instead Le stuck the piece of scone in her mouth and began putting jam on another.

Gale fell silent, remembering the sting of Le's palm, remembering that this woman was not afraid to lash out. But she also remembered the anxiety in Ella's voice: *That article comes out and says they are trouble-makers . . . And they're in our house. You've brought them to my house.* She didn't agree that the Nguyen women were troublemakers, but she had to concede Ella a point. They were in her house. And if they wanted to stay, they owed the Alden women an explanation.

"Le," she said gently. "We've invited you to our home. You are welcome to stay as long as you need to. But I wish you would tell us more about yourselves."

Le's butter knife slid over the scone, once then back again. She placed the buttered piece on her plate, contemplating it, her hands folded in her lap.

After a long pause, she spoke. "Okay. You want to know why I gave up my job as a hotel chef to work in a tiny restaurant in a backwood town? Tuan taught me that word—*backwood*. Tuan lived in Chamblee, in Atlanta, but he wanted us out here. It was safe in the backwood. Safe for my mother, safe for Chau. More important, it was safe for Tuan's baby. He had a wife and a baby boy. He wanted to bring them to Statlers Cross to live with us. I don't want my boy in the city, he said. Too many boys end up dead in the city. Gangs. Drugs. But his wife didn't want to leave her family. Her family came over from Vietnam, wanted to stay right there in Chamblee, right there with other Vietnamese families. They felt safe there—they could go to Vietnamese churches, Vietnamese stores."

"But something happened to them." Nadianna's voice was soft. "Something happened to them in the city?"

Le looked at her, a flinty gleam in her eye. "Happened to them? Hell, yes. The slut took off with another man, stole the baby. Tuan didn't know where. Her family said California. Tuan wanted to go to California to look for them. But he didn't have the money. I told him to forget about them. They are better gone."

The kitchen was hushed, the warmth from the stove dissipating to a stuffy coolness. Gale shook her head. "That's awful, Le . . ."

"Not so awful. She was awful."

"I know. But Tuan's baby—"

"If it was his. I don't believe it. He was chasing a—" She paused, trying to come up with the word. Finally she snapped her fingers, angrily. "A ghost. Chasing a ghost."

"Okay. But do you mind telling us what made you come to the U.S. to begin with?"

"Tuan brought us. It wasn't good there. My father was killed in the war. My mother was a spy for the Vietcong. But she was accused of treason at the end of the war. It got bad for her. She was tortured by both sides. You Americans don't understand that war, what you left us with. She was lucky she lived; many others didn't. She couldn't get a job, couldn't make money. Even all these years later, she only worked as a cleaner. I got a job because of a friend. I changed my name. Tuan decided to leave. He said we could make a lot of money in the U.S."

"What about Chau's father?" Nadianna asked.

"What about him? He doesn't matter."

"So what about Tuan? What kind of job did he have here?"

Again the shrug, causing Gale to wonder if this was

a common Vietnamese gesture or if Le had picked it up as she had picked up scones and scrambled eggs. "He worked in restaurants, too."

"As a chef?"

"No. A deliveryman."

"Le," Gale said slowly, "have you told the sheriff about all this?"

Le's eyes grew guarded. "About all what?"

"About the baby, about Tuan's job. You know, when someone is murdered, the detectives need to know all they can about the victim so they can figure out what might have happened."

If Le had started to open up, she instantly shut down. "Americans like to blame everyone but Americans," she said. "Tuan isn't dead because he was Tuan. He is dead because he was a goddamn gook. It could have been me, it could have been Chau. It didn't matter, as long as it was a gook. Or don't you know that about Americans, Gale Grayson? Don't you know that about your kind?"

The Statlers Cross United Methodist Church didn't usually have meetings on Thursday nights, but the drift to the church must have seemed natural to this Bible Belt culture. Ron Goddard sat in the back pew, a small notepad tucked into his coat pocket. This was a linguist's dream, he thought, a community gathered to react to its culture's hallmark. Southerners together to discuss a crime of hate. The only thing more apt would have been a lynching.

It had been Tim Murphy, Darrell's father, who had called him. *I know how much my son meant to you. I know how much you meant to him. Darrell was always going on about you, about how smart you were, about how you understood so much. I just wanted to thank you, sir. Thank you for treating my son with respect.* Then he had told him about the prayer meeting that would take place at the church later in the evening. *That awful thing that happened to those women. We all need to pray about it as a community.*

Tim Murphy was present, playing the mayor's role but made haggard by his grief. He stood at the front of the sanctuary, slightly to the left of the altar, in a bundle of men who shook his hand or patted his back. Goddard looked around and noted that most of the people who had decided to come were men. There were a few women—the nosy and outrageously coiffed Reebe Vaughter with her bland husband Andy; Joile Watkins, the minister's long-faced wife; Nellynne Langley, whose broad hands helped stock the goods at her husband's store; old Ilene Parker, the fainthearted soul who hadn't wanted to help him in the early days of his research because she didn't want to intrude on the "privacy" of how people talked. As he watched her, Ilene glanced toward him. For a second she seemed frozen, but she hastily looked away. Frail thing. It was interesting to Goddard that in the two months he had been here he had been permitted into the circles of so many residents. And being in the circles allowed him to hear so much. Southerners loved to tell their stories. He could recite some of these people's stories back in their own words.

He heard a footfall behind him and turned to see Sally Robertson enter the sanctuary. An odd bird, that. Attractive, in a young, educated, proper blonde sort of way. He knew a hundred of them at university, up and coming with their eye on the prize. But this one wasn't in academia. This one was escorting diners to cloth-covered tables. The fact that they were her tables didn't seem much of a point. As he watched, she searched the pews for a friendly face before resignedly settling for the empty pew opposite him. She was achingly lonely, anyone could see that. No wonder, what with being childless and her husband away so much. Probably, in the scheme of things, Sally had less going for her than Nadianna.

Tim Murphy was at the pulpit, his hand raised to settle the congregants' murmurs. He looked like a hump-backed bug, a beetle of some sort, in his wrinkled black suit. "I want to thank you," he said. "I want to thank you for coming tonight, to be a community asking to understand. And I want to thank you for a more personal reason, for coming to join in prayer to help my family and me. To pray for us as we ask the Lord to help us bear our loss . . ."

He inhaled deeply through his nose, fighting back tears. Goddard counted back the days—only three nights since Darrell was found murdered. No, Tim shouldn't be here. He should be home grieving with his wife. This was too soon for him to be acting the part of elected official.

Ted Stevens, the church's lay leader, hurried up to the pulpit and started to escort the elder Murphy to his seat. After passing him off to other solicitous hands, Stevens returned to the pulpit and looked out over the pews.

"Let us pray."

The prayer went on for five minutes, roiling with images of heavenly host and weeping sinners. Mothers were sorrowful in Heaven; fathers were ripped open with guilt and anguish. By the time Ted Stevens, gangly and silver-haired, finished his opening prayer, Goddard wasn't sure if he had been talking about paradise or punishment. And as he quickly jotted down notes on his pad, taking full advantage of everyone's closed eyes, he realized that Ted Stevens probably didn't do a great deal of differentiating between the two.

"Amen," Stevens finally intoned, and Goddard repressed the urge to applaud and shout bravo.

It was time for the real minister to mount the pulpit. John Watkins, Goddard thought, could more easily be married to Sally Robertson than to his glum-faced wife. This was another figure cut for academia—the square jaw, the fair complexion, the well-tailored suit. Methodists must be strange, to put their best-dressed offerings in their smallest churches. Goddard would wager money that their best-dressed were also their weakest. Watkins had never struck him as a strong man. If this isolated rural church were a member of some other denomination, it might be relatively easy for a dynamic leader, a man of action, to take power and literally whisk the church away. He knew of it happening. It was interesting to speculate whether or not it could happen here.

From the pulpit, Watkins looked out over the congregation from behind tortoiseshell glasses.

"We are all gathered here in grief today," he said. "Tomorrow is Darrell Murphy's funeral, and tomorrow we will come together again to give formal expression of our sorrow. But tonight I wanted to give us the opportunity to share a different kind of sorrow—our discomfort and uneasiness, and downright anger about what has happened to our peaceful community."

There was a slight rustling among the congregation. Perhaps the good people of Statlers Cross didn't feel any discomfort or uneasiness. But that wouldn't be right. Ron had seen the fear in Nadianna's eyes, had seen Halford's disheveled appearance as he returned from the Nguyens' house. And he had talked with Stuart Keast's grandmother, seen the resignation and cold-stone determination in her face. There was a lot of discomfort and anger in Statlers Cross. The question was where it would find its outlet.

Watkins's minister face looked wistfully out at his parishioners. "Who would like to begin? Let's talk about what we're all feeling."

Goddard slipped his notepad up his sleeve, where he could reach it without drawing attention. This man was obviously a novice. No one with his full faculties would ask a group in a volatile emotional state to talk openly about their feelings. Not in this situation. Not with three men dead and a family run out of their home. As alarmed as he was by the minister's approach, he also knew that what he was about to witness was a linguistic South he couldn't access from books, and perhaps not even from isolated interviews. He wanted to kiss John Watkins for being so naive.

"Come on now," Watkins urged. "It's better if we talk these things out."

Tiny Ilene Parker rose from her seat. "I just want to say that I feel badly about what happened to the Nguyens. It was a horrible thing for someone to do. And I feel badly that I didn't help more. I don't know if you realize it, but those girls slept out in their front yard last night. I should have invited them in, but I didn't. And I've asked the Lord to forgive me for it."

Watkins nodded sympathetically. "Sometimes we know what's right and can't bring ourselves to do it. But ours is a forgiving God. That's where we take our comfort."

Ilene sat, and the congregation shifted uncomfortably. Ted Stevens spoke from his seat. "Ella's taken them in. So don't worry about them, Ilene. They're okay until they find another place."

Across the aisle from him Sally Robertson drew a deep breath. Goddard turned to her, expecting her to rise, but she stayed silent and seated.

"I think we should talk to the sheriff's department," Reebe said. "Alby might have some ideas on what we can do."

"Like what, Reebe?" Watkins asked.

"Oh, I don't know. Like an interim place for them to stay. To get clothes, some food . . ."

Another sharp breath from Sally. This time she spoke. "But they have clothes and food, Reebe. Their house wasn't burned down. They can return."

"Well, I know that, Sally, but would they want to? Obviously if they're staying with Ella it's because they don't want to go back home. I'm just suggesting we ask Alby his advice on what they should do."

Sally's face had turned pink. "I'm not trying to be a problem here, Reebe, but don't you think that should be up to the Nguyens to decide? As far as I know, and probably as far as any of you know, they are planning to return to their house. Why would they need the sheriff's help?"

An awkward silence filled the sanctuary. Finally, Stevens cleared his throat. "Listen, this is just between us, right? Dr. Goddard, sir, you understand that what we're discussing here tonight is just between us. We're neighbors trying to figure out what to do. You with me?"

Goddard raised his hand in supplication. "Absolutely, Ted. I'd like to be part of the discussion, but if you'd prefer I leave—"

"Oh, no," Reverend Watkins interposed. "Everyone is part of our community. Ted, did you have a point to make?"

"Yes, I think we need to face up to some facts." He turned back to Sally. "I heard you fired Le, Sally."

"I haven't fired her. I may have to replace her . . ."

"I'm not saying I'd blame you. You're running a business, and what's best for your business is going to be best for us as a whole. But it does put the Nguyens in a tenuous position. What kind of work do you think she's going to find around here? And it's not like they paid for that house free and clear. They got a mortgage

on that place in excess of a thousand dollars a month—
I know, because my wife sold them the property. How
they gonna pay that without a job? And I guarantee that
brother of their's didn't leave insurance money."

"And then there's the damage to the house," Reebe
Vaughter put in. "I wonder if they kept up with their
homeowner's insurance payments."

"That's a good question. In fact, I think one of us
should just call the bank and talk to them about it. I
mean, the condition of that house should be of interest
to the bank. First they paint it that godawful color, and
then this firebombing. The bank has a vested interest
in the condition of that house. I'm going to call them
tomorrow and see what they have to say."

Sally's back was rigid. Goddard looked at her knuckles, pearly as they gripped the pew in front of her. "Say
about what?" she asked. "What business is it of yours
what the bank has to say?"

Stevens stabbed his finger at Sally. "Now listen
here. I think you've done some good things for this
community—you fixed up that old house of yours, and
you turned that old empty photography studio into a
business. We're real grateful. In fact, I would think you'd
be particularly concerned about the Nguyen property.
What do towns like us have to bring in revenue? It ain't
factories and big businesses, I tell you that. It's *charm*,
Sally. And you're part of that. You come in and start fixing up Main Street, and then other shops do the same.
Coop here has his little store that people like to come
to because it reminds them of their childhood, or even
their grandmother's childhood. We got all those new
families that have moved outside of town, and you think
they came here because they thought we were a bunch
of low-class rural trash? Nosirree, they came because
they saw the charm in us. If you think charm's not a
commodity, you don't know your own business. And the

Nguyens are threatening that charm. They've trashed that house so that we all look like trash. If you think that's not of interest to their bank and my bank and your bank, then you just don't know how the world works."

Sally looked aghast. "I can't believe what you're saying."

"What am I saying? That we need to look out for ourselves? That we need to know what our strengths are as a community? Our strength is we *are* a community. I'm not being prejudiced here. I'm not saying we need to watch out for the Nguyens because they're Vietnamese. I'm saying we need to watch out for them because they are breaking the rules. They come in here and try to fit in and be a part of our town, then I say great. Let 'em come. But they come in here with their own rules and their attitudes—well, no ma'am, that ain't right. We gave them the chance to fit in and they damn well threw it in our face. I'm going to go ahead and say this because I know many of you are thinking it: I'm ready to get them out of town any way possible."

Sally's face was ashen; the flesh had sagged so that she looked suddenly old. "Are you insane?" she breathed.

Ted Stevens came out of his pew. "Insane? By God, I am not insane. I evidently understand things better than you. But you're insane if you think we can just sit by and do nothing. Two of our boys were murdered." He swung his arm out toward Tim Murphy. "That man lost his son. You gonna tell me I'm insane when there's a murderer loose? You gonna tell me it doesn't have anything to do with those women? You damn well better believe it does. Whatever those Vietnamese are up to, they dragged our boys into it. And by God, I am not going to stand here and do nothing!"

The Reverend John Watkins held up his hands,

which were shaking with either nervousness or alarm. Does he realize now he's made an amateur's mistake? Goddard wondered.

"All right, Ted," the reverend said. "I think we understand the scope of the problem now. Why don't you sit down? Perhaps now's a good time to pray."

Stevens took long strides down the center aisle, the old wood of the sanctuary floors creaking under his weight. "You pray without me, Preacher. Praying's only good if it gives the courage to act."

23

Daylight skimmed the horizon when Gale finally fell asleep. Halford had gone home at midnight, bleary-eyed and concerned and protesting that he ought to stay the night—he could sleep on the parlor couch, he had argued, near the front windows so he could hear anyone who might come up the gravel drive. She hadn't reminded him that if anyone wanted to break into the Alden house, they would do it through the French doors in the den, that isolated funny room that jutted out from the main house like an exclamation point. No one inside would hear the breaking of the glass; entry would be unnoticeable. But then, the people who liked making a point in Statlers Cross didn't seem much interested in stealth. Screeching brakes and flames seemed more their style.

In the end, Halford had left, but she doubted he strayed from his sentry post by Ron Goddard's kitchen window. And she herself didn't go to bed, either. Despite her brave assurances to Halford that regardless of somebody's willingness to hurl firebombs at the Nguyens' house, no one, absolutely no one in town was going to cross that line with Ella Alden, she knew she wouldn't sleep. She had spent the night on the parlor couch, straining to hear every sound, her heart pounding at every snap in the dark.

It had been Sally's visit that started their vigil. Sally's face had been haggard when she knocked on the Aldens' door at ten. Everyone in the house had retired with the exception of Gale, who sat with Halford in the parlor. Sally had pushed past Gale without an apology.

"This is going to sound terrible," she began. "You're not going to believe what I just heard."

But the sad truth was Gale had no problem believing it. It always, she suspected, started with a meeting. It must have taken a meeting to decide to vandalize her cottage in Fetherbridge two years before; it must have taken a meeting to decide to run her out of the village. And it must have been at a meeting, in some dark room beside a pub, that members of In Gaia's Name convinced a young poet to kill a barrister and thereby set up the events that ended with Tom's suicide in a church.

But Sally had been badly shaken. A few minutes after she arrived, Ron Goddard walked over, and together they related what had happened at the church. "I can't think that Ted meant any actual harm," Goddard kept murmuring. "I'm sure he wouldn't do anything illegal."

"But there are probably plenty of ways to legally harass an immigrant," Gale said. "Fear of deportation alone is bad." It had been one of her own fears, the fear of isolation, compounded by the fear of being forced to return to a country one had willingly left. But she had left home for what, in the frank light of reflection, had been romantic and rebellious reasons. The Nguyens had left for their own well-being. The Nguyens had left to truly pursue a better life.

"It was no doubt just hotheaded emotion," Goddard said. "I've met Ted Stevens. He strikes me as a passionate man about many things—"

"I know Ted Stevens, too," Sally interrupted. "He is hotheaded. He's not a bad man, but he acts before he thinks."

"Then give him time to think, Sally," Goddard insisted. "It's an emotional time for everyone—that's why people came to that meeting, to work through their emotions."

"John Watkins shouldn't have conducted that meeting," Sally said bitterly.

"I'm sure he did it thinking it was better to air feelings than to let them fester."

"Then he's a fool. He did it because he's naive and thinks meetings are things where college students gather to solve world problems. He doesn't have a clue what the rest of the world is like."

They all had fallen silent at that. It would have been a hard call, Gale thought, and in her own youth, she would have probably done as the young minister had, believing in the innate goodness of man and the strength of the community to heal. But she had lived through too much to accept that at face value anymore. Community, she had learned, was a far more complex creature than that.

Sally and Goddard had left not long afterwards, Goddard insisting on following Sally in his car to ensure she got home safe. Then the long talk until midnight with Halford, the mixed emotions of leave-taking as she explained to him that she knew he could protect them; she simply didn't want him to. And finally, at dawn, snatches of fitful, gritty sleep.

It was the phone that awakened her. From the kitchen, she could hear Nadianna's voice, polite at first, then slightly argumentative.

A hesitant knock on the parlor door, and she opened a sleep-filled eye to see Nadianna standing there with the portable phone in her hand.

"It's a man," she said. "He says he's Sarah Gainer's lawyer. He wants to speak with Ella, but she's still asleep and I ain't waking her."

Gale struggled to sit up and held out her hand. "Let me talk with him."

The lawyer said his name was James Whitfield; Gale conjured up a grainy newspaper image of a carefully dressed African-American man, youngish, with closely cropped hair and horn-rimmed glasses. Vaguely, Gale recalled that Whitfield had been appointed by the courts to represent Sarah. She wondered if he was doing it of his own volition this time around.

"What can I do you for, Mr. Whitfield?"

"Miss Gainer would like to speak to Ella Alden."

"I'm afraid that's not possible. Ella is my grandmother. And she's ill. She's in bed on medication, and I'm not going to disturb her."

A hand went over the receiver on the other end of the line. Several seconds passed before Whitfield's clipped voice returned.

"I've spoken with my client, Mrs. Grayson. If Sarah can't talk with your grandmother, she'd like to talk with you."

"What on earth for?"

She heard a sigh, deep but controlled. "Can I talk you into coming to the jail and meeting with me for a few minutes?" Whitfield asked. "It'll be difficult for me to give you an explanation over the phone. But it has to do with your grandmother . . . and why Sarah was camped out in her fields."

"Then she needs to talk with Sheriff Truitt."

"Ah." A pause. "It has to do with that as well. I know this is unorthodox, and if there's something I can do to convince you . . ." His voice became more relaxed, conversational. "Listen, I realize you're a professional woman, and this will eat into your work time. What if I do some bartering with you? If you will take time to come up and speak with my client, I will do some pro bono legal work for you. Anytime, you name it. I will owe you."

"Is it that important?"

"I have no idea. Sarah won't talk with me. And I've advised her not to talk with you. But she's insistent. What do you say?"

"If she says anything incriminating, I'm going straight to Alby."

"I'll make sure she understands that. So I can count on you in about an hour?"

"About an hour," Gale repeated. She rubbed her eyes as she punched off the phone. Jesus God.

Seventy minutes later she was dressed in jeans and a sweater and gripping James Whitfield's outstretched hand in the jail's visitor room. "This isn't normal, is it?" she asked.

"Between you and me, Mrs. Grayson, Sarah Gainer is not normal. I thought I would never see that young lady again when she was sentenced, and I can't say that I've missed her. But she called me yesterday, quite upset, and I've agreed to represent her—for now. But if I find out she had anything to do with that firebombing or those murders, I'm walking."

"Do you believe she's innocent?"

"I don't honestly know. She's an interesting case. She readily admits she has not reformed her racist beliefs— hell, I've met few honest people who have—but she swears she didn't have anything to do with these crimes. It's hard to dismiss someone who looks you in the eye, says she thinks you are naturally inferior, but insists that she's innocent. It would be much smarter of her to lie to me on all counts, don't you think?"

"Why does she want to see me?"

"You ask her. She won't tell me."

"Am I going to be alone with her?"

"No. I'll be in there, too. But she's told me that I have to sit in the corner." His smile was wry. "Like a good 'boy.'"

He motioned to the receptionist, and the door buzzed. A young bristle-haired deputy appeared and escorted them to another room, this one furnished with a table and three chairs. He left them and in a few minutes returned with Sarah Gainer.

She had been allowed to bathe. Her hair shone cleanly in the gray grunge of the room, a dark strawberry-blond color that Gale always associated with Elizabeth Tudor. She had it pulled back into a ponytail, and if it hadn't been for her orange coveralls, she would have looked like a fresh-faced coed, one who eschewed make-up but couldn't quite let go of the good-girl look. She seemed frail, and Gale was surprised to see how delicate she appeared. Not what she had imagined reading all those newspaper accounts. Racist women were supposed to be rawboned things. Racist women could slaughter and eat hogs.

She looked shyly at Gale and licked her lips. But she didn't speak.

"Sarah," Whitfield said from his corner. "Perhaps you need to tell Mrs. Grayson why you wanted to talk with her."

"Call me Gale, Sarah. What can I do for you?"

Sarah Gainer's voice was higher than Gale expected. "I wanted to talk to Miz Alden—"

"My grandmother's not feeling well. I don't know when she'll be up and about. If you want to talk to one of us, it's going to have to be me."

"You interrupted me," Sarah said firmly. "I was going to say that I wanted to talk to Miz Alden, but I will talk to you instead. I don't know if you can help me as much as she can, but maybe so. My mother always put a lot of stock in Miz Alden. She said she was tougher than a copperhead but fair, and that was more than she could say about most people. Well, I want to talk to someone who's fair. Do you reckon you can be fair with me?"

"I can be fair, Sarah. But that's really all I can be, do you understand? I don't have to agree with you, and I certainly won't protect you if I feel you've done something wrong. Your lawyer has explained to you that I will probably go see Sheriff Truitt after I talk with you, and anything the sheriff asks I will answer. So be careful what you tell me, Sarah. Don't tell me anything you don't want the sheriff to hear."

"You know the sheriff? You friends with him?"

"I know him, yes."

"You like him?"

Sarah's eyes had an odd gleam to them, like a child playing tricks. "Like him?" Gale asked. "Yes, I like him. I trust him. I would go to him if I had a problem."

Sarah leaned back in her metal chair, apparently satisfied. "Then I want to tell you what I know. And I want you to go tell the sheriff what I tell you. I want him to hear it from you."

"Why don't you tell him yourself?"

"Because he won't believe me. I'm not sure you will either, but you'll be fair. You'll listen to me fair. The sheriff won't do that. His nigger deputy won't do that. I don't even think Mr. Whitfield over there will do that. They all think I'm a white trash little girl and I'm stupid. And it don't matter what I say, they're gonna hear a stupid white trash little girl saying it. But Miss Ella wouldn't do that. And I don't think you will, either."

Gale shook her head. "I don't understand, Sarah. What do you want to tell me?"

"I didn't have nothing to do with burning that

house. And I didn't have nothing to do with those kill-ings. The sheriff says it was my gun—"

"Your gun was used in the killings?"

"My gun was *stolen*. Stuart's little nephew stole it. I know the day he did it, too. He had come over to help me put up some beans, and I bet you the little fucker stole it then. I don't know why. Stuart could have got-ten him all the guns he wanted."

"Was Stuart running guns?"

Sarah's eyes got hard. "I don't know about that. But he could've gotten a ten-year-old boy a gun if the boy'd wanted one."

"All right. So your gun was stolen. What else you want to tell me?"

Sarah licked her lips again, studying Gale. "You ever hear of Marcus Siler? He lives on Highway 441, cou-ple miles down from your grandmother's house. Yellow trailer? You've driven past it a million times. You'll see it next time you drive down there. You just never paid any attention. He and I date sometimes." She paused. "He found the bodies."

Gale chose her words carefully. "What was he doing in the woods?"

Sarah averted her eyes from Gale's gaze. "Hunting, like he said."

"So he didn't know he was going to find the bodies?"

Sarah let out a laugh. "You mean, did he shoot 'em and then go back and find 'em? Hell, no. You think he's an idiot? He came upon 'em, just like he said."

"And he didn't have another reason for being in those woods? They're awfully remote, Sarah."

"Which is why they're such good hunting."

"Okay. So why are you telling me this?"

Sarah took a deep breath, letting it out as if she were blowing out smoke. "You're gonna be fair with me, Miss Gale?" Gale nodded. "All right, then. Marcus didn't have nothing to do with those killings. He didn't even know Stuart and Darrell. But he did burn them Vietnamese out. He told me he was going to do it. I tried to talk him out of it. I don't like them Vietnamese none, but they never hurt me. I told him to just splash paint on their house, but he said they already done that themselves. He wanted to burn 'em out."

"So why didn't you tell anyone? You could have stopped him."

Sarah gave a snort. "Yeah. Like I could stop Marcus Siler. I might have stopped him for one night, but what about the next? He was going to do it. I just wanted to make sure nobody got hurt."

"So is that why you were hiding in the bushes behind the house?"

Behind Sarah, Whitfield leaned forward· in his seat.

"Yeah." She ran her finger along the edge of the table, not looking at Gale. "He told me what night he was going to do it. I thought if I was there, I could get help. Or maybe help them people out of the house. But there was a man there. . . . He didn't need me."

"Why didn't you warn the Nguyens in advance?"

Sarah looked at her as if she were daft. "You don't get it. Marcus was going to throw that bomb. Wasn't nobody could stop him. I warn them, they leave one night, they come back, he does it then. Besides, they wouldn't believe me. They'd call the police and I'd have been arrested for harassing them."

Gale caught Whitfield's eye over Sarah's shoulder. There might be some truth in that. The avowed racist knew her place.

"So it was Marcus's truck, the one with the ram taillights?"

"Yes'm. You can tell the sheriff to run a check."

"Okay, Sarah. What else did you want to tell me?"

Tears sprang into Sarah's eyes. "I don't want them to let me out of jail. You've got to convince the sheriff not to let me out of jail."

Gale fought to keep the surprise out of her voice. "Why not, Sarah?"

"It's not safe. I'm afraid they're gonna kill me. That's why I was in your grandma's fields. I thought they were gonna kill me."

"Who, Sarah? Who was going to kill you?"

The tears fell fat on her narrow hands. "I don't know who. That's why I'm so scared. Stuart and Darrell, they weren't bad. I don't know why they're dead. They must have been into something . . ."

"Like what?"

"I don't know." She was almost wailing. "I don't know, Miss Gale. Stuart was into the Nazi stuff like me. When I got out of jail, I told him no more, I wasn't doin' it no more. And he understood, he really did. I wanted to lead a normal life, I didn't want no more jail time. And that was okay with Stuart."

"What about Darrell? Was he in the neo-Nazi movement, too?"

Her lips were quivering as she looked at Gale and nodded.

"What was Darrell doing in Ella's fields the day he was murdered, Sarah? Do you know?"

She shook her head. "No, ma'am. But they used those fields a lot. I know those fields like the back of my hand. That's why, when I needed a place to go, I went there."

"Why did they use those fields, Sarah? What were they doing?"

"They used the fields because they bordered the woods. The woods made a real good meeting place.

Don't ask me any more than that, Miss Gale, 'cause I don't know. Honest."

Reaching into his pocket, Whitfield pulled out a crisp white handkerchief and handed it to Sarah. Still sobbing, Sarah blew her nose loudly. Gale and Whitfield waited in silence while she calmed down.

In a few minutes, her sobs had subsided, reduced to occasional gulps. "So now you know why I wanted to talk to you," she told Gale. "I want you to go to your friend the sheriff. I want you to tell him I ain't done none of it. And I want you to make him promise that he won't let me out of jail until he finds the killer."

As Sarah wiped her face, Gale noticed for the first time a light bruise on her cheek.

"Did you get that hiding out in the fields?" she asked gently.

Sarah reached up and drew her finger along the bruise. She scowled. "No'm." She twisted and tried to touch her back. "I got another one there. And one on my side. It was them Keasts women. They liked to beat the shit out of me."

"Rosen and Bethy? Why would they do that?"

" 'Cause I said that Jud boy stole my gun, like I told you. They didn't like that. So they tried to beat me." She winced as she touched her rib cage. "It wasn't normal."

"What wasn't normal?"

"The way they acted. When I come up on them, they were laughing. You think that's normal, laughing when your grandson's been murdered? That's part of what made me go beserk about Jud. Why would they be laughing like that?"

"People have different ways of reacting to grief . . ."

"I'll say. And I'll tell you something else. Don't you believe everything you hear about them Keasts, about how they're so pure and independent. I liked Stuart, but I wouldn't give you two toots for that Bethy. Someone ought to ask why, when her brother's been murdered, she's on his cell phone making dates."

"Making dates? You sure?"

"I heard what I heard. You go tell that to the sheriff."

24

The inviting scent of cinnamon and oranges greeted Nadianna as she opened Ron Goddard's back door and hollered through the screen: "Hello! Anybody up for some work?"

Goddard sat at the kitchen table, a notebook open in front of him. From deeper in the house Nadianna could hear a shower, the pipes making a noise her father used to liken to that of a cow stepping on its udder. Goddard grinned at her as he pushed back his chair and walked over to unlatch the screen.

"Always up for some work," he said. When she turned her face to his, he kissed her lightly. "You look cheerful and rested. I guess nothing disturbed your sleep last night."

"Not mine. I feel great. Gale looked like something the cat dragged in this morning. She told me what happened at the meeting last night. It must have been a doozy."

"It was at that. Would you like some tea?"

"Love some. I came over to see if I could get started on those tapes you wanted me to look at. Guess you were in the mood for company this morning."

"Absolutely. I was thinking about calling you. I'm hoping I can talk you into going with me up to the

Keasts tomorrow morning, just to take a look at the place."

"Will they want us up there? So soon after Stuart's murder?"

Goddard shrugged. "I think it might be good for them. When I was up there last, Bethy—you know Bethy, don't you, she's about your age—anyway, she asked if I would come again. She thinks it would be good for her grandmother. And I hate to sound all academic and objective about this, but grief can be a good time for a linguist. People talk excessively following a death, and their guard is down. They aren't worried about how they sound. So considering Bethy's plea, I think we ought to go." He looked around her, as if searching for something. "Where's Michael?"

She rolled her eyes. "Oh, don't worry. That house is busting out in women. Ella's in bed with 'nerves,' and Gale had to go to Praterton, but there's Le and Phoung. Phoung said she'd look after Michael. Chau and Katie Pru have become fast friends, and thanks to the thicket witch, they're not likely to wander into the fields again."

Goddard's eyes twinkled. "My, that is a lot of women. You even have women in the woodpile, so to speak. You'd think men barely exist around here."

"Oh, they exist. Just hard for them to get through the door right now. Daniel called early this morning, just to make sure we made it through the night. But Gale was gone by then. She wasn't happy about it, either."

"The trip to Praterton? Not bad news, I hope. I know Ella's not been feeling well . . ."

Nadianna waved her hand dismissively. "Oh, no, nothing to do with Ella. Sarah Gainer's lawyer called her. Now if you ask me, there is nobody more unlikely to be called by Sarah Gainer's lawyer than Gale. Oil and water, that's what Gale and Sarah would be."

"Gale knows her, then?"

"I don't think so. Gale couldn't figure out what Sarah wanted to talk to her about, and the lawyer wouldn't tell her. Ticked her off plenty, I can tell you. She's trying to get this book written and things keep cropping up and getting in the way."

The tea was warming her up, and Nadianna found herself thinking that if she ever had pleasant memories, she would want them to include this tea and this man—sweet, frivolous, and playful. She smiled at him happily.

Goddard returned the smile, then leaned forward conspiratorially, his elbows on the table. "Listen, I may be totally wrong in this, and Lord knows I'm no anthropologist or psychologist, but I sense a changing of the guard going on in your household. Gale seems to be coming into her own, don't you think?"

"What do you mean?"

"I mean, Ella's always seemed to be the one everyone turned to, but she is getting older. Now Gale seems to be coming to the fore. Might mean some friction."

"There's always been friction between Gale and Ella . . ."

"I know. Two strong personalities. But I sense in different ways. Gale's more . . ." He paused.

"Quiet, maybe? Determined?"

"Deliberate is what I was thinking. Reflective. I get the sense that Ella is more set in her ways and sees things only in her way, while Gale is more receptive. And more widely experienced, of course, having lived in the U.K."

Nadianna took another sip of tea. At the other end of the house, the pipes stopped squeaking as the water was turned off. "Gale is reflective all right. Sometimes I think too much so."

"Really? In what way?"

"Well, everything has to be so carefully thought out. Everything has to be reasoned. Sometimes I think

Ella and I are closer in the way we think. I believe in intuition. I know scientists don't think it exists, not in people anyway, but I listen to what I first feel about things. I mean, what is intuition but a wisdom that's been built up over generations? I react a certain way because of my mother, and she reacted the way she did because of her mother. It's like making a pearl—each generation builds around the one before until you go from a piece of grit to this beautiful thing. That's intuition." She laughed as she lifted the mug. "Maybe that's where the phrase 'pearl of wisdom' comes from. Wisdom is just layers of reaction all around a pitiful piece of dirt."

"And Ella believes in intuition, too?"

"She believes in history, which may be the same thing. She believes in honoring the past. And because of that she acts the way she does, almost by second nature. She wants to be open, but there are some lines she just won't cross. You take the Nguyens, for instance. She'll take them in, but I guarantee you that after they've gone home, she'll never invited them over for dinner. That's a line she can't cross. We all have lines we can't cross, don't you think?"

"Are yours the same as Ella's?"

Nadianna thought a minute, wanting to get the words right. "I won't be pushed around anymore. I had enough of that growing up. I won't be thought of as the ignorant little mill girl anymore. I'm proud of my heritage and the people I come from. That's one of the reasons I don't see my father and sister much. They still see themselves as mill people, and they won't let me be anything but their idea of what that means. To them it means polite, hardworking, accepting. I want to be the first two, but not necessarily the last. I'll accept what's good for me and my son, but I'll be darned if I'm going to sit by and put up with anything that's bad for us."

Goddard smiled and laid his hand over hers. "You're a wise young woman, Nadianna."

Nadianna felt the heat rise in her face. "No, I'm not. I'm just learning all the time. I'm learning a lot from Gale. She's teaching me to be open to new ideas. Which is odd, considering she's been closed for so long."

"You mean regarding the way she feels about Daniel?"

She looked at him, surprised. "You know about that?"

"Hard to miss it. It's obvious he's in love with her. But I don't know about her. What do you think?"

A hair dryer's whir sounded; Halford was almost finished getting dressed. "I think she loves him," Nadianna said quietly as she turned her palm up to grasp Goddard's hand. "But Gale's a tough nut to crack. It's all that deliberate thinking she does. She hasn't let go of her past. I'm not sure he has a chance."

The toxicological reports on all three murder victims lay on Truitt's desk. Evidence of alcohol in the blood-streams of Murphy and Keast, and both had eaten meals within two hours of death. Nguyen's results were different: No evidence of alcohol, and the man's stomach was virtually empty. "He probably hadn't eaten food in two days," the pathologist had said. "If then."

But Truitt wasn't nearly as disturbed by what wasn't in his stomach as what was—traces of iron oxide. During the time that he hadn't eaten any food, Tuan Nguyen, either voluntarily or by force, had ingested rust.

"What does that mean?" Haskell asked. "What could the man have eaten?"

"Let's put this one together, Craig. We have a man we know was bound and shot execution-style. The men

found shot with him had evidently enjoyed a meal of—"
Truitt scanned the reports "—peas, potato skins, beef,
and maybe beer well within the time frame when Tuan
had eaten nothing at all. But Tuan has two things those
men don't have—tiny punctures in his mouth and rust
in his gut."

"My God," Haskell breathed. "You saying that the
holes in his mouth . . ."

"Maybe something metal. What's metal and rusty
with barbs?"

"I can only think of one thing—barbed wire."

"That's a good starting point for me. We need to
get someone out to those woods and see if they can
find something barbed wiredy."

"I'll take care of it." Haskell rose to leave, then
paused. "I have one question. The autopsy report said
his mouth had been washed out. Why?"

"The only thing I can think is to get rid of the evidence. Wanted the rust out of the mouth, didn't reckon
on the stomach. Has Mrs. Grayson left yet?"

"No. She's still in with Sarah."

"Make sure she sees me before she leaves, okay?"

"Yessir."

Nine minutes passed before Truitt heard a knock
on his door and Haskell ushered in Gale Grayson. She
looked fatigued, with pink half-moons under her dark
eyes. He nodded Haskell out the door and turned his
attention to Gale.

"Have a seat. I just wanted to chat with you before
you went home."

Gale sank into the chair and for a moment rested
her head on his desk. "I don't want to be anyone's
Mother Confessor," she said, slumping against the back
of the chair.

"She confessed something to you?"

"She did. And she did it knowing full well that I

would tell you everything. In fact, she wants me to tell you everything. Her lawyer wants me to tell you everything."

"Why not her?"

"Because you are a man and you won't listen to her."

"God, she's a bigot about more things than race, then."

"It would figure."

"Okay, shoot. What have you been sent to tell me?"

"The Ram belongs to Marcus Siler. He threw the Molotov cocktail at the Nguyens."

"My friend Mr. Siler. So did he know Keast and Murphy?"

"She led me to think not, but to be honest, Alby, I got the impression she was lying about that. But she did tell me that Stuart and Darrell were members of a neo-Nazi group. And that they were using Ella's fields and the Kirby woods as meeting grounds."

"Why not somebody's house?"

"I don't know. But what she's worried about most is that you're going to release her from jail. She wants to stay in. She's afraid she'll be killed if you let her go."

Truitt stood, whistling idly through his teeth. If Keast and Murphy were involved in anything illegal in those woods, Siler was in on it, too. It would explain how he happened upon the bodies, even, perhaps, the odd way his car had been parked, wedged between two trees. And if Siler was in on it, chances were his terrified girlfriend was, too.

Gale interrupted his thoughts. "And she wants you to check out Bethy Keast. She says Bethy's 'not normal.' "

Truitt let out a hoot. "They should hold a convention. But I'll visit Bethy again. Anything else?"

"One other thing. I don't think Ella told you, but

she saw Darrell's car parked out in our fields Monday morning. Behind a thicket of kudzu. She says it looked hidden."

"What, she's just remembering this?"

"No. She knows she should have told you. But it's taken her a while to accept that perhaps Darrell was up to no good. You know Ella—her ability to judge people and know what's going on all the time is important to her. If she misjudged Darrell, she's going to have to rethink a lot of self-perceptions."

"Did she notice anything else?"

"Not that I know of."

"I'll need to talk with her."

"She's ill."

"Really? Anything serious?"

The fatigue seemed to darken in Gale's eyes. "I don't know. John's going to check her into the hospital next week for tests. She's been acting a little off ever since she heard of Darrell's death."

Truitt sighed. "You know I wish the best for her. Hopefully it's nothing."

"Hopefully. Thanks." A pause. "Did you hear about the meeting at the Statlers Cross Methodist Church last night?"

"What meeting?"

"It was ostensibly a prayer meeting, for everyone to get together and pray about the murders and about what happened to the Nguyens. But it turned ugly. Evidently, emotions got a little out of hand. Some comments were made about running the Nguyens out of town."

"Jesus. But the Nguyens are safe at your house."

"For now. But they can't stay forever, Alby. And if there's something serious wrong with Ella . . ."

She studied him, her eyes pleading, confused. She wanted some guidance from him, some leadership. "Gale, what you're doing for those people is kind. It's unbelievably kind. But you don't owe them that. Your first responsibility is to Ella and Katie Pru." He stopped, realizing that her odd family extended beyond biological lines. "And whoever else you wish to make a part of your circle. But we have services for people like the Nguyens. Don't feel guilty if you have to send them on their way. They will be okay."

Even as he said them, he knew his words rang hollow. He could hear it in his own hesitant tone; he could see it reflected in the skepticism in her eyes. Tuan hadn't been okay. Why in the world should either one of them expect that his survivors would be?

25

"I need lacy socks."

"Here are some lacy socks."

"I need pretty black shoes."

"I got the pretty black shoes. But you can have my pretty blue shoes. They'll fit you."

"I need something else. It's not right."

"I have an idea. Let's go to my Grandma Ella's room, but we got to be quiet."

Katie Pru took Chau's hand, and together they walked to the doorway of Katie Pru's bedroom and peeked into the upstairs hall. No one was there. From downstairs they could hear a radio—Katie Pru knew that either Chau's mother or grandmother was listening to it because the radio was usually never on—and from another part of the house they heard a slow, high-pitched singing.

"That's my grandma," Chau said. "That's what she sings when she wants me to go to sleep."

Katie Pru was wondering if Chau's grandmother was trying to sing Chau's mother to sleep when she remembered baby Michael, who would be drowsy and a little fussy by this time in the afternoon. As they listened, the singing trailed off, and all they could hear was the radio, a faint song with a strong beat. Michael must be asleep, she reasoned. Which meant that soon, someone would come to check on her and Chau.

Chau's hand in hers, she led her friend down the hall to the shut door of the last room. Here she paused and pressed her ear against the door. She couldn't hear anything—she didn't know for sure if it was possible to hear anything, but she had heard about children pressing their ears against doors in books. Putting her finger to her mouth as a warning, Katie Pru turned the doorknob and the two girls went into the room.

The lights were off and the curtains drawn, so it took her a moment to make out the figure of her sleeping grandmother in her huge wooden bed. She tried to listen for her grandmother's breathing, but all she could hear was the steady rhythm of the radio, farther off now. She dropped Chau's hand and headed for the Big Thing, where Ella kept all her hats.

The Big Thing had a proper name, but Katie Pru could never remember it. To her it was just a huge piece of furniture with doors that swung open to reveal drawers of nightgowns and rods of hanging clothes. Grandma Ella's house had no closets, so every room had a Big Thing, even her own, but nobody's was as big as Grandma Ella's. It was so big Katie Pru could hide in it, which was something she did regularly when she wanted to jump out and scare her grandmother.

But right now she was not interested in scaring anyone. Right now she wanted to finish dressing up. She motioned to Chau to join her, and when she did, Katie Pru slowly, dramatically, opened up the Big Thing's two huge doors.

She heard Chau gasp. Satisfied with the response, Katie Pru pulled out one of the bottom drawers and, using it as a ladder, climbed in the Big Thing and started throwing out hats.

Grandma Ella had explained once that her sister Nora, who died long before Katie Pru was born, had loved hats. "She had a hat for every time of day, every season," Grandma Ella had said. "She even made her own hats. Proper ladies wore hats in those days, Katie Pru. If you had lived back then, you would have been a proper little girl, and you would have worn hats. Gloves, too."

The only gloves Katie Pru ever wore were mittens, and the idea of wearing those in anything but a snowstorm wasn't something she understood. But hats . . .

One by one hats thudded to the ground as Chau gleefully gathered them up. It was too dark in here to try them on; they would have to sneak them back to her room.

From the bed, Grandma Ella shifted. "Gale?" she murmured sleepily. Then louder, "Gale?"

Immediately, they heard footsteps below and the sound of someone mounting the stairs. Chau's eyes grew big. They couldn't get caught in here. They didn't want to get punished.

Katie Pru slapped the hats out of Chau's hands and gestured her into the Big Thing. Light from the hallway shone into the room as Katie Pru climbed in beside her and pulled the Big Thing's door shut.

She heard her mother's voice, soft. "Ella? You all right?"

"Come here," Grandma Ella said. "I need to talk to you."

There was a rustle of bedclothes, and Katie Pru imagined her mother climbing into bed with her grandmother, just like her mother climbed into bed with her when Katie Pru had had a nightmare. "You need to be sleeping, Ella," her mother said. "John said the more rest you get the better."

"I've not slept well all night." Grandma Ella's voice sounded muffled, far off. "I keep having bad dreams."

"It's the medication. You know how it does that sometimes."

"I heard voices last night. Who all was here?"

A pause. "Just Sally and Ron. And Daniel. But they didn't stay late. I'm sorry we woke you."

"Things are going bad, aren't they?"

"Why would you say that?"

"I always know more than you do. I know this isn't nerves . . ."

"Let's wait for the doctors to—"

"And I know someone's gonna get hurt. One of us. Maybe all of us. You shouldn't have brought them home."

"Ella, you need to get to sleep. I'll check on you later."

"No. You need to listen to me. Darrell lied to me. There was something going on in those woods—"

"Ella, I already know that. I spent the morning with Sarah Gainer. She told me about some of the men in the town meeting in the Kirby woods. They used our fields, too. Alby's looking into it. You don't have anything to worry about. I have a feeling this whole thing is about to come to an end."

"Well, this is where I know more than you, Miss Lady." A pause, and what Katie Pru thought was a chuckle. "Remember when Nora used to call you Miss Lady? It used to drive your mother crazy. 'Don't call her that. I don't want my daughter to grow up with that kind of idea in her head.' She figured she could raise you not to be Southern. That's funny, isn't it?"

"Ella." Her mother sounded the way she did when she was telling Katie Pru for the last time that there were no monsters under the bed. "Get some more sleep."

"I knew Tom would hurt you. I could tell he was lying to you. How could I tell he lied to you and I couldn't tell Darrell was lying to me? Huh. Must be my age."

"Tom didn't lie to me at first, Ella. He didn't get messed up in all that business until after we were married, in England. There were several years when he didn't lie to me at all."

"You are so naive, Gale. People don't grow bad. It's in them like a bad gene. Tom was rotten from the beginning. You just couldn't see it. Like I couldn't see Darrell. Wonder what he did in my fields?"

"I don't know."

"Then you need to find out. Something was going on. And there's more for you to worry about. Katie Pru knows."

"Knows what?"

"She knows about the fields. She doesn't understand it yet, but she will. Just like she knows about Tom. You're going to have to worry about that. We're all going to have to worry about what we're passing on to her."

Three of Truitt's deputies had been out since midmorning, scouring the Kirbys' woods for discarded barbed wire. But when the call came through to Truitt, he was asked to come not to the woods, but to the Alden house.

He exchanged only the mildest of greetings with Gale as he trudged past the house to join the group of khaki-dressed men in her yard. He followed Haskell down an overgrown path, past large mounds of briars, past the area where Sarah Gainer had set up camp, until Haskell came to a stop.

"Look here, Alby," he said. "Look where someone's broken through this overgrowth here."

Truitt stopped and examined a place off the path where a large hole, big enough for a man to climb through, had been hacked into a wall of briars. "Interesting, Craig. Is that all you've got to show me?"

"No, sir," said Haskell. "If you'll follow me . . ."

Haskell pushed his muscular frame through the opening, holding back tendrils so that Truitt could come through. Inside a variety of vines twined overhead, forming a small room. "Bet foxes live here part of the year," Truitt said. "This is a regular little den."

"Bet they haven't been here recently," Haskell answered. "Look at this."

Crouching, Haskell stepped over to the far side of the thicket and pulled aside some vines. In the gloom, Truitt could see the brown lines of a barbed wire fence.

"It's the fence that marks the Alden property from the road on out about five hundred yards," Haskell said. "The thicket grows over it here. When we searched it, we found that it's down in several places, but this is the only place we can find where it's been cut."

Truitt pulled out his penlight and shone it on the wire. "My, my. You are absolutely right. Nice little eighteen-inch piece. No rust on the fresh places. Might be relatively recent."

"I'm just thinking that of all the places to cut a barbed wire fence, if you were doing it for honest reasons, why would you do it here, where it would be hidden?"

"Good question." Truitt looked around the interior of the opening. "I wonder if you can see this from the Alden house."

"I dunno. Want me to check?"

"I'll check. I gotta talk with them anyway."

Gale watched Truitt and his men from her back porch. And they were literally men, she thought as some of them rounded the corner in the path and stepped out into the cleared yard. There must not be any female deputies in Calwyn County. She wondered if that was Truitt's subtle preference or a lack of womanly interest.

She held the porch door open as Truitt broke ranks with his men and came toward her. His eyes were grim.

"Can we go inside, Gale? I need to ask y'all a few questions."

She directed him toward the den, the one room in the house where the sounds were self-contained. It was their most vulnerable point of entry, but it was also the most private. As she passed the parlor door, she raised a cautionary hand to Halford. Not that it mattered. When he saw Truitt, Halford stood, a look of concern crossing his face. Obviously, Truitt's body language was readable to all.

Truitt caught a glimpse of Halford as he passed the parlor. He stopped. "You know what, Daniel? I need to talk with you, too. Do you mind coming in here with me and Gale?"

The three of them entered the den, and Gale flicked on the lights. "Okay, Alby. What did you find?"

He motioned them to sit on the sofa, but he kept standing, his hands in his trouser pockets. His suit coat was rumpled from his tromp through the fields, and his hair was windblown.

"I want both of you to think back to Sunday night, early Monday morning," he said. "Did you see or hear anything unusual?"

Gale and Halford exchanged glances. Sunday night. Gale tried to focus. Halford had come in that morning. They had spent the afternoon relaxing, ate dinner on the porch. And that evening . . . She strained to think of that evening. She and Halford had walked across the railroad tracks to the old mill, so she could show him the inspiration for the book she and Nadianna had authored. They had sat on a large stone inside the mill's burned-out hull, talking long past midnight. Then they had returned to the house and their respective bedrooms. But no, she couldn't remember anything unusual.

That didn't satisfy Truitt. "Take your time and think about it, Gale. Think about anything you might have seen or heard, no matter how you might have dismissed it at the time."

When Gale finally gave up, shrugging, Truitt turned to Halford. "Daniel, you're trained to pay attention to such things. Do you remember anything at all?"

Beside her, Gale felt Halford stiffen, but he lapsed into thought. He shook his head. "I don't know what you're fishing for, Alby, but I can't come up with anything. Nothing unusual stands out."

Truitt hunched his shoulders, obviously frustrated. "I want you to think some more. Come on, guys, if anyone can do this, it's going to be the two of you."

Gale turned at a rustling sound at the door. Ella stood there, still in her bathrobe, the blue comforter from her bed wrapped around her.

"They may not know what you want, Alby," she said, "but I do. It was about ten-thirty Sunday night. I heard cries. At first I thought they were owls. Katie Pru came into my room because she thought they were someone crying. I told her an owl story, about what impressive birds they were, and sent her on to bed. But the cries didn't stop, and I knew they weren't owls at all. Darrell had gotten rid of all my owls."

Her chin was lifted, her skin pale, almost translucent. For the first time Gale realized with a jolt that Ella was truly . . . old.

"Why didn't you tell me, Ella?" Truitt's voice was sharp. "If not when it happened, why didn't you tell me once we found those bodies?"

"Because Darrell convinced me it was nothing. I called him Monday morning to ask him what the sound might have been, and he told me it was probably a fox giving birth. And I accepted that. But I remembered later about his car being out there and him not mentioning the first thing about it. Don't you figure if I had said, 'Darrell, I think I heard someone crying in my fields last night,' that he would have said, 'Oh, Ella, don't worry. I was out there last night hunting and didn't hear nothing but some foxes.' But he didn't say that. He didn't mention being out there at all. That's when I realized he must have been up to no good."

"But Ella," Gale said. "Daniel and I were outside about that time. Surely if there was someone crying in the fields we would have heard it."

"Would you? You were over the railroad tracks, inside the stone walls of the old mill. You wouldn't have heard a thing. But Katie Pru and I did. And I didn't do a damn thing. Because I believed in a young man who would lie to my face and smile the whole time he was doing it. He played me for a fool, Gale. He played me for an old damn fool."

Suddenly, Ella's mouth went slack and she crumpled to the floor. As Halford placed his fingers at the pulse on Ella's neck, Gale heard Truitt behind her punching in numbers on a phone. And all she could hear from herself was the name *Ella, Ella,* over and over again.

26

Donna Crow had a smoker's voice, even though as far as Sally knew she had never smoked. It was that feature that identified the speaker as soon as Sally answered the phone.

"Sally? I'm so glad I found you. I called the tearoom but no answer. The girls and I were wondering. You planning on opening the Rose Cross tonight for business? Seems like an awful lot of work without help."

For a brief moment, Sally had the idea that Donna was volunteering, that the MMMM's had surveyed the situation and decided that soulmate Sally needed their help and they would man the cash register and bus the tables. But in the next sentence, her hopes fell.

"Because we were thinking . . . We have a little investment club going, nothing big, just something we do to build up our assets . . ."

Again a surge of hope. Was Donna about to suggest they would be interested in investing in the tearoom? She could afford to hire several new people, maybe even expand into the empty hardware store next door . . .

". . . and we were wondering if you would like to become a member. We contribute a hundred dollars a month—like I said, nothing big. We're each responsible for researching a company and recommending it, or not recommending it, for investment. It's Sue, Honey, and myself—in fact, we call ourselves the Money-Manic Militant Moms, just as a takeoff. We rotate hosting the monthly meetings. Tonight I'm on. What do you say? Would you like to join?"

Sally stammered as she tried to push aside the numbing sense of foolishness she felt. Like Donna Crow would ever bus tables; like the den mothers of Sag Harbor Estates would invest in a tiny mom-and-no-pop diner like the Rose Cross. She was an idiot.

"Well, actually, Donna, I was planning on closing the Rose Cross for tonight. I still haven't found help, and brunch is one thing, but dinner is something else . . ."

"See? That's what we were thinking. So you want to join us?"

"I don't know. I wasn't really looking to invest . . ."

"That's what we said. Then we started doing this and we've done damn good. Impressed the hell out of our husbands—they thought this was just for fun, but it's become serious. That's why we're so particular about who we invite in. And we're inviting you."

The last line was spoken slowly, each word emphasized. A hundred dollars wasn't much, Sally thought. It might actually help her to diversify; she had plowed all her own money into the tearoom, and she had learned during the past week that any bump could throw a small business into crisis. Besides, she had to admit that part of her was flattered. They were inviting her in. In matters of money, the MMMM's wouldn't do anything lightly.

"Seven-thirty?" Sally asked. "Do I need to bring anything?"

"Just your checkbook, doll. And be prepared to stay a while. We've been known to yack until midnight. It's not *all* business, you know."

Sally ate a quick dinner and spent too much time fretting over what to wear—did Donna's tone of voice indicate that the meeting would have a professional or casual feel?—before settling on a white velour pantsuit with silver jewelry that was noncommittal enough to reflect the atmosphere around it. At seven-thirty it was already dark when she spied the signature lighthouse and pulled into the Sag Harbor Estates subdivision. She was struck by how the houses sparkled. Her home, no matter how proud she was of it, would never have the jewel-on-the-promenade look of these brick-and-plaster edifices. She fought back a twinge of envy. Her little house had its share of class; she had made sure the colors were appropriate if not altogether authentic. But it wasn't like this. These were people who had arrived at a particular station in life and were proud to proclaim it. These were people comfortable with themselves. These were people whom life had treated damn well.

Donna's house was at the end of a cul-de-sac, a two-story brick with a multipeaked roofline. Chandeliers glittered from two Palladian windows, and boxwoods manicured in the shape of spirals bordered each side of the covered stoop. Pulling her respectable Chrysler sedan into the curved driveway, Sally parked behind a more respectable Mercedes SUV. No wonder these women's husbands were delighted that the Money Manics had turned into something serious—with these folks, finance was a serious subject.

Donna greeted her at the door with a champagne glass in hand. "Welcome to our newest member," she said. "We're about to toast you."

Sally slunk into the house behind her hostess, afraid to touch the white walls, to put her farmhouse-familiar shoes on the taupe carpet. But Donna seemed impervious to her discomfort, and led the way into the great room.

The two other MMMM's were present, and with growing uneasiness, Sally realized that despite her efforts she had managed to overdress. Jogging suits, and not particularly nice ones, were evidently de rigeur at these meetings. Honey rose up on her knees from where she was sitting on the floor and struggled to the coffee table to pour Sally a flute of champagne.

"We've been meaning to ask you forever," she said as she handed Sally the glass. "But we figured you'd be too busy with the café and all. Tonight looked like a perfect time to get you with us." She raised her glass. "To the newest Money Manic. May your business savvy and insight serve us all."

The women raised their glasses and laughed as they went through the complicated moves of clinking. The champagne was sharp in Sally's throat. She smiled as she sat on the sofa next to Sue.

"Thank you," she said. "But I don't know how much business savvy I have to offer."

"Oh, you'd be surprised," said Sue. "I think as women we tend to naturally downplay our abilities. The truth is we sometimes know more than we give ourselves credit for. You should see our portfolios. If we were smart, we'd open our own firm."

"We're better off this way," said Donna. "Just coming in under the radar. Picking our stocks, making our money. Why should we worry with commissions and licenses and shit when we can pocket all the gold ourselves?"

The women laughed, and Sally took another sip. Her nose felt warm and tingly, and she began to relax into the camaraderie. She had settled into the sofa cushions, enjoying the banter, when another thought occurred to her.

"I won't be able to meet on Friday evenings. I closed the Rose Cross tonight because I couldn't find a replacement for Le in time, but I hope to be open again at night soon."

"Really?" said Honey. "How soon?"

"Maybe next Friday. That may be optimistic, considering how far out this is. It's hard to get a qualified chef to drive this far. But it shouldn't be impossible. And besides, I can do some of the cooking. I'm not as good as Le—"

"Was Le really that good?" Donna reached over from her side chair and dipped a chip into some salsa. "I got the impression you taught her everything she knew. Thought she was a quick learner."

"She was. I did . . . well, I taught her the particular recipes I wanted. But she was an accomplished chef in Vietnam. She worked in a hotel."

Honey hooted. "Is that like being an accomplished doctor from Guam?"

"No, seriously, Le is very good. I had a particular idea for the kind of cuisine I wanted. She learned the recipes very quickly."

"But she's not coming back."

"No." Sally felt a wave of sadness as she stared into her champagne glass. "I don't think she's coming back. She's given me every indication that she doesn't want to."

"I can't say I blame her," said Donna. "I can't say I'd blame her if she packed up her family and left."

"That's true enough," agreed Sue. "First her brother. Now her house. I'd have to think good and hard about staying."

The group fell silent. Then Honey scooched forward on her haunches and lifted the champagne bottle aloft.

"I'm giving everybody seconds," she announced. "These meetings are supposed to be fun. Let's stop talking about the Nguyens and their troubles. They're their troubles, after all. My daddy always said 'trouble follows trouble,' and well, that seems to be the Nguyens all over."

"It certainly doesn't help that they've chosen to live in the buckle of the Bible Belt," said Donna. "They could have chosen a more tolerant location. That was one thing Jim and I discussed for a long time before moving here—we might get twice the house and zero the congestion, but it's bound to be like moving back into the 1950's. And sure enough, the first time we drove through Statlers Cross, we kept expecting to see Andy Griffith coming up from the fishing hole. We realized *we* were going to be the diversity around here. The token Yankee city folks."

"But that's the difference between you and the Nguyens, Donna," insisted Honey. "You understood you had a choice. You could have stayed in the city where there are more of your kind, but you opted to come here. And besides, unless you open your mouth, no one knows you're a carpetbagger." Her wide blue eyes twinkled as she grinned at Donna over her champagne glass. "All the Nguyens have to do is walk out their front door for folks to know they're not from around here. They've chosen a tough lifestyle for themselves."

"That's right." Sue nodded. "There's such a thing as disaster waiting to happen. When the Nguyens painted their house that color, they were courting disaster. They might as well have hired the Mormon Tabernacle Choir to sing naked in their front yard. I'm not saying that Le's brother deserved to die, but let's face it—a lot of their kind end up dead. I'm not saying it's right, but I'm saying it's a fact. Look at how violence increased in the parts of Atlanta where the immigrants moved. Why do you think we moved out here? I looked at the schools my daughters were going to, and I thought, no way are they going to date any of those brown-faced little boys. I'm not going to have any brown-faced grand-babies in my house. I'm not a bigot—"

Honey snickered. "You, Sue, *are* a bigot—"

"No, I'm not. I just got tired of having neighbors

with names I couldn't pronounce. I got tired of living in a place where nobody but me celebrated Christmas. I got tired, for God's sakes, of not being able to call it Christmas—damned 'winter break.' Winter break is for skiing, not celebrating the birth of Christ. So we put our house on the market and got the hell out of there. You can imagined how thrilled I was to see that they'd followed me out here."

"I don't think it was you personally," commented Donna dryly.

"No, but they followed my sentiments. They didn't want to live in what they'd created, either. So instead of sticking around and cleaning it up, they packed up and moved. Every time I go to the tearoom, I can look down the street and see the roof of that goddamned house . . ." She gave an exaggerated shudder. "It makes me ill."

"I have a toast," declared Honey. "To all us city expatriates who moved here for a cleaner way of life. Here's to being free, white, and over twenty-one. Or at least to being free and white. To hell with being over twenty-one."

She held the bottle out and began refilling the glasses. Sally placed hers on the table and stood. Her face felt cold; her hands ached.

"I'm sorry that I'm going to have to leave, but I've got some business to take care of."

"Can't stay away from the tearoom after all, huh?" teased Donna.

"Oh, I can stay away from the tearoom. But I can't stay in this room with you. I'm a businesswoman, and my establishment is always open to you. I hope you bring your friends. But if I ever hear in my restaurant the kind of crap I've just heard in your home, I'll throw the goddamned lot of you out on your bigoted asses."

She turned and left them stunned in their seats. Her pulse beat in her temples as she pulled out of Donna's driveway and made her way past the dazzling rows of houses. At the subdivision entrance, she stared up at the lighthouse before signaling left. *What a crock,* she thought. *They hate immigrants, but they couldn't think of anything indigenous to name their damned retreat.*

She drove down the Main Street of Statlers Cross, past the locked door of the Rose Cross. At the end of town, next to the old burnt-out mill, she mounted the railroad crossing. At the summit, she looked out over the Alden house, its windows ablaze with light. The dashboard clock indicated it was only eight-thirty. Late, but perhaps Ella and Gale would forgive her this last transgression.

Her knock was met by Nadianna, her eyes big in the porch's yellow light.

"I'm sorry, Mrs. Robertson," she said as she held out her hand to usher Sally inside. "I thought you might be someone else. Gale and Daniel are at the hospital. Ella had a stroke this afternoon."

"My God! Is she all right?"

"I don't reckon you can really be 'all right' after a stroke. Gale called a little while ago to say that she was stabilized. She said the doctors think it was minor. But she'll be in the hospital for a few days."

"I'm sorry, Nadianna. I won't bother you now. I just had something to discuss with Le, but it can wait."

From the parlor Sally saw a slender shadow move across the doorway. Le entered the foyer. With a shock, Sally saw how tiny she had become, as if in two days she had shrunk from a woman to a child.

"What do you want, Sally?" Le asked.

"This is a bad time, Le—"

"This is a bad time for the Aldens. It might not be a bad time for me."

The comment was as hard as a punch. Sally studied her former employee. The analogy of the child had been wrong. The quiet, hardworking woman who hunched over the counter and rarely spoke to her boss now had a steely set to her shoulders. Her eyes were stern. But they weren't hateful. Sally saw something else in them. Fortitude, maybe. Determination. It was the look of a woman who had crossed seas to get what she wanted. It was, Sally realized, the look of a businesswoman.

"Le," she said. "I'm going to go to the Rose Cross and put on a pot of coffee. We need to talk. For starters, I'd like to offer you my home until you feel comfortable returning to your own. But mainly, I'd like to ask you to become my business partner."

27

Alby Truitt called early Saturday morning to tell Le that her brother's body had been released by the state crime lab and was ready for burial. Nadianna had stayed in the background as Le took the call, busying herself with the breakfast dishes and spooning globs of applesauce into the baby's mouth. At the table, Katie Pru and Chau ate cereal and bananas, but if they were aware of the somberness of Le's call, they bravely ignored it. They took turns shoveling huge spoonfuls of cornflakes into their mouths, then opening their jaws wide to gross each other out.

After hanging up the phone, a dry-eyed Le disappeared upstairs. Nadianna didn't know how the woman did it, how she seemed to remain so composed. Except for the flashes of anger, it wasn't apparent she had lost a brother at all. Nadianna's own grief was always torrential. It took months for the steeliness to come.

Katie Pru and Chau had now added sound effects to their displays. Milk dribbled down their chins as they opened their mouths wide.

"Ahhhhhhhhh," said Katie Pru.

"Ahhhhhhhhh," said Chau.

"Both of y'all are worse than Michael," Nadianna said, taking a paper towel to their faces. "Eat right or get yourselves upstairs and dressed."

Eating right didn't appear to be an option; the girls exchanged glances and hopped down from the table. Nadianna heard their guffaws as they clattered up the stairs.

She sighed and flung herself down into Katie Pru's seat. It was only nine A.M. and she was already exhausted. Gale had spent most of the night at the hospital, dragging in near daybreak. Halford was still asleep in the parlor, not having wanted to disturb Goddard by bumbling in so late. Le had returned even later than Gale. For most of the night, Nadianna had felt like she was manning a train station.

The prognosis on Ella could have been better, but it also could have been worse. The stroke had left her with slurred speech and partial paralysis on her right side. It would be days or weeks before the doctors knew how permanent the damage was. It was hard for Nadianna to conjure up a picture of a confined Ella. It would probably be hard for Ella to do so, as well. Nadianna had no problem imagining the anger in Ella's eyes every time she had to ask for assistance. What was it Goddard had called it—a changing of the guard?

The phone jangled her to attention. Goddard's voice was cheerful.

"Ready to go? I've got my notebook and my tape recorder juiced up."

She had to fight to understand what he was talking about. Then she remembered. The Keasts. They were supposed to go to the Keasts this morning.

"Gee, Ron," she said. "Is there any way I can beg out? Gale didn't get home from the hospital until four A.M., and someone needs to watch the kids. Besides, Le just got a call that Tuan's body's been released and now she's got to focus on the funeral. The Keasts probably got the same call. Maybe they don't need the intrusion."

The silence on the other end of the phone was palpable. Goddard cleared his throat.

"Nadianna, if you need to stay home with the children, I understand—"

His stress on the word "children" flustered her. Behind her, Michael squealed and banged his spoon on his tray. "No, it's not that . . ."

"—but it would be . . . beneficial . . . if this project had some priority. I'm not trying to be an ogre, I understand the situation with Ella, I really do . . ."

"No, no, you're not being an ogre. I just thought the Keasts would like some time alone."

His voice became soft, sincere. "The Keasts have had time alone all week. How many visitors do you think they've had? Other than the time Daniel and the doctor came by, I bet I've been their only visitor all week. Maybe the minister made it up there, once. The Keasts are among the loneliest people I know. They will welcome us with open arms, I assure you, particularly if they're having to think about the funeral now."

Thinking about the funeral. That would mean talking about it, especially if they had a sympathetic ear. Nadianna could see Rosen Keast's lean face, could imagine her mouth move as she spoke the words: *my boy's funeral.* She could see it in black and white. It would make a stunning photograph. It would capture so much of what the rural South was about.

She knew Goddard's conflict. She, too, had been in a foreign country for a limited amount of time, anxious to capture what experiences she could for the sake of her work. She understood the powerful discord between compassion and practicality—yes, she could feel for these people, but she also had a project to do. Her responsibility was to her work. And he was right: If she was going to take this project on, she had to be professional about it. No sloughing off work because there was no one to keep the baby. The Alden house was practically a dormitory. There had to be a free woman somewhere.

"Can I have thirty minutes?" she asked.

"Absolutely. It'll give me time to fix us some tea for a thermos. I find that it's cold up there, and I'm not always too sure about drinking the water. And don't worry, Nadianna, I don't think we'll be more than a couple of hours."

As Nadianna rang off, a disheveled Halford, barefoot but dressed in trousers and a rumpled shirt, slumped into the room. He smiled at her as, without a word, she poured him a cup of coffee.

"I look that bad, do I?"

"Awful. Don't imagine you slept well on that old horsehair sofa."

"I've slept in worse places. Gale down yet?"

"No, although I expect with Katie Pru and Chau banging around she will be soon."

"I'm going to run over and shower and then come back. I imagine she'll want to go back to the hospital."

Nadianna grimaced. "Daniel, I have a favor to ask. Could you watch the baby, just for a couple of hours? I told Ron I'd go with him to the Keasts today—just to get a feel for the place, maybe take some preliminary shots."

Halford looked at her through the steam from his coffee. "The man has odd timing. Does he know about Ella?"

She felt herself color. "Yes. And I suppose I could have been firmer with him. But this is important, Daniel, and I don't want to blow—"

He held up a hand. "It's okay. We'll work out something. Tell you what, you let me shower and I'll take care of Michael all day if you need."

"About Gale and Ella . . ."

"We'll work something out. Don't worry." He rose and put his cup in the sink. As he passed by the high chair, he rested his hand on the baby's head. The baby slapped the tray with his palm. "If Gale wakes up, tell her I'll be back in a bit."

But Gale wasn't up by the time thirty minutes had passed, and Nadianna, anxious not to get in Goddard's bad graces, bundled up the baby and threw a bottle and some toys in the diaper bag. After confirming that Le would keep an eye on the girls, she grabbed her camera bag, strapped the baby into his carrying seat, and, hoisting the diaper bag over one arm, scrambled outside to Goddard's house.

She could hear the sound of Halford's hair dryer as she entered the back door. She started talking as soon as she saw Goddard's expression at the sight of the baby.

"Don't worry. I'm not taking him with us. Daniel said he'd watch him. I'm just going to plunk him in Daniel's bedroom, give him instructions, and then I'll be ready to go."

The drive up to the Keasts' place was a difficult one, the engine in Goddard's car churning and whining up the rutted slope. Nadianna had never been on this property. One time, she remembered her father taking some venison to give to the family, but she couldn't remember the circumstances. They were a family the people of Statlers Cross knew to leave alone. The fact that a university professor from a foreign country could have befriended them was still a wonder to her.

The house looked deserted as they topped the hill and entered the compound. The whole scene struck Nadianna as drear and scraggly—the house shingles loose and curled, the bare twigs of trees like skeletal bones against the overcast sky. She shuddered as she climbed from the car and placed her foot on hard, dried dirt. This was a place neglected long before death. She could only imagine what kind of decay lay in wait.

The boards sagged under her as they mounted the wooden steps to the front porch. She heard no sounds from the inside of the house, just the sigh of the breeze through the leafless trees.

"Do you think anyone's home?" she whispered.

"I would think so. Where else on earth would they be?"

Where else indeed, and she realized that she had never seen Bethy at the store, never encountered her at the post office, or the gas station or the host of other places where townspeople ran into each other. For the first time she wondered if her father's gift of venison had been more than a neighborly gesture, if within that generation there had been a secret agreement for everyone to do their part in keeping this family alive.

Bethy's blue eyes bore into Nadianna as she opened the door, but as soon as she saw Goddard, she relaxed and swung the door wide.

"Grandmama wondered if you were comin' today. She been lookin' for you to come up the road."

"Of course I was coming. I figured this would be a difficult day. The sheriff been by?" At Bethy's nod, Goddard shook his head and laid his hand lightly on her shoulder. "This is going to be tough, burying Stuart. You're going to have to be strong for Rosen. You're going to have to be strong for her and that son of yours."

"Oh, I'm plenty strong, Mr. Goddard," the young woman answered. "Whatever we need to do, I can do. Stuart taught me a lot about things. I know a lot. I can run this place. Me and my boy can run it."

"That's fine, Bethy." He held his hand out to Nadianna. "Do you know Nadianna Jesup? She lives with Ella Alden. She's come to help me with my work. She's a photographer, much better than I am."

Bethy eyeballed Nadianna. "She's gonna take our picture?"

"The same as with my video camera, except better. Trust me, Bethy, it won't be any different from if I were doing it myself except she knows what she's doing."

Bethy evidently did trust him because she stepped back from the door and motioned them both in. Easing her camera bag over her shoulder, Nadianna slid into the room.

Rosen Keast, tall and white-haired, stood by the open fireplace, braiding her hair. When she saw Goddard, she smiled, her eyes sad.

"I can have my boy to bury," she said. "But the preacher don't think they'll let me do it up here."

"I suppose there are laws that determine where you can bury these days," Goddard said.

"Shame. He needs to be up here with me."

Nadianna wondered where all the other Keasts were buried, if there were a family plot somewhere on this tangled hill. But she didn't say anything, trying instead to look quiet and compassionate.

"Who's the pretty girl?" Rosen asked.

"Nadianna Jesup. She lives—"

"I know about Nadianna Jesup. Knew her daddy. He was a good man. Married a bad woman, though. Years back." She studied Nadianna until Nadianna felt awkward and turned away. "You don't look like your mama. Good thing. Looks carry a lot of badness."

"I came to see if you needed anything, Rosen, to see if I could be some help," Goddard said.

"Liar. You come to hear me talk."

"I always come for that. But I come for more. You know that."

"Uh-huh. That's what Stuart said. But he never telled me what."

"Stuart was my friend. I was his."

"Friends is good to have."

The conversation dwindled there, Rosen's eyes still on Nadianna. This wasn't what Nadianna had expected, this languid talk of badness and friendship. She had expected more grief. She had expected a louder pain.

From the corner of her eye, she saw Bethy lean over Goddard. "I gots somethin' to talk with you about," the young woman whispered. "Come here."

Goddard went with Bethy, leaving Nadianna alone with Rosen Keast. The woman had finished braiding her hair, and it hung in long ropes on either side of her face. Her smile belied the deep sadness in her eyes.

"You messin' with him, girl?"

Nadianna's lips parted in shock. "Messin'? With Ron?"

"You have messin' in your blood, I can tell you that. So you messin' with Mr. Goddard?"

"No, ma'am. I wouldn't . . . we're here to work—"

Rosen took one of her braids and began wrapping it around the crown of her head. "Good. 'Cause I want to tell you what I told Bethy about Ron Goddard. Nice-talking man, kind eyes, but you would be messin' with a snake."

Truitt was ready to leave his office to interview the newly jailed Marcus Siler when his desk phone rang. He picked it up, irritated that Blaire had ignored his orders to direct all his calls to Haskell.

The voice on the other end was hesitant. "I've been trying to reach you." Ilene Parker sounded slightly miffed. "You haven't returned my calls."

"I didn't get your messages, Miz Parker. I apologize. It's been busy around here. But you've got me now. What's the problem?"

"I realized it at the church meeting Thursday night. I was looking at all the men in the pews, most of them dressed nicely, but, well, dressed the way men around here dress. Then it dawned on me."

"What dawned on you, Miz Parker?" Truitt tried to keep the irritation from his voice.

"The figure I saw hunting around the back of the Nguyens' house the afternoon it was bombed. It was Dr. Goddard."

"Ron Goddard. You sure?"

"Yes, sir. Nobody else in Statlers Cross has clothes like that. It's the colors. They're just slightly different. Even his shoes are different."

"All right, Miz Parker. Thank you very much."

"But there's something else, Sheriff. When I realized it was him, it put me in mind of Tuesday morning. I saw him outside Tuesday morning. But not in the Nguyens' yard. Further back, in what would be the Aldens'. I didn't think much of it at the time, but now I'm thinking I've seen him around back there before."

"You mean searching, like he was at the Nguyens'?"

"That's why I didn't put it together before. I didn't get the impression that he was searching for anything at the Aldens'. I got the impression he was checking their fences."

28

The baby Michael kicked his fat legs, making the bells on his carrier jingle lightly. Halford knelt beside him and squeezed his sock-covered toe. A squeal, and Michael tilted back his head to give Halford a gummy grin. Bubbles and a motor noise, and his arms batted around like helicopter propellers. Babies, Halford decided, aren't half bad.

The phone rang, and he tickled Michael's stomach before answering.

Gale sounded tired. "I understand you have baby-sitting duty this morning."

"Yep. Thought I'd do a load of wash and bake some cookies while I'm at it."

"Funny. Will you be all right?"

He looked down at the gurgling bundle gyrating in his carrier. "I think we can manage. Nadianna left us a bottle and a bunch of toys. I suspect Ron's got some Mozart or some sort of brain music around here. We'll be fine."

"Good. I've got to run Nadianna's camera up to her—I just found it in the kitchen; would you believe she left it?"

"She seemed a bit flustered this morning."

"And then I'm going directly to the hospital. Phoung

said she would look after Chau and Katie Pru. Thank God those girls are getting along so well." A pause. "I'm sorry, Daniel. Tomorrow's your last day. This isn't how I intended your visit to be. It was supposed to be . . . I don't know . . ."

"Slow and sultry?"

"Something like that."

"I'll take what I can get."

"Thank you. I'll see you when I get back. If you need help, Phoung's here. Le's gone to Atlanta with Sally to finalize the memorial arrangements."

"Don't worry about me and Michael. I think we're becoming pals."

He hung up and, gazing down at Michael, felt a tug of regret. This wasn't how he had envisioned his visit, either, although he had to admit he wasn't sure what the vision had originally been. To spend time with Gale on her native turf, to maybe understand exactly the nature of the tie between them? If so, the trip had been a success. He had seen Gale waltz between the pecan trees her great-great-grandfather had planted, kissed her full and passionately in rooms inhabited by so many Alden ghosts. He knew the nature of the tie between them. He loved her. It would hurt like hell to leave.

"Life isn't easy, old boy," he told the burbling baby. "But you don't want to hear that, yet."

More kicks, and a huh-huh sound that seemed to indicate the child wanted to play. Halford unlatched him from his carrier and picked him up. Michael cackled with delight.

"How about some music, sport? Let's see how Dr. Goddard's tastes run."

A CD player rested on a beat-up cabinet in the corner of the room. Halford opened the cabinet drawer but found nothing but a ramble of papers. Clutching Michael in the crook of one arm, he knelt and opened the doors.

This was more promising—only a couple of CD's but scores of audiotapes, bound together by rubber bands. He glanced at the CD's—the Brodsky Quartet, Brian Eno. Interesting. He picked up a bound block of audiotapes and read the label on the first one—Rosen Keast, September 22. These were the tape recordings of Goddard's interviews. God, he hated to think of the transcription hours they would require.

He bent down further, taking care that Michael's head didn't bang into the cabinet. No more CD's. Reaching deep inside, he felt around, just to make sure. He liked the Brodsky Quartet, but he wasn't sure how they'd go down with an eight-month-old.

His hand hit a larger object, and he pulled out a lone videotape. Odd that it wasn't with its mates in the spare bedroom. He looked at the label. No words, just a mark that looked vaguely like a sun with a dagger through it. He stared at it, incredulous. He knew this mark. He just hadn't seen it in five years.

Gripping Michael, he popped the tape into Goddard's VCR and turned on the television. The machine hummed; the blue screen popped into action.

It was a cottage, the black-and-white kind that had become exceedingly rare in southern England. A white fence bounded its garden.

"My God," he murmured. "My God."

A slightly pregnant Gale appeared in the cottage door. She didn't wave at the cameraman, wasn't, Halford felt certain, aware that a camera was on her. She looked up at the sky as if judging the weather, then closed the door behind her. Moving down the garden walk, she passed through the gate and disappeared from the frame.

The tape went into a gray sizzle, then another sequence flickered into life. Another day—Gale wore different clothes—and this time Tom was with her, closing the door behind them. They both left through the gate.

Halford picked up the remote and fast forwarded. Another day. Another. Gale grew increasingly pregnant. The last image was of her in a wool coat, the belt tied above her bulging belly. This was very much the way she looked the first day he met her, the day Tom committed suicide.

He stopped the machine; the tape spit out. The baby tugged at his nose and laughed. Without stopping to wrap the child up, Halford grabbed the tape with the In Gaia's Name insignia and was out of the house, determinedly tugging at the rusted-nail latch on the barbed wire gate.

29

Nadianna found Goddard in the Keasts' kitchen, one leg hiked up on an old dinette set's dented metal chair while Bethy sat at the table. In his hands he held a stack of money.

When he saw her, he casually handed the money to Bethy. He smiled at Nadianna. "What's wrong?" he asked. "Rosen kind of spook you? She did me the first time I met her."

"No," Nadianna said. "I just need to go home. I left something at home."

"What?" His expression was quizzical, friendly. "You lugged that huge camera bag up here."

She searched for an answer. "My light meter," she said. "It's dark in here. I'll need my light meter . . ."

"I thought cameras were so sophisticated now that photographers didn't need light meters. Shows what I know. Well, let's forget the picture-taking today. Let's just get familiar with each other. It will make the future sessions more comfortable. Don't you agree, Bethy?"

Bethy nodded, her washed-out blue eyes on Nadianna. Nadianna glanced down at the money still in Bethy's hand.

"What's that for?" she asked.

"The money?" Goddard shrugged. "I didn't tell

you? Well, you know how I agreed to pay you for your work—I also pay the Keasts. I couldn't very well expect them to put up with hours of my questions and taping without compensation, could I? They—I just prefer that the payment be in cash. No problem, I hope."

"No . . . no. Listen, I really do need to get home. I shouldn't have left. Ella's in the hospital, Le's having to plan her brother's funeral. It was selfish of me—"

"Selfish? I don't think so, Nadianna. You have to put yourself first sometimes. And this is very important to you. You said so yourself."

"It is important, but not today, okay? Ron, really, I need to go. I need to get home to Michael."

Goddard was watching her closely, the light from the overhead bulb shining comically off his forehead. "Daniel has Michael. Don't worry about him. If you're going to work for yourself, you're going to have to learn to leave that child with others."

His gaze made her uncomfortable. She picked at a hole in the hem of her sweater. "I know that. But it's asking too much for Daniel to keep him today. Daniel needs to go to the hospital with Gale. He's leaving tomorrow. He needs to be with her today."

Goddard gave her a wan smile. Taking his foot from the chair, he abruptly left the room, returning a few seconds later with her camera bag. He rummaged through it, and with an "Aha," lifted out her light meter.

"You didn't leave it. But the interesting thing is you do seem to have forgotten your camera."

Nadianna felt relief sweep through her. "I *knew* it was something . . ."

Goddard placed her camera bag on the table and pulled out a chair. "Have a seat, Nadianna. I think we need to talk."

Reluctantly, she sat. He stood over her and Bethy, his arms crossed, a slight smile on his lips.

"Remember what you told me yesterday, Nadianna? Remember what you told me about not wanting people to push you around anymore? Remember about being proud of your heritage, about wanting to hold your head up as a 'poor little mill girl' without having to live up to people's stereotypes of you?"

Nadianna nodded, confused. "Yes. I remember all that."

"You have a chance to be part of something, Nadianna, that will give you back the pride in your heritage and the promise of your future. You can be that girl who illuminated the mill culture with her talent. You can be acclaimed. And you can do it without the baggage of Gale Grayson."

"What are you talking about?"

He leaned over her so that she could smell the sour odor of digested tea. "I am talking about you going out on your own. Without Gale. She's only going to hold you back, Nadianna. I've seen a hundred women like her at university—they want to be your mentor, they want to see you succeed, but just wait until they discover that their protégée is more talented than they could ever hope to be. God, you've never seen such revenge. Spiteful women, those frail academic types. Ivory towers, don't know the real world at all. And they will hate you for your authenticity, for the realness of your life."

"But that's not Gale," Nadianna stammered. "She's not like that."

"Isn't she? What if I told you I've known about Gale longer than you have? It's true. I knew Tom before he and Gale got married. I never met her in England, but I kept up with Tom, followed his writing career, followed hers. I know how she was perceived in England, and believe me, she's not the poor victim she paints herself to be. She's tough as nails, is Gale Grayson. And she will turn you and that baby out on your pretty white arses if she thinks it's in her best interest."

Across the table Bethy watched her, every now and then nodding. "Them Aldens think their crap don't smell. I always did hate them."

"Bethy, you don't even know them. What are you talking about?" She looked from Goddard to Bethy. "What have you been telling her? What in the hell have you been doing up here?"

Goddard knelt beside her and clutched her hand. "Nadianna, listen to me. Think for once about what's best for you and your baby. You don't owe anybody anything. The only thing you have to do in this life is to give Michael a better life than you have. I can help you do that. Be my partner, Nadianna. You can't imagine the opportunities that will open for you."

Nadianna's throat constricted. She tried to pull away; he tightened his grip.

"You have a gift, Nadianna. Has Gale ever told you exactly the height of your talent? Forget Dorothea Lange, forget Walker Evans. You could be better. The fact that Gale hasn't told you that should make you suspicious. Well, I'm telling you that. You are more talented than those photographers. You could be hanging in museums one day, be the subject of college classrooms. All you need is the proper exposure. The proper support. I can give you that, Nadianna. I can give you that as well as a family to belong to."

He slipped his other arm around the back of her chair so that it felt like he was embracing her. His lips brushed hers roughly. "You can be my eyes, Nadianna. I hear the voices, I hear the passion, but I can't bring the images to life. Look at Bethy. What a beautiful, poignant face. Some people might look at that face and see poverty and ignorance, but do you know what *you* would see? Elegance and nobility. Pride. Resilience. The characteristics of a proud and worthy race. You could bring the poetry of the visual to my work, Nadianna. I need you. And I could make you famous. Don't think that there aren't millions who would buy your work, because there are. Millions of people who want to see the beauty of the white race before it disappears. Millions who would use your images as their flag as they fought back."

His breath filled her mouth, her nose. She couldn't breathe. She pushed her head back, trying to escape him, but he came closer, his face filling her vision.

"You can have everything you want, Nadianna. And more importantly, Michael could have his own future—not the future a bunch of politicians and goddamned lazy immigrants decided was to be his."

From far off she heard the crunch of tires on gravel. Bethy must have heard it, too, for she jumped up and hurried to the window.

"It's the Grayson woman," she told Goddard. "She's getting out of a car."

Nadianna shoved Goddard with all her strength. "Gale!" she screamed.

Goddard fell back against the table. Nadianna flung herself through the doorway, heading for the front door. She grabbed the knob; the door whipped back against the wall from the force of her tug, and she was out of the house, stumbling down the wooden stairs.

"Gale!" she screamed. "Get out of here!"

Gale appeared suddenly from the side of the house. Nadianna ran toward her.

A bullet whistled by her head. She grabbed Gale and slammed her to the gravel as a second slashed overhead.

They lay flat for only an instant. The shooting stopped, but Nadianna could hear the creak of someone walking deliberately down the porch steps.

She jabbed Gale and they started crawling toward Gale's car. Nadianna's heart pounded. Gravel bit through her jeans and scraped her palms. They scrabbled over the drive, footsteps crunching the ground behind them.

"Stop it, ladies." Goddard's voice was cool. "I have a gun. It's great to be in America."

Gale rolled over to face him. "Ron—"

Another shot, and Nadianna heard Gale grunt and fall beside her. Horrified, she twisted around, facing Goddard from the ground.

"Are you insane?" she screamed. "What did you shoot her for? Why did you do that?"

"To get her out of the way," Goddard replied evenly. "So you could think clearly. Now, listen to me, Nadianna. You have a fairly stark choice here. You can pack up Michael and come work with me, or I can kill you here and now. What's it going to be? Do you have a life ahead of you or not?"

Tears blurred her vision. "How could you do that? How could you shoot her?"

"How? Pulling the trigger. Want to watch me do it again?" He fired the pistol again, and Nadianna heard it hit a soft mark. "Don't make me shoot you, Nadianna. I've had to shoot two of the people I trusted this week. I'll make it three without blinking an eye."

"You're sick," she sobbed.

"No. I'm a practical man with a very clear vision. I've been at this a long time, Nadianna, longer than you know. Tom was a colleague of mine. And I don't mean at university. We pretty much founded In Gaia's Name. We started out focusing on ecology, but we grew to so much more than that. The issue is much more complex than recycling and birth control. It's about the future of this incredible planet, God's most wonderful creation. You know what Tom was good at? I think Americans call it *schmoozing*. He made contacts here in the U.S.—with gun sellers, with white supremacists. What we discovered is that in the network of terrorists, all kinds of lines get crossed. We work with this group here, they help us there. We had us a neat little conglomerate going. Then I'll be damned if the man didn't have a fit of conscience. Had to be the pregnancy. Little Katie Pru. He couldn't go on. He mucked it up. And in the end he killed himself. Idiot."

He knelt down beside her, the pistol at her cheek. "Don't be an idiot. Do what is in your best interest, Nadianna. Choose life. Choose life for Michael."

"I'm not a white supremacist," she whispered.

Goddard shrugged. "I'm not either. I apologize for that. I misread you. I don't do that often, but every now and then . . . I thought that would be the way to reach you. It was the way to reach Darrell and Stuart. If you listen for people's hate, you'll always find the key to controlling them. I needed a guns operation here in the States. What better place than a small hick town with a reputation for wanting to be left alone? I thought I might take over the church, use it as a base." He looked regretfully at Gale's body. "But I'll have to leave now. Two bodies I might be able to get away with. Three, and this one the love of a Scotland Yard detective . . ." He shrugged. "Will you go with me?"

Nadianna trembled so badly her teeth cut her lips. "Where . . . will we go?"

"Going isn't the problem. You still have your passport. All you need is the baby's birth certificate. We'll be fine. What I will have to do is make sure it is safe to leave. You'll have to help me hide Gale's body. And then I'll need you to gather up her notes and computers. It was those damn memoirs of hers that brought me here in the first place. I have no idea what she knows or doesn't realize she knows. Those will have to be destroyed."

"What about the Keasts? They'll tell on you."

He laughed. "The Keasts are set for life. In a few weeks they'll have more money than they know what to do with. They'll probably use it as toilet paper. Stuart was a very savvy gun dealer." Goddard looked momentarily sad. "He let his hate get in the way. Stupid." He turned his gaze back on Nadianna and nudged the nose of the pistol deeper into her cheek. "Well, Nadianna? What is your choice? Do you choose life?"

Her tongue was thick in her mouth. "I choose life," she said. "I choose life."

"Of course. I read people so well. It's all a matter of listening. I know what people are saying even when they don't know it themselves. And since I first met you, you've been saying you wanted something *more*. You wanted your own future. Well, given the state of the world today, there's only one way to assure your future, and that is by taking it. Sometimes that means taking another dumb bastard's away from him."

He moved away from her and stood. Stepping back, he held out his hand.

She didn't hear where the bullet came from; she saw only where it found its mark. Goddard's chest exploded in front of her. Blood flung through the air and splattered in her face. Goddard reeled, his eyes wide and uncomprehending, before collapsing beside Gale.

Dazed, Nadianna looked up to see Rosen Keast on her front porch, a shotgun held tightly in her hands. As Nadianna watched, the gun dropped to the ground, and the old woman sank to her knees. She clutched at the fraying planks of the porch, pulling up long splinters with her fingers.

"My boy!" The wail bounded around the house, echoing between the twigs in the barren trees. "You killed my boy!"

Within seconds, the Keast grounds were full of men. They swarmed around Nadianna, lifting her to her feet, dragging her down the hill. She looked over her shoulder to see Halford and Truitt bent over Gale.

"Please, God," she mumbled, "please—" And suddenly she knew nothing to say except the words her father had taught her as a child. "The Lord is my shepherd, I shall not want . . ."

EPILOGUE

Thursday

Halford didn't want to take roses. Too many people had already sent roses—Gale's editor, her agent, the Calwyn County Arts Council, and the Chamber of Commerce—until the room was overflowing with them and the nurses had to bring in wheeled tables to hold them in the hall. Halford had always arrived flowerless. When she remembered flowers from him, he wanted it to be with joy.

So today he arrived with a small basket of clay dolls, each made in bright colors and sporting an outrageous clay hat. Katie Pru and Chau had spent hours on them, giggling in Sally Robertson's den. Doll-making had seen them through Gale's absence, Tuan's memorial service, Ella's slow arrival and her ascent into her bedroom for recuperation. "They're fine as rain," Sally kept assuring him. "Honest, Daniel, they're bucking each other up. Children are amazing. You and Nadianna look after the grown-ups—I'll take care of the little ones as long as you need me."

He wondered, in truth, how long they would need her. The bullet had split Gale's collarbone. She claimed she had never lost consciousness, that she had been aware of all that Goddard had said. He wondered. There appeared to be lapses in her memory, as there were in

Nadianna's—some things don't bear keeping close in the mind. But he couldn't imagine that anyone could feel a second bullet plug the ground a fraction from her head and not flinch or cry out. Gale had not. She had lain stone still on the Keasts' dirt, feigning death, until he had laid his fingers against her cheek.

She was awake in bed and writing on a portable table when he entered the room. She put down her pen when she saw him.

"Gifts from giggling girls." He set the basket on the table. "I think the one in the blue hat is supposed to be Katie Pru. And, ah, the handsome one in the green is me."

Gale laughed. "Yes, she looks rather stern and serious. But I think it's the mustache that gives her away. They're marvelous."

He pulled up a chair and sat beside her. "I have news and more news. Rosen Keast is out on bail."

She looked at him in astonishment. "How on earth would she get out on a murder charge?"

"Good lawyer, sympathetic judge, low bail. I believe you know her lawyer—James Whitfield, Sarah Gainer's counsel. His argument was that Rosen could be excused for killing the man she just heard confess to murdering her grandson. The judge apparently agreed. He wasn't so nice to Bethy, however. She's still locked up on illegal gun-dealing charges. Jud's been placed in foster care."

"God, it's so hard to believe. Stuart was buying guns for Goddard to ship to the U.K. . . ."

"It has a kind of beautiful logic to it when you think about it. Alby and I were up until dawn this morning going over everything. Marcus Siler has evidently spilled his guts. Goddard's main point in being here was to monitor your memoirs, to destroy them if he had to. He didn't know what you knew, what Tom had told you before he killed himself. You weren't a threat as long as you were scared and isolated. But then you started making a life for yourself, and that life included publication. A very noisy act, that."

"So he wasn't a linguist from the University of Leeds?"

"Oh, yes, he was. And he was here on a grant. *There's* the beautiful logic in it. He was here to legitimately do what he claimed he was doing—to record and analyze a Cornish-derived American Southern dialect. However, while he was here, he could watch you, buy a few guns for the cause, and even establish a little power base in a small southern town that could continue to keep his group fed with arms and propagate its mission. No point in killing two birds with one stone when you can kill five."

"And Tuan?"

Halford sighed. "Tuan, I'm afraid, was a classic victim. Goddard evidently thought he could reach some of the young men in this county by appealing to their racism. What he didn't reckon on was the extent of their hate. According to Siler, Darrell and Stuart wanted to kill an immigrant. Simple as that. Tuan was in town frequently to visit his family. They kidnapped him, took him to the thickets in Ella's fields, tortured him, and shot him. That wasn't the kind of allegiance Goddard wanted. You don't want fellow terrorists who kill for fun—too risky."

"So what did Goddard do when he found out?"

"All we have is Siler's version. He was supposed to meet Keast and Murphy at 'the meeting place,' the place in the woods where they usually rendezvoused with various gun runners. When he got there, he parked in his usual spot, off the path in what looks like an impossible space, but he claims he could zig-zag his car to the highway in less than five minutes if he needed to make a quick getaway. Keast and Murphy were already there in Murphy's car. According to Siler, they were drunk, talking about the kill they'd made. He thought they'd shot an illegal deer. Instead, he looked in the backseat and saw Nguyen. Evidently, it scared the hell out of him. He knew Goddard would be furious. When he heard another car coming down the path, he hid. He heard the gunshots, but he didn't return to the scene. He ran to the highway and called the police from the market."

"So Goddard shot them."

"By all accounts. Alby's men found a cache of guns in the attic of the Greene house. One of them is a close match to the gun used to shoot Murphy and Keast."

"God. So that was Goddard's grand plan, to get a group of locals to serve as a power base?"

"It's not that unusual, really. Truitt explained this to me. His friend Wiley Dawkins wasn't surprised at how it all came about. White supremacy groups sometimes target isolated churches. A leader moves in anonymously, slowly works on the prejudices of the group. When he has their allegiance, he takes over the church. Voilà— instant organization. Apparently, when Ted Stevens attacked the Nguyens at the prayer meeting, Goddard believed he had the lay leader's allegiance. He was ready to make his move, to ask members of the church to break away and set up their own 'mission.' But he misread Nadianna. For all his listening skills, he wasn't necessarily an astute observer of human behavior."

"Not all humans, anyway." Gale fingered a red flower on one of the doll's hats. "I thought In Gaia's Name was defunct. I thought when Tom died, the investigation shut them down. Isn't that what you told me?"

"That's what I thought. That's what we all thought. In all of Tom's papers, in all our interviews with informants, nobody mentioned Goddard's name. They were smarter than us, Gale. Frequently terrorists aren't— they get stupid with their cause—but these people were. It was like they put up a fire wall. We could ferret out part of the group, but enough protections were in place that the other part remained concealed. It could have been that Tom and Goddard were the only two who knew about the other half's existence. I don't know."

"So there will be more investigations?"

"Oh, yes. I've spent quite a bit of time on the phone. New Scotland Yard is going to start the investigation, but in all likelihood it will be handed to MI-5."

"Like the last time."

"Yes, like the last time."

Gale closed her eyes and slowly leaned into her pillows. Tears formed at the corners of her eyelids. He let her be silent.

"I heard what Goddard said about Tom," she whispered at last. "When I became pregnant, he got soft."

"Does that help at all?"

Wiping her nose with a tissue, she handed Halford the paper she had been writing on.

We learn to protect ourselves, we women of political betrayal. We have all manner of armor. Perhaps the final armor I will choose, the one I will wear daily, the one I will rear my daughter in, pay my bills in, go to grocery stores, PTA meetings, lectures in, is the armor of nonjudgment. In the end, I may not be able to judge my husband. Did he kill himself out of cowardice, because he didn't want to face what he had done? Or was it, finally, an act of parenthood, that ability every parent has to sacrifice his flesh for his flesh.

"I don't think he knew about the tapes," she said thickly.

"He may not have."

"Which means that Goddard didn't trust him. And if that's the case, perhaps he had reached the point where he didn't trust Goddard, either. Perhaps by killing himself, he thought he was removing the danger from us."

"That could be, Gale."

"So maybe the legacy he left for Katie Pru isn't hopeless after all."

"Not if it's mitigated. Not if she's surrounded by people who love her. And she is."

She sniffed loudly, and he helped her pull herself up on the pillows. "You said you had more news."

"I met your doctor in the hall. You're going home."

"Today?"

"This afternoon. Up for it?"

"Lord, yes. I've missed Katie Pru." She paused. "But I don't look forward to going back to the house. So many people—"

"Not to worry. The Nguyens have returned home. Nadianna called a second prayer meeting at the church Tuesday night. Made everyone promise to leave the Nguyens alone and to befriend them if they could. Yesterday, a group of women went into the house and patched what they could of the damaged room—new paint, new curtains. Ilene Parker organized it."

Gale gave him a wan smile. "You better watch it, Daniel. You're beginning to know everyone's name."

"Lady, I have met more fussy Southern women in the past week. You have no idea how tranquil you've had it. We've had to keep the brigades from marching in here and forcing you back to health."

"Le's not worried about finding a job?"

"Le's not worried about much of anything right now. Seems Tuan had an insurance policy. Left Le and Phoung a tidy sum of money. Which they've both decided to invest in a little Southern-Vietnamese tearoom in Athens, in partnership with Mrs. Sally Robertson."

"That's wonderful! So our little family is back to being Nadianna, Michael, Katie Pru, Ella, and myself." A shadow passed over Gale's face. "Is Ella okay this morning?"

"Ella is cranky this morning. She doesn't like to be down, Gale. It's going to take some adjustment on her part. She's never going to be able to manage those stairs without assistance. Want some unsolicited advice? You might want to turn that peculiar little den of hers into a bedroom."

"So the damage from the stroke is permanent?"

"So says the doctor. But I wouldn't put anything past Ella. She'll probably be climbing trees by summer."

Gale was silent a long time, gazing past him at the wall of red roses. "You know, she's resented having all of us with her these past months. She never said much, but she did. We needed her, and that took away her independence."

"She's going to need you now. There's something to be said for dependence."

"Isn't there, though." She held out her hand for his. "So, tell me," she said softly, "who is going to head up that investigation at Scotland Yard?"

He brought her hand to his lips and kissed it. "Hell if I know. Some fresh-faced inspector with promotion on his mind. If he—or she—handles it right, it'll make his damn career."

"They don't need you back right away?"

He ran his finger down the heart line on her palm. "They may not need me back, period. I've been discussing things with Alby. He's putting out some calls. There might be a need for an experienced Scotland Yard detective in this state. I called the Greenes yesterday. They're looking to rent that house again. They're afraid it might be difficult to do so, considering its recent history."

"You can think of someone who would like to rent it?"

"Perhaps," he murmured. "If it wouldn't be an intrusion."

She stroked his cheek. "I can't believe it would be. It might make coming home a lovely experience, after all."

ABOUT THE AUTHOR

TERI HOLBROOK is a former journalist who lives in Atlanta with her cartoonist husband and their two children. She is the author of three acclaimed mysteries, *A Far and Deadly Cry*, *The Grass Widow*, and *Sad Water*.